LAND WHERE
I FLEE

Also by Prajwal Parajuly

The Gurkha's Daughter: Stories

LAND WHERE I FLEE

I FLEE

PRAJWAL PARAJULY

Quercus

New York • London

Quercus

New York • London

© 2014 by Prajwal Parajuly
Map © 2013 by Raymond Turvey
First published in the United States by Quercus in 2015

ISBN 978-1-62365-457-3

Library of Congress Control Number: 2015931872

Distributed in the United States and Canada by
Hachette Book Group
1290 Avenue of the Americas
New York, NY 10104

Manufactured in the United States

10 9 8 7 6 5 4 3 2 1

www.quercus.com

For Gangtok and Kalimpong

and

for Advik Vyas Sharma, who, at 1.5 years, laughs when I read out the most serious parts of this book to him.

Author's Note

The *Chaurasi* is a curious event—not many Nepali-speaking Hindus in India, especially people of my generation, know much about it. This could be partly because few people live to see their 84th birthday. When I referred to texts, priests, and people in the know about why the 84th birthday was a landmark event—and not, say, the 83rd or the 85th one—I was frequently given answers in the form of one or some combination of the following: there being 8,400,000 species on Earth, the soul having 8,400,000 births, and the 8,400,000th birth taking the human form. Besides the numerical connection brought about by 84, these responses weren't entirely convincing. Also, some sources dismissed the 8,400,000 link as hogwash. A somewhat satisfactory, if rarely cited, explanation lay in the significance of the lunar calendar and the numbers 108 and 1,008—especially auspicious in Hinduism. With 12 full moons a year, it takes 84 years for one to witness 1,008 full moons. The 84th birthday is, thus, celebrated as a day of gratitude to the moon. All four of my grandparents lived past 84. The grandfathers spent their *Chaurasi* their own ways—the one in Nepal participated in three-day-long celebrations, and the one in India had a simple *puja* for a few hours—while the grandmothers forewent theirs on account of sicknesses.

For some insight into the Nepalese words and phrases used in the book, please consult the glossary on page 313.

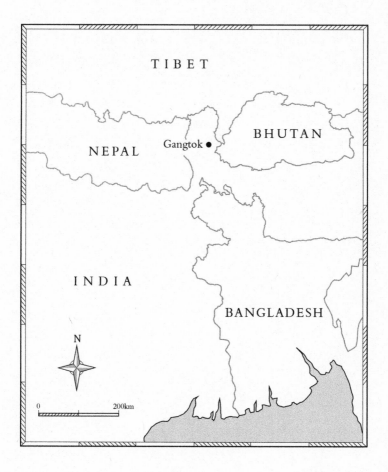

TIBET

NEPAL   Gangtok ●   BHUTAN

INDIA

BANGLADESH

N

0   200km

The factory looks like a heritage hotel.

As though it houses not drudgeries and machinery and yards of uninteresting linen but priceless artifacts.

Its exterior yellow, light and cheerful, with bay windows gleaming and inviting; the main door, intricately embellished with carvings of lords Ganesha, Shiva, and Hanuman in terra-cotta; two trees—guava and orange, one on either side of the building—standing guard.

Ropes of Buddhist prayer flags strung high up between the two trees—blue, white, red, green, yellow—flapping, fluttering, almost flying. The inscriptions on them—symbols, sutras, mantras—sending out positive energy. Keeping evil forces at bay.

The cutouts of the couple advertising the factory's products on the garage door: once clad in Western clothes, now wearing Nepali outfits.

The male is in cream *daura-suruwal*. His top, the *daura*, button-, collar-, and cuff-less, the flaps in its front held in place by the only visible pair of strings across the chest. The pants, the *suruwal*, snug-cuffed, tapered, their excess length gathering at the ankles. The woman, formerly depicted in a black dress, is now wearing *gunyu-cholo*, her green *gunyu* a sari with its loose end tucked into the front. The blouse, her red-and-white rhombus-patterned *cholo*, bulging at the chest but otherwise similar to the *daura*.

The topiary on the marigold-covered lawn spells out: NEUPANEY TEXTILES. The squash climbers on the trellis conceal stenciled inscriptions that reveal: NEUPANEY GARMENTS EST. 1984. A polished copper plaque by the entrance of the building announces: NEUPANEY APPAREL, INC., KALIMPONG, GORKHALAND.

ONE

The Problem
with Reunions

Blowing thick, circular smoke that mirrored the slowly accumulating cirrus clouds in the sky, Chitralekha surveyed the scene unfolding before her from the balcony. Her choice of cigarette—the kind that found favor among the servants, coolies, and construction workers of Gangtok—confounded her doctor as much as the way she smoked it: she puffed on the tobacco wrapping held in an O of her forefinger and thumb. Her technique may have been considered uncouth, and the tobacco flakes in the *beedi* might pose more harm than those inside an ordinary cigarette, but Chitralekha preferred relishing her poison the way she did. Like the ring that for more than seventy years had swung between her nostrils, stretching the septum, the *beedi* represented the familiar. With so much change imminent, she found comfort in the familiar.

Her grandchildren, who lived in various countries whose names she could barely pronounce and whose shores she had no intention of visiting, would be here soon for the *Chaurasi*, her eighty-fourth birthday, the preparations for which were in full swing. The garden

around her cottage was abuzz with activity. The priest
was not satisfied with the length of bamboos that would
be used for the sacred kiln and expressed his discon-
tent in a nasal voice together with a perpetual thudding
of his walking stick. The eunuch servant, who swept
the driveway more for Chitralekha's comic relief than
to actually contribute to the bustle around her, wasn't
happy with the priest and made her disdain known with
loud, off-pitch singing that drowned out the old man's
drone. A few painters, mostly oblivious to the disagree-
ments surrounding them, lazily splashed the walls with
vertical patterns that often became zigzags. Chitralekha
did not like the look of the walls now. The chipping
layer of red the workers were trying to paint over was
too strong for a coat of white to dilute it; they'd have to
paint twice, maybe three times. A jeep tottered a few
days prematurely into the driveway with a thousand
marigolds that the eunuch would soon have to sew into
garlands to be festooned from the roof and to deck the
windows.

"We need competence around here," the Brahmin
priest whined. "We all talk too much."

"Aye, the Brahmin thinks *we* all talk too much," the
eunuch retorted. "A Brahmin thinks we talk too much.
Soon he will tell us we eat too much sugar."

"It's useless talking to your kind of people, Prasanti,"
said the priest while squinting at the terrace to lock his
eyes with Chitralekha's. He failed because she looked
away. "All you do is talk, talk, and talk."

"Oh, and I sing and dance, too!" Prasanti shouted.
"Sing, dance, and clean while you stand there and order
everyone around. Don't forget I am of the Brahmin
caste, too, Pundit-*jee*."

"You should be out on the streets singing and dancing with your kind. Were it not for the generosity of Aamaa here, you'd not have a home."

"And were it not for the kindness of Aamaa here, you wouldn't have a *rupiya* to feed that bulging stomach of yours, Pundit-*jee*. We're both the same."

The priest looked up at Chitralekha again. She knew he expected her to intervene, but she was enjoying the exchange too much to put a stop to it. She had taught Prasanti a lot of things, but the eunuch had taken it upon herself to puncture the Brahmin's ego on a regular basis, and to mediate just when a performance this flawless had been delivered would be a shame. It was important that the priest be put in his place because every festival brought about a resurgence in his belief that he was irreplaceable. This translated into a general disregard for the opinion of everyone around him—he found fault with matters as trivial as the height of the pedestal on which he was to be seated during ceremonies and made purchases Chitralekha seldom authorized.

"What has the world come to?" The Brahmin shook his head. "A half-sex thinks she and a priest are one and the same."

"Yes, this half-sex has to prepare for the arrival of Kamal Moktan now," Prasanti said. "I am a *hijra* who knows important people—unlike you, Pundit-*jee*."

"Yes, to be sure, he must be coming all the way from Darjeeling to see you."

"To see Aamaa, but at least I get to greet him."

"He must be looking forward to that."

"As much as I am to seeing you leave."

It was time for Chitralekha to make her presence felt.

"Prasanti, show some respect to Pundit-*jee*," she said. "He will leave only after you've served him tea."

This would do it. The *hijra* had done well. The priest's self-importance was sufficiently deflated. He would not insist on seven-hour-long ceremonies and outrageous donations. With this minor issue taken care of, Chitralekha could now prepare for her meeting with Kamal Moktan, who headed the new political party that promised the residents of the neighboring Darjeeling district their beloved Gorkhaland, a separate state from West Bengal, of which they were now an ill-treated part. Moktan had infused the Gorkhaland movement, largely stagnant since it hit its crescendo in the eighties, with new hope. He probably needed to talk to Chitralekha about making the movement bigger and better.

Chitralekha would have preferred to meet with Moktan up on the terrace, but it would be too noisy. Prasanti had already laid claim to a makeshift storeroom in the west corner of the rooftop that now housed a huge cauldron of rice-flour batter prepared by her voluble recruits—two miserable, pitch-dark girls from the neighborhood—that they would soon fry into *sel-rotis*, those crispy doughnuts that Chitralekha had no great fondness for and from which she could seldom escape during festivals and celebrations. It'd be interesting to see how the politician would react to his earnest solicitation for donation being punctuated with guffaws from the trio inside the storeroom, but the rare October drizzle that looked as if it would arrive in a few minutes was as much a deterrent to a meeting on the terrace as the clanging of utensils and the giggling fits that had already begun.

Her office was a mess. Prasanti had wiped clean all the pictures on the walls but had conveniently ignored the hillock of paperwork that had built up on the desk. The ashtray was overflowing with *beedi* butts. The cleanliness of the office didn't matter much to Chitralekha as long as the photos on the walls—two of her with the governor of Sikkim, one with the chief minister and a few with various important people—were spotless. She noticed with consternation that a picture she had long before relegated to the cupboard, the one with the ex-chief minister whose chances of coming back to power were as high as those of Prasanti's giving birth, was enjoying pride of place between the photo in which she was shown receiving an award from the governor and another in which she and the tourism minister smiled gaily into the camera. Prasanti could be so useless.

"Prasanti!" Chitralekha called out, her voice echoing through the house. She repeated the servant's name a few times, aware that the eunuch feigned deafness when she felt like it.

"These *sel-rotis* are so round." Prasanti walked in, coughing, a few minutes later. "Even rounder than my head. But the smoke is killing us."

"Don't talk too much, Prasanti. Why have you hung this picture up?" Chitralekha rapped at the offending frame, almost knocking it down and wishing it would fall when the picture managed to stay put.

"Was it not to come out?" Prasanti innocently asked.

"Why would it, fool? Why would you find a picture from the cupboard and hang it up?"

"All these photos you've taken are with ugly men. I wanted a picture of you with a good-looking man. He is the only handsome man with whom you've been shot."

"And why would I, an eighty-three-year-old widow, want a picture with a handsome man, Prasanti?" Chitralekha could feel her fury abate.

"They are better than these ugly men. Some have no hair, and this one has more hair sprouting from his ears than he does on his head. This one could braid his nose hair with a rubber band."

"So, you hung the other picture up?"

"Yes," Prasanti answered impudently. "I want pictures with handsome men, so must you."

"But Basnett will never come to power. How would a picture with a loser like him make me look good?"

"Good for you, then—at least other women won't take pictures with him."

Chitralekha stifled a smile, ordered Prasanti to consign the picture to where it belonged, had her abort the task midway, and asked for the photo to be propped back up in its new home.

"See? You like his handsome face, too, don't you?" Prasanti giggled.

"No, I don't. Go make *sel-roti*. You'll waste a few hours putting that silly picture back in the cupboard."

Moktan was late. The meeting was scheduled for three, and Chitralekha had specifically told the politician's jabbering assistant that she didn't like to be kept waiting. It would be another fifteen minutes before a fleet of cars slithered into the driveway carrying Moktan and his entourage, their black Nepali hats perched pharisaically on their heads.

The bell chimed. Prasanti had been instructed not to open the door until she counted to sixty twice. Chitralekha walked to the foyer so she could hear better.

"Is Chitralekha Aamaa there?" one of the men asked.

"She's in a meeting," Prasanti answered.

"I am Kamal Moktan," Moktan said.

"I am Prasanti."

She had been trained well. The men laughed. Prasanti giggled with them.

"I have a meeting with Aamaa."

"She had a meeting with you at three. She waited until 3:05, but when you didn't come, she took another meeting. She's busy. Why don't you wait in the garden?"

One of the men was quick to quip, "The rain has stopped, sir. The sun might be out at any moment. It's better to wait out in the warm than inside."

Five minutes lapsed, then ten. Prasanti brought the men tea and Good-Day biscuits. "She will be out in another five minutes. She told me she was meeting with only you," she told Moktan. "The others will have to wait here."

Prasanti had done her job, once again redeeming herself in her mistress's eyes. Kamal Moktan would be malleable now.

"*Namaste*, Aamaa," Moktan said sincerely, straightening his jacket at the entrance of Chitralekha's office. "Sorry I was late. The roads are bad because of the landslides in Rangpo, you know."

"Yes, I know. The last time our chief minister was here, he told me he always started an hour early to see me because he didn't want to keep me waiting. Starting an hour early even when he lives in Gangtok is practical."

"I'll take note of that," Moktan said, taking a seat. "I am sorry if I was late, but we enjoyed the tea and biscuits outside."

"So, why did you want to meet me?"

Moktan rubbed his hands together as though warming them. The action bored Chitralekha even before all the verbosity tumbled out. She had had enough experience with politicians to know that this one had a long speech planned, and she'd have to find her way out of it. The Nepali-speaking people of Darjeeling were stupid to rest their hopes on this man to get them a separate state.

"You know the Gorkhaland movement sometimes needs elderly people to encourage the youngsters, especially an elderly person as respected as you in society." There'd be a lot of repetition, a little flattery, allusions to her old age and the wisdom that came with it, her generosity, and how important she was. "You haven't given us your full endorsement since we started. I understand that you are from Sikkim now, but we all know your roots are in Kalimpong, and that's where you own your first and most symbolic factory. Unlike most people in Sikkim, you haven't chosen to distance yourself from the great cause of Gorkhaland. We would be highly obliged if you'd give a speech about the importance of Gorkhaland and how I'd help achieve it because of my devotion to its people."

"Why me?" she asked. "It's interesting that you should ask me."

"I have a cousin's cousin called Rajeev."

"I am glad I know his name."

"He completed his engineering degree from Manipal in Rangpo. All his friends from Sikkim already have government jobs. He was among the top students in his class—got better scores than even the Bengalis. He's yet to find anything. We just have no jobs in Darjeeling—no prospects, nothing."

"I can't find him a job in Sikkim if he's not from Sikkim."

"No, no, that wasn't what I was going for. If in this speech you could ask people like him—educated and unemployed—to support the movement and tell them that they will find jobs when Gorkhaland happens, which we can attain only if we receive their full support, I'd be really grateful. There is too much cynicism among the educated."

Sizing up the man before her, Chitralekha concluded that he wasn't worth inviting to her *Chaurasi*—he wasn't a long-term politician like Sikkim's Subba was. He'd probably be blinded by power, do something stupid, and spend his life absconding or rotting in jail. But at almost eighty-four, she didn't need to think long-term. She was already the oldest member of her extended family on all sides—her father's, her mother's and her husband's—and she was conscious of her mortality. At the most, she had ten years to live. Currying favors with Moktan wouldn't get her anywhere in the long run; from now on, she was all about immediate gratification.

"What do I get out of it?" she asked.

"What would you suggest? We keep hearing rumors that you'll stop being directly involved in your business, that one of your grandchildren will take over, but aren't they all abroad? I have a lot of respect for your decision not to step down even at this age. You are an inspiration to all of us, you see. But please do not ask us for money because we rely on the blessings of people like you to keep ourselves financially afloat."

"Just two months ago, I gave two *lakhs* to your organization. I am not donating any money unless I see a return on that." She lit her *beedi*. It was a habit no amount of amassed wealth would help her get rid of. She

also understood that it intimidated most men of power
when she smoked in front of them. Her white sari,
the loose end of which demurely covered her white hair,
and smoking just did not go hand in hand.

Kamal smacked his lips. "Do you have any suggestions on how we could help you?"

"This Gorkhaland movement is going nowhere,
Kamal-*jeeu*. We have waited long for something to happen. There's too much vandalism, too much hooligan-
ism. We need to inspire the people, inflame them. Ask
any person from Kurseong or Kalimpong if they have
faith in Gorkhaland, and they say no."

"Now, even if someone like you says that, we are
doomed. We have been doing our best. Just last month a
meeting with the West Bengal minister of—"

She cut him short. "Meetings don't achieve anything.
Look at us right now. We have met for the past five minutes, but we haven't talked about anything useful."

The politician's forehead furrowed. "Do you have any
suggestions, then?"

"Yes, we need to instill a sense of oneness in our people. Why don't you mandate that everyone should wear
the Nepali costume—*daura-suruwals* and *gunyu-cholos* and
topis—certain days of the week, especially during festivals and important national holidays? Look at you—
you wear a Gurkha hat, but where's your *daura-suruwal*?
You, more than anyone else, need to set an example.
Let's declare one date—how about the first day be during *Tihaar*, say, sometime next week?—as the date for
everyone to wear only Nepali clothes in solidarity."

"That's a good idea. We would like to do that."

"Yes, another time for dressing up could be the day of
the conference. And I'll come to it, too."

"It's a good plan—but perhaps next week is too early."

"It's not. This movement requires urgency. It has to start now."

He looked at her as though surprised at the lack of caveat. "Is that it, then?"

She glanced at the clock and then at her watch. "That's it, but by now you know that my factory in Kalimpong will be the supplier of all the Nepali clothes to the stores. The clothes are ready. All you have to do is make your announcements. We even have custom-made *daura-suruwal*—no other factory has manufactured the outfit before. Your men will take care of all those stores that don't buy their clothes in bulk from my factory, right?"

Moktan's eyes lit up—Chitralekha couldn't make out if it was in indignation or admiration. She procured a package from under her desk and unwrapped it. In it lay a set of cream-colored *daura-suruwal*.

"Yes, I can do that," he said.

"Good," she said, wiggling the outfit out of its package. She untied all the four pairs of strings, even those on the inside, of the top. "And ten percent of our profits will be donated to your cause—whether your cause is killing people or getting them their state, I don't know." Next, she focused her attention on the pants.

"It's Gorkhaland," Moktan said. "A few casualties occur along the way, which is unfortunate, but what revolution didn't have people die for it? Those who die are either villains or martyrs."

"Yes, and you are the hero." She chuckled while holding up the *suruwal* for her guest to inspect. "Your men down there make too much noise. The next time you come to visit me, can you come alone? Let's plan a

meeting three months from now. You could also pick up
your donation then."

Moktan brought his hands together in supplication
and perhaps as a precursor to a long-winded speech that
Chitralekha would have to prohibit.

"Look at these photos, Moktan-*jeeu*—what do you
see?"

The politician turned around. His eyes fixated on
the picture of her with the ex-chief minister, but he was
quiet.

"That's who I am, Moktan-*jeeu*," Chitralekha said. "I
am your friend for a lifetime if you've earned my trust.
I don't care if your party is not in power. I don't care if
you will never be reelected. I'll forever be faithful to you."

Moktan listened in silence.

"You'll give yourself an opportunity to earn my trust,
will you not?" Chitralekha looked him in the eye. And
then she broke into a smile, one that birthed a multitude
of lines on her face. "You will see to it that your picture
will be standing there among these, won't you?"

Moktan nodded and told her he would have to rush to
a meeting with I. K. Subba, the chief minister of Sikkim,
who had publicly announced his support for the separatist movement. "We Gorkhaland people have so much to
be thankful for in people like you and him, Aamaa," he
said. "For too long we've been under the oppression of
the Bengalis. Gorkhaland as a state has to happen. We
have to have a separate state just as you people in Sikkim
do. Thank you so much for giving us hope."

Once Moktan left, Chitralekha summoned Prasanti
to banish Basnett's picture to the cupboard.

"She now doesn't want to see a mere picture after she
saw such a macho man in person," Prasanti teased, tying

her shoulder-length hair, receding around the temples, in a chignon. "How old is he? Are you sure his caste is Moktan? He looks like a Newaar to me. His eyes aren't small enough to be a Moktan's eyes. By the way, the fatty priest is still around, retching poison into anything within reach."

Chitralekha smoked another *beedi*. The meeting was a success. She would turn eighty-four in a week. For most of her life, age had meant nothing. In fact, like most women of her generation, she did not even know when her actual birthday was. But this was different. It was a slap in the faces of those diseases that killed you before you reached your prime. Eighty-four was special, for she was now among the very few who had survived that far. To most people, like her pathetic husband, living to that age was an unattainable dream. It was time to go now—maybe stick around for a few years and then die peacefully. Her biggest fear was of outliving one of her grandchildren, and, going by the surgeries, aches, and pains they complained about, she wouldn't be at all surprised if she lived to see at least one of their deaths. She didn't want that. She had witnessed too many people dying—her husband, her son, her daughter-in-law. She wouldn't be able to withstand another tragedy. She had bargained with God that at least this quarter of her life would be devoid of sadness. And she'd see to it that he kept his promise.

•

Bhagwati could have prevented the pot from toppling over, but her wandering thoughts had betrayed her.

"Help!" she screamed. "The spaghetti water spilled on me."

She braced herself for the generous sprinkling of innu-
endos that would come her way in the distance that she
had to limp between the dishwasher and the kitchen
entrance. Brian, the busboy whose presence triggered in
her the same reaction as did the peccadilloes of the ruf-
fians outside the refugee camps, was nowhere to be seen,
but Bhagwati had become skilled at discovering creepy
figures lurking inside walk-in freezers or behind bulky
kitchen equipment, and even in her pain, she looked over
her shoulder, lest someone jump at her. Two weeks before,
when she allowed her thoughts to compare somewhat
unfavorably the *Dashain* festivities in Bhutan to those in
Gangtok, a mouth had come dangerously close to breathing hot, putrid air against her shoulders and neck. That's
what she got for daydreaming about Hindu festivals in
Christian America. She had to constantly be on the watch,
or she'd find her body parts and the busboy's coming
together in unwelcome interaction.

The cook rushed to her as she fell to the floor. The
pain was unbearable.

"Good thing the water hadn't come to a complete
boil," he said, grazing his hand over the burn. "Brian,
could you get me a Band-Aid?"

"It's a burn." Bhagwati winced. "I think I need
a cream—something with aloe—more than I need a
Band-Aid."

"I don't know where the fucking first-aid kit is," Brian
said with a snicker, and he swaggered outside, only to
emerge a few seconds later with a box. "I don't know how
to open this damn thing. She only works here like us, and
now we're all becoming her damn slaves."

By now, a substantial crowd of kitchen staff had
gathered around the reclining Bhagwati and the gently

comforting cook, and each offered his own diagnosis and prescription. Between a suggestion to rub toothpaste on the affected area and another to use a pack of ice arose an idea that a long, passionate kiss from the cook might help alleviate Bhagwati's pain. Raucous applause signified approval from the bystanders.

The cook handed her a tube from the box. Bhagwati concentrated on squeezing the cream out of the small tube and applied it to her ankle. The burn didn't seem as severe as the pain was.

"It's just a first-degree burn," someone said, before the manager commanded the crowd to disperse. "She'll be fine."

"Damn, refugee," the cook said to her softly, ignoring her grimace. "Damn, you can only be happy you weren't hurt by a pot of fully boiled water."

"Thank you," Bhagwati said. "Could you please ask Brian not to bother me today?"

"Don't worry about him. You be careful around boiling pots. Be thankful I was here. The last time someone from your world burned himself, he applied some butter. Crazy man."

Bhagwati still had a stack of dirty dishes to negotiate, but the story about this other person from her world intrigued her. She wanted to ask the cook, whom she was still hesitant to call by name because of its numerous silent letters, if that burned man had been treated as badly as she was. The manager—suited, limp-wristed, but otherwise a kind man—was already looking at her with impatience, so she dashed off to tackle the plates, which, in between the accident and its treatment, had trebled in number.

Days like today took her on an endless question-and-answer session about whether life had actually changed for the better since she'd left the refugee camps of Nepal. When she and other Nepali-speaking Bhutanese were herded out of Bhutan because they weren't Bhutanese enough to be Bhutanese, they wouldn't let go of the hope that Nepal would take them in, but their ancestors had been gone from Nepal and been in Bhutan too long for them to be Nepalese.

Life in the refugee camps of Nepal was supposed to be better than living in fear of persecution in Bhutan, but it wasn't. Day in and day out, she and the other refugees struggled as noncontributing members of society, loathed by the Nepalese outside the camps—the Nepalese from Nepal; the real Nepalese—because the refugees' desperation had attracted enough Western attention for countries such as America to come to their rescue. The campers had survived years clinging to a thin reed of hope that someday America, Australia—any country where life was better than in the camps—would whisk them away. When America finally did, life didn't get any better.

"All that beauty wasted on a Damaai," her grandmother had said about her in more than one phone conversation, adding a colorful word or two to describe her husband's low caste. But she was used to her grandmother's barbs—they didn't hurt her the way people's behavior toward her at work did. In the kitchen of Tom's Diner in Boulder, Colorado, she was often invisible, which was preferable to being the recipient of uninvited caresses. The first female dishwasher, the waiters and cooks had cheered the minute she walked in. All this she bore for the low-caste Damaai husband of hers—a nameless, identity-less, stateless Damaai.

Refugees didn't belong anywhere, but she especially belonged nowhere. Who was she? Born: a

Nepali-speaking Indian with a dead father from Sikkim, a dead mother from Nepal, and a live grandmother from Kalimpong who was married into Sikkim. Postmarriage: a Nepali-speaking Bhutanese who had lawfully relinquished her Indian citizenship so she could belong. Post the ousting of 106,000 Nepali-speaking people from Bhutan: an inhabitant of a state of statelessness in the refugee camps of Nepal. Post America's magnanimity: a refugee now in America with a shiny green card that would probably never land her a job commensurate with her expectations.

She could have gone back to Sikkim and exploited her grandmother's connections to reestablish her Indian identity, but her husband was too proud to give in. In the beginning, he, like thousands of others, had languished in disbelief that his country would actually turn him away, but Ram had done enough harm to the monarchy with his column in an underground Nepali newspaper. Incredulity gave way to expectation, which was gradually usurped by hopeless resignation. After living that way for a decade and a half, Bhagwati had stopped questioning the purpose of life.

At least in Boulder she was making a wage and trying her best to become a functional part of society. Despite efforts ranging from picking up Dzongkha, that Bhutanese language so different from Nepali, to cultivating reverence for the king, Bhutan had never felt like home, and these days even Gangtok seemed alien, as though it had decided to grow up and old without her. The shiny new city with the pedestrianized square, like Pearl Street here, wasn't what she'd left behind. Now, when she saw pictures of her hometown on Facebook, she felt no familiar stirrings. It was like staring at a photo of her long-dead parents.

Brian placed a new stack of plates beside her. The dishes had been piling up, and she was woefully behind. She'd have no time to drink her coffee, and she willed the bitter pangs of remorse stemming from the looks the manager flung at her to go away. She wasn't about to peg the accident to her negligence, to her drifting mind—not today, at least.

"Hey, refugee, what's going on?" the line cook yelled. "Why are the dishes so slow?"

Bhagwati didn't answer but hurried along to scour off a plate some breadcrumbs that an excess of maple syrup had rendered immobile. The old Christian busboy, who usually scraped the plates before he brought them to Bhagwati while extolling the virtues of Christ, manned the counter today. She'd have to deal with Brian's handi-work, and that entailed getting rid of every uneaten morsel of food left on the dishes.

"Plates not coming fast enough!" someone shouted. "No food if no plates. Where do we put what we fucking cook?"

Bhagwati loaded some dishes into the washer, wish-ing someone would turn down the heat.

"Damn, refugee, are we okay?" Brian said. "We are running outta plates."

She paid him no attention. Brian would probably do what he'd done three days before—tell the manager that she had been painting her nails. To corroborate his story he had obtained a bottle of nail polish that he claimed to have heroically confiscated from her.

But he hadn't.

"Damn, at this rate, you'll be fired," he hooted.

A grain of rice clung stubbornly to a plate. Had Brian been doing his work instead of breathing down her neck, her workload would have been reduced by half.

"Damn, girl, the rice don't want to leave you."

She stayed silent. And then, as he turned to leave, Brian's hand touched her back, as if by accident. But Bhagwati knew better. She slapped him.

"You!" she shrieked. "Stop touching me with your filthy hand!"

Brian winced and yelped. A waiter, the line cook, and the Christian busboy came by to inspect the scene. Just the day before, Brian had gone past her, deliberately brushing his arm against her behind. She had said nothing then. Last week, it was something else. She looked around, hoping at least the Christian busboy would cheer her on, as he, too, had on numerous occasions complained about Brian's disrespectful ways. But the old man's face reflected disbelief, and his revulsion—like everyone else's—was not directed at Brian.

"Bitch." Brian walked away. "What's this country come to, taking in immigrants like you? You can't take jokes, man. You don't understand the language; you don't do jokes."

The next batch of plates arrived surprisingly well-scraped, and complaints about the dishes not coming out soon enough abruptly stopped.

If this was how things worked around here, maybe she should continue behaving the way she just had. She wondered about how difficult life was for a barely educated refugee in this country. She had, at least, received an excellent English-medium education in Gangtok. Her husband had gone to a government school in Bhutan and was nervous about his English, so she forgave him for not being able to hold down a job for more than a few days. Often, she, who was confident in her language abilities, didn't understand the way Americans spoke—did they really

have to twist and turn their tongues all the time? Hardly
had she celebrated the victory of having understood something when off they'd go, curling their tongues, making
incomprehensible whatever little she had gathered until
then. Fifteen years at the camp had rusted her brain.

"These seem to be the last plates of the day," the cook
said. "The boss wants to see you in his office after this."

She looked up in surprise at the calm tone and found
the absence of any epithets strangely jarring. That's what
her life had become: she thought something was amiss
when she wasn't summoned as a refugee.

The manager treated her well, but his consideration
toward her was always obscured by the others' hostil-
ity. Perhaps he had called her in to apologize for Brian's
behavior. Maybe he'd even get rid of the devil.

"There's been a problem," the manager began, maintaining negligible eye contact.

She said nothing.

"There were reports that you were violent with him,
B. We've a zero tolerance policy toward violence. Here's
a message for you: do not come back. You can return
your uniform shirt when you pick up your last paycheck."

If she were to look at the positive side of things, at
least she didn't have to disclose her profession to everyone she would meet at her grandmother's *Chaurasi*. She
wouldn't be lying when she declared to relatives that she
didn't work.

The apartment complex where Bhagwati, Ram, and
their sons lived at Thunderbird Circle housed enough
Nepali-speaking people to shatter the myth about Boulder's monochromatic personality. The other Nepalis

resented people like Ram and her: the Bhutanese refugees who had decided to uproot themselves from Denver, where they were originally settled by America, to Boulder for better opportunities. Hated almost as much as the refugees were the Diversity Lottery winners from Nepal. Then came the professionals—diligent graduates of American universities, working harder still to climb the immigrant ladder one visa status at a time—who maintained a safe distance from the first two categories, guided in no small part by a mixture of scorn and envy. A handful of South Asian students with the resources to afford the state university's private-school-like fees or the brains to lend themselves to the school's teaching-assistant workforce comprised the remaining residents. Rumor had it that the two couples sharing the one-bedroom in 208 were illegal.

Bhagwati waved at the allegedly illegal wives sunning themselves in the courtyard and bolted for the mailbox before they could approach her with a question about her sons' braces, which were paid for by some NGO. Today was the last day she needed to be reminded how lucky her family was for having so many things done for them by America. In the last few weeks, the tone of the letters from Chase and Citi had grown especially aggressive, so Bhagwati decided against opening her mail.

In 213, sprawled on the flowery bed sheet that covered the carpet was a headphone-bedecked Ram repeating, "Thank you for calling Doe-mino's. How may I help you?" over and over again. When he noticed her, he removed his headphones and smiled.

"Got the Doe-mino's job," he said in halting English, and then, moving to the comfort of Nepali, he added, "I am practicing how to answer the phone."

"That's nice." Bhagwati faked enthusiasm. "At least one of us will be working."

"You're back early," Ram said. "Did you take a half day?"

"No, I quit," Bhagwati lied.

Ram was quiet.

"It was getting too much. The man had begun touching me."

"What will you do when you get back from India?"

"Look for a new job—something that requires more qualification than the kind of jobs illegals do."

"A hotel?" Ram asked. "Front desk?"

"Reservations, perhaps. No standing up required. When do you start?"

"This afternoon. 'Thank you for calling Doe-mino's. How may I help you?'"

"That's fine. Now change the 'doe' to 'da.' It's not Doe-mino's but Da-minos."

"Da-da-da," Ram repeated. "I'll have to end practice soon. Aatish will make fun of me if he hears."

"You should tell Aatish you're doing it all for him and Virochan. You didn't have the good fortune to go to school in America the way they do."

"I'll stop now. Will you join me to pray before I head to Doe-mino's?"

How ironic it was that her husband, an untouchable, the lowest of the low castes, an upsetting by-product of the heinous system that her ancestors had helped create and propagate, should be so full of piety. He knew the *shlokas*, memorized elliptical Sanskrit mantras, read the Gita, and understood what festival was celebrated for what reason. He was combative when she, a Brahmin, dismissed Hinduism's many superstitions, made her analyze and reanalyze these beliefs, and furnished her with the scientific reasoning behind them, which she grudgingly acknowledged. And yet, he could never become a priest. He'd never be allowed near the altar of most Hindus. He was a casualty of Hinduism who had chosen not to be a victim. An untouchable who had no shame about his low caste as much as he did of robbing his Baahun wife of hers on account of her marriage to him. A bigger Hindu, a better Hindu, than she or anyone she knew. Ram Bahadur Damaai—whose kind the Christian missionaries had been targeting for centuries and whose family had stood firm in their devotion to Hinduism, naming their child after a Hindu god; Ram Bahadur Damaai—of the tailor caste, the father of her half-caste children who would, thankfully, not be taunted in this country for carrying in their bloodline accusations of incest and consanguinity; Ram Bahadur Damaai—responsible for the biggest blemish anyone had brought on her family, for belonging to a family of tailors, of alterers and cutters, for altering family dynamics in a way that could never be unaltered, for ripping grandmother from granddaughter in a way that could never be re-hemmed; Ram Bahadur Damaai— who gave her two sons in whose DNA were Damaai blood and Brahmin blood, one infiltrating another, poisoning another, the two sons her grandmother would never touch, whose presence would desecrate her ancestral house; Ram Bahadur Damaai—the untouchable kicked out of Bhutan along with Brahmins, Chettris, and Newaars, the man for whom she had given it all up and never regretted it—was a better human being than any of her family members would ever be.

And as her husband stood in front of the makeshift altar—a shelf in their closet on whose surface sat a

motley arrangement of colorful gods and goddesses—
sonorously reciting the Gayatri Mantra, the Hanuman
Chalisa, and the Ganesha Mantra, chants coined by the
very Brahmins who had determined his legacy and the
identity of his sons and grandsons—Bhagwati Neupaney
Damaai, with a bell oscillating in frenzy in one hand,
prayed the hardest she had in her thirty-seven years. For
a long period she had put off thinking about the enor-
mity of the impending reunion, but it was here now.
She'd be seeing her grandmother after eighteen years—
for the first time since the elopement—and she needed
to fortify herself with all the prayers of all the religions
in the world.

●

The love of Agastaya's life hardly fulfilled the require-
ments that an ideal match was expected to satisfy. First,
the person he desired to spend the rest of his life with
wasn't a Brahmin—not the upper-echelon Upadhyay
Baahun, nor belonging to the lower orders. Second,
as the first son and grandson of the Neupaney family,
Agastaya, it was understood, would marry a Nepali,
no matter from which side of the border. Nicky, even
after all these years together, was still prone to Nepal-
Naples/Nepali-Napolean malapropisms and was easily
the most American American Agastaya had come across.
And third, it was important that whomever Agastaya
intended to bring into his clan be from a prestigious,
well-known family. Nicky belonged to a broken one
from rural Ohio, a descendant of a line of rednecks who
could barely trace their ancestry beyond two generations
and among whom the divorce rate hovered precariously
close to one hundred percent. A less important requisite

that the freckled, pale, and skinny Nicky fulfilled over-whelmingly was the fairness criterion.

Despite being from his family and being witness to what his sister's inter-caste marriage had done to it, Agastaya was sure that most of the issues that disqualified Nicky from being the perfect life-mate could be worked around. In the face of the big problem, this insurmount-able problem, the mother of all problems, Nicky's race, nationality, and questionable family background were hardly worth losing sleep over. No one in the family knew about Nicky. No one among the Neupaneys knew that Agastaya was in a relationship. Registered Nurse Nicholas Zachary Wells, you see, was a man, and the man had just threatened his boyfriend with the effec-tive termination of their relationship if they didn't some-how adopt a baby soon and if his own concealment from Agastaya's world continued. That Nicky should choose to drop the dual ultimatum five minutes before Agastaya was to leave for the airport was a quintessential Nicky trait. In the three years that they had been together, Agastaya had noticed with growing awe his lover's scheming skills evolve and expand. The silent treatment hadn't yet begun. It would once they neared the airport.

"I've never been in a relationship where I was hidden for so long," Nicky said, getting into the waiting cab. "I feel like the other man. Even Mormon Rob's crazy fam-ily knew I existed."

"It's just my grandmother's birthday, Nicky. Even if you were to go to the party, it'd be boring."

"We can't even fly together."

"We will fly together when we return. And before that, we shall see the Taj Mahal. Doesn't that get you excited?"

"I'm not sure the stupid king who built the Taj Mahal would have built it had he had to keep his wife hidden from everyone."

The Indian cabbie, while making a turn, stole a furtive glance at them in the rearview mirror. "Indian?" he asked.

"Napolean-Indian," Nicky answered for Agastaya and bitterly laughed.

The driver nodded, as though he comprehended the frustration behind the hyphen. The spirited shaking of his head could have convinced anyone that the driver had long been a willing audience to Agastaya's many rants on the unfairness of having to stress his nationality every time he mentioned his ethnicity.

To leave New York was to leave an identity behind. And Agastaya had many identities. In Gangtok, he was the pressured orphan grandson of a woman who considered her other grandson long dead. In Pondicherry, he was the medical student proving that his belonging to Sikkim—a state still favored by the education god, for she endowed on its residents one precious medical-school seat after another—wasn't the only reason he had found his way into the prestigious Jawaharlal Institute of Postgraduate Medical Education and Research. In New York, he was the high-flying oncologist in a clandestine three-year relationship with a nurse who he sometimes suspected had gossiped about their affair with other nurses. Shedding one cloak and donning another as he traveled from place to place was second nature to Agastaya. He was now mentally preparing himself to give up his New York self for several days—at least until Nicky joined him in Delhi after his grandmother's *Chaurasi*. He hated the compulsion to be that supple.

"What are you mostly looking forward to?" Nicky asked, his mood lightened by the taxi driver's deep understanding of Agastaya's Napolean-Indian existence.

"Eating barely edible oranges on the terrace."

"And I thought you'd say you'd enjoy spending time with the family."

"It's family. You can't do with them, and you can't do without them."

"What about the nephews?"

"You know I love kids as much as I love snakes. Bhagwati isn't bringing her sons."

"You also hated animals, but once we got Cauffield, you liked him. I now think he likes you better than he likes me."

Agastaya was nervous about where this conversation was meandering. He'd have to nip the topic before tempers flared, although he was thankful that his boyfriend had decided to temporarily drop his favorite issue of being nonexistent to Agastaya's family.

"What will you do while I am gone?"

"Oh, you know, cheat on you, foolito," Nicky said. "Go to Splash, pick up a hot Brazilian who possibly wants children."

"We've talked about that."

"Your stupid grandmother doesn't know about me. Okay. I can't attend her stupid eighty-fourth birthday—I can accept that. Even your stupid siblings don't know about me—I can live with that. I can't upload a harmless picture of us on Facebook—I haven't complained about it. I've one desire, one burning desire, and I can't even have that?"

"I've told you time and again that we aren't adopting kids not because I don't want anybody to know about us but because I can't stand them."

"You couldn't stand dogs, either."

"Yes, had I not liked Cauffield, we had the option to return him. We can't do that with a child."

"Think about it. Spend time with your hundred different cousins and their children. You'll have a different opinion."

"I don't want a different opinion. The kid will grow up with no mother. I grew up without one. I hated it. It was embarrassing."

"You also grew up without a father."

"Yes, it sucked, and you know it."

"You grew up in a different culture than our child will. Sikkim and New York are different places."

"Yes, let's call attention to the cultural differences between us, as if your friends don't do that enough."

"I didn't mean it that way."

"Of course, you didn't."

This should have been a ride full of chitchat, of bittersweet good-byes, of plans for Agastaya's thirty-fourth birthday in the palaces of Udaipur, of excited last-minute changes to the itinerary they had meticulously planned for after Nicky joined Agastaya in Delhi in a week. It'd be Nicky's first visit to India. Agastaya hoped that his boyfriend would gain a deeper sense of where he came from out of this tour. Maybe Nicky wouldn't be so upset anymore when Agastaya reprimanded him for never finishing anything on his plate. Nicky would perhaps be more understanding of why Agastaya was just not comfortable holding hands in public. All these, however, were trivial issues. If Nicky didn't bounce back and forth between the very private nature of their relationship and the desire to start a family, Agastaya would gladly settle for a lifetime of his lover's letting half his $33 carbonara go to waste. He'd even be swayed to give Nicky a peck in a semi-deserted alley.

Nicky's paternal instinct, latent all the while Agastaya and he had been together, had suddenly surfaced since one of his many old lovers adopted a Belarusian boy. A few months before, when Nicky volunteered to babysit the child, Agastaya had been forced to spend a Saturday night in the toddler's sniveling company, and he'd found in the baby's abundant demands, cries, and screams a reiteration of everything he disliked in children. With children in the picture, your life was no longer your own.

"You could babysit Anthony's child all you want with me gone," Agastaya said in a spirit of generosity, although he'd have preferred for Nicky to stay far, far away from father and son.

"I'll see him and Anthony Junior the day after," Nicky said. "It's Tony's twenty-ninth birthday and Tony-the-Second's third. How cute is it that they have the same birthday?"

"You didn't tell me anything about that."

"I would if the talk about the child's cuteness didn't make your eyes go glazy."

After all the words Agastaya had minced, the concerns he didn't voice, and his effort at civility, he and Nicky were back to where they'd started.

"How about we talk about the child once we get back?" Agastaya asked, compensating for the insincerity of his intentions with a softening of the voice that he found pathetic.

"That's fine, but promise me you'll be less cynical of kids."

"I'll try, but wouldn't I be lying to you if I said I'd do that? You know I'm incapable of feeling that way."

Once their car reached the Triborough Bridge and they found the Manhattan skyline loom imposingly beside them, they both fell quiet. During their initial dates, they had often walked the Brooklyn Bridge and stood in silence, hand in hand, staring in wonder at the majesty of the city they called home. They hadn't needed words, which could only diminish those moments. New York had the capability to render them both mute, as it did right now in its sun-setting glory, and sights such as this one made Agastaya feel that his problems were insignificant, that even if the car crashed and he died, the city would go on, the world would go on, life would go on. It was so easy to embrace the notion that difficult times would pass, just as everything did, when you were overcome by such emotion. Impermanence was a beautiful thing.

"I'll miss you," Nicky said, hugging him, when the buildings became dots behind them. "I'll miss your stinky socks and the disgusting hair on your back."

"I'll miss you, too," Agastaya replied, genuinely moved. "I'll miss your abs and the awesome hair on your head."

"I'm thinking of cutting it."

"Don't. For me."

"I've already done so many things for you. I think it's time my needs took priority."

"You're right—you should do what you want," Agastaya said with a sigh, trying to distract his irritation by looking at the puffy cheeks in the pictures of Hanuman, the monkey god, that adorned the car's dashboard.

"I also don't have to take orders from you."

"You don't, and I don't expect you to." Noting that his tone, too, had mimicked Nicky's, Agastaya added, "You'd look good no matter how you wear your hair. You'd look good bald."

"That's what Anthony used to say."

Feeling his temper escalate, Agastaya pointed at the dashboard and asked Nicky, "Are my cheeks bigger than Hanuman's?"

"They probably will be in India. All that greasy food—ew. Who is this fellow, anyway?"

"Our monkey god."

"With a face like that, I hope to God he found his goddess."

"He didn't. He was a Brahmacharya." Agastaya stopped himself before the grind of explanation pushed him into dangerous territory—quagmires that he had until now managed to pull himself out of with minuscule success.

"Oh, now I am supposed to understand what that means?"

"He was a bachelor." It was just Agastaya's luck that his attempt at humor should somehow come down to nuptials and commitment.

"Like we will be, thanks to your principle that I should be hidden under your bed forever," Nicky said.

In response, Agastaya verified that his passport was in the laptop case. A mixture of guilt and relief enveloped him as they pulled up outside Terminal 1 at JFK. Nicky had been insufferable the last few hours, and the idea of a week with his grandmother and siblings didn't seem as unpleasant as it had yesterday. Agastaya would shrug off taunts about being past his prime, brave judgment on his singlehood, and fake curiosity in matches that would never come to fruition. After the few hours of hell he had been through with Nicky, he'd breeze through them all.

•

The one advantage of having her immobile father-in-law tag along with her and her husband everywhere, besides their being able to exploit handicapped parking spots, came to light at the London airport. A surly attendant wheeled Bua everywhere, with Manasa and Himal close behind, as they averted their gaze from other passengers while bypassing them to find their seats on the plane. The decision to travel economy was in part fueled by this preferential treatment they knew would be meted out on Bua and, in the process, on them, irrespective of what class they flew. If the attendant was expecting a gratuity, Manasa wasn't going to dispense any.

"How much should we tip her?" Himal asked in the safety of Nepali. "She looks like she needs it."

"For service that bad? She deserves nothing."

"It could've been worse."

"That'd be pushing Bua into a wall."

Her father-in-law, now comfortable in a bulkhead seat, handed a one-pound coin to the attendant, whose presence was perpetually announced by regular beeps on her cell phone. She grimaced at the coin, took it, and, folding the wheelchair, left without a word.

"The two of you argue about everything," Bua said. "It's a long flight ahead. In economy, it will be even longer."

The other Air India 130 passengers would soon filter in. It was best to feed Bua his *jaulo* now. Manasa steeled herself for some resistance from her father-in-law in the form of a jibe about his life being reduced to eating watery porridge every meal of the day. Once the perfunctory remark was doled out and ignored, she brought a spoonful of liquidy rice close to Bua's mouth, willed it open by forcing the spoon against the lips, allowed him a minute to chew the food, and then repeated the process

several times. By the end of the feeding, the major-
ity of passengers were in their seats. Bua's swallowing
some colorful pills with orange juice sipped through a
straw ended the nightmare, and Manasa seated herself in
between her father-in-law and husband, whose role during the entire feeding process didn't go beyond smiling
apologetically at the passengers who walked by them.

Once the plane took off and her father-in-law was fast
asleep, Manasa attempted fiddling with the entertain-
ment system. A few seconds later a loud, booming voice
attributed the TV's unavailability to some technical difficulty; she'd have to make do without the ridiculousness
of a Bollywood movie. The insouciance with which her
co-passengers received the news surprised Manasa. Unlike
many of them, who dozed off, she found that sleep, especially when she was in motion, never came easily to her.
The snoring of her father-in-law complemented the aircraft
hum—louder, she was certain, on this flight than on any
other—and Manasa's request for earplugs was met with a
frosty half nod by a flight attendant way past her prime.
When a pair didn't materialize even fifteen minutes later,
Manasa gave up and flipped through a copy of *The Hindu*
that was stuffed in a pouch by the window. She stopped at
the obituaries, plumbing one notice after another for details
on the cause of death. One, especially, caught her eye:

*Kanthamani Ramaswamy, 69 years, Retired Joint Secre-
tary Education Tamil Nadu passed away on Oct. 15 in
Chennai after a short illness. Greatly missed by his wife,
son, daughter-in-law, and grandchildren.*

Manasa smiled. The obituary made very little sense. First,
the idea of a short illness, a non-incapacitating disease, a

sickness that didn't just bring your life to a screeching halt
but also impinged upon the dreams and ambitions of your
family, was unfathomable. This must have been a last-
minute attempt made by the person who sent in the obituary to feel good about Ramaswamy's wretched life. Perhaps
the tribute was written in a hurry, before friends and family
filed in to condole and commiserate. To Manasa, short ill-
nesses didn't exist—she wasn't living in a world of benign
fevers and colds anymore. Her existence was dictated by
severe paraplegia—not her own but her father-in-law's.
The way it had sent her own life spiraling out of control,
one would think she was the one paralyzed, and in a way
she was, for her father-in-law's condition had become her
own; in her attempt at making sure his life had some movement, hers had come to a standstill.

Sometimes she wished she had a debilitating sickness—at least then she wouldn't have to be son, daughter,
wife, live-in nurse, caretaker, housekeeper, perhaps soon-
to-be-shit-wiper (Manasa had not, not yet, been subjected
to the humiliation of encountering her father-in-law's private parts) rolled into one. The obituary stated that Ramaswamy was greatly missed by his daughter-in-law. This
South Asian notion of filial piety expanding to the in-laws
was the most forced, hypocritical thing about their society.
You were expected to develop feelings for your husband's
parents the day you got married. Perhaps the reason she
enjoyed family sagas on Star Plus so much, despite being an
Oxford-educated former Deloitte consultant, rested purely
on the drama that played out between in-laws.

"What's so funny?" Himal asked earnestly, looking
up from *Secrets*, his preferred reading at the moment.

"Nothing," Manasa said, still laughing. "Just reading
the obituaries."

"How do they infuse you with so much joy?" Himal smiled.

"I enjoy reading them."

"You're morbid," Himal said, resting his head on her shoulder.

"This one's son-in-law is mourning him." She jerked his hand. "They must have been so attached."

"Not here, please," Himal pleaded.

"I'm just asking you to read the obituary, Himal. Why do you think everything I say is so snide?"

Himal read the paper quietly.

"I wonder if Kumaramangalam's son-in-law washed, clothed, and fed his father-in-law," Manasa said. "If he stopped going to work because his wife's high-profile hedge-fund career couldn't afford to be derailed."

"He can hear, Manasa. At least wait until he's out of earshot."

"No, he can't," Manasa said.

"How do you know?"

"Should I tell you how? Because he falls asleep within exactly three minutes of taking his pills. He wakes up exactly six hours later, and the first thing he does is say something negative about the way he's been taken care of. But how would you know that, Himal? You haven't quit your job to look after him."

"Manasa, he's an unwell widower."

"Yes, and looking after my paraplegic father-in-law is my sole responsibility. I am no different from Kaali."

"Who's Kaali?"

"The neighbor's servant—the one with the bad lip who's constantly hovering around your family home in Kathmandu."

"Do you know she's had surgery? She looks much better."

"You should marry her, then."

Manasa felt herself get tearful but controlled the urge to weep when two aging flight attendants, apparently competing with each other on who could be more discourteous, served them drinks. The temptation to guzzle everything out of those tiny gin bottles was acute, but she settled for an orange juice. Then, drawing a connection between her father-in-law's drink of choice and the one before her, she felt as though the juice was incomplete unless half a dozen pills supplemented it. She couldn't drink it.

"Why aren't you drinking?" Himal asked.

She didn't answer his question. "I wonder if Bhagwati would've put up with all this, and she got married when she was barely out of high school."

"She and you are different people. I understand you do it for me. I don't think I show my appreciation enough."

Himal was right. He did not show his appreciation enough. The lack of alignment in what he expected his wife to be to his father—everything—and what Manasa initially thought were a daughter-in-law's responsibilities— nothing beyond being polite and charming—could have unraveled any marriage. She had tried to make hers work, although no amount of speaking in a clipped, upper-crust British accent and having a fancy hedge-fund career could erase the boy from Kathmandu, a boy brought up by a mother and a fleet of illiterate nannies over whom he had reigned. Himal might have tried to curb it, but he came from a world in which women were different from men, and remnants of this past were everywhere in his present. It was evident in the get-togethers in which men and women formed separate groups, the former to drink and the latter to whip up accompaniments; in the number of times her husband's family marveled at her Oxford background—a degree that prestigious despite her being a woman!—while casually dismissing Himal's Cambridge one; in the easy reception of her father-in-law's second marriage to Himal's mother because he had as much property in their village in Illam as he did in Kathmandu—the justification was that he needed a second wife to look after all their land in the countryside because there was no way he could concentrate on his political career when he was straddling two places.

The Ghimirey family—that famous Ghimirey family that she had been married into in a ceremony attended by every important person from Sikkim and Nepal, by the clan's own admission the richest and oldest Baahun family of Nepal ("We and the Ranas are about the same; they squandered their wealth, and we built up on ours until we fell out of favor with those Maoists"), claiming among their recent ancestors Gazadar Ghimirey, the astrologer who had predicted the downfall of the monarchy in Nepal fifty years before the media had—wasn't very different in its antiquated beliefs from her driver Nirmal Daaju's family in Gangtok.

The marriage, now six years old, had been a source of vindication for her grandmother. "They even know about Bhagwati," her grandmother had gleefully exclaimed. "They know of what she did to this family, they know of the caste of her husband and yet they want you and only you for their son."

Himal nursed a vodka and Sprite. "I'd like some," Manasa said, and she grabbed the glass from his tray. "What's in it that women can't drink?"

"You're making things awkward, Manasa. What if Bua saw?"

"He won't. He's asleep. Do you think your family was so desperate to get you married to me because they wanted an Oxbridge-educated bride? Let's face it—I am no beauty like Bhagwati."

"Could be," Himal uneasily said.

"But the Ghimireys don't care so much for their wom-enfolk's education. Why should they have chosen me?"

"Well, I wanted an Oxbridge-educated wife. I wanted to marry you more than they wanted me to marry you."

"We know your opinion doesn't matter, Himal. It's the family's that takes precedence. I wonder if I'd have married you had I known it would come with having to be a governess to your father."

"Emasculate me, Manasa. As if you haven't done it before by making fun of me with my cousins."

"Himal, I told them about that foul-smelling dis-charge from your ear. How's that insulting?"

"You took such a personal issue and made it public."

A stewardess threw dinner their way, accosting Manasa with effluvia originating from her armpits.

"That's how bad your ear smells. Worse. You need surgery."

"With Bua around, how's that even possible?"

"You keep forgetting that Bua hardly takes half an hour of your day. That's no reason not to have an operation."

"Wouldn't Bua like some food? Should we wake him up?"

"I've told you, he sleeps six hours, Himal—if only you knew your father better."

•

By the time they were disgorged into the shiny new T-3 in Delhi, Manasa had promised herself she'd never fly Air India again. Bua, still hurt by his request for whiskey being rebuffed by a rude flight attendant, had dictated a long letter of complaint to the CEO, which Manasa, being the dutiful Ghimirey daughter-in-law that she was, meticulously jotted down. Bua was firm that she mention all his past titles at the end of the letter. That took more than half the page.

Once her father-in-law had grasped from *Namaskaar*, the in-flight magazine, that Air India was a government-owned airline, he decided that he'd have to address the letter to the president of India. Then good sense prevailed. He complained that the president wasn't going to read his letter, so he tried flushing it down the commode when brushing his teeth, which clogged the toilet. A flight attendant used the bathroom after Bua and Manasa returned to their seats and informed all her co-workers who the perpetrator of the overflow was. Each and every attendant then glared at them as she passed.

Bua snarled that the women's treatment of him would probably change if they knew he was a former home minister of Nepal, to which Manasa didn't have the heart to reply that these air hostesses, long inured to the possibility of getting fired from their cushy government jobs, would probably not care if he was the king of the damn country. Nepal meant little to India—an indigestible piece of information for those in Himal's family, who were of the opinion that their antagonism toward the *dhotis* of India had to be reciprocated somehow. Her in-laws failed to see that India was too busy dealing with real problems, such as China and Pakistan, to worry about its landlocked neighbor. For the better part of the two hours after he woke up, Manasa patiently listened to Bua's rant about the colorful Nepali hat on his head nettling the flight attendants while Himal nervously read *The Hindu.*

"Should I talk to them about it?" Manasa finally offered.

"No, you don't," Bua replied. "I will. What will they think of me? An invalid who needs a woman to speak for him."

"I think it'll be easier if a woman approaches women."

But Bua was adamant about not being defended by a female.

This was where her husband came from. A family clinging to its past because its present had become unpalatable. The son of a man self-exiled from his country under the pretext of his paralysis, when Maoists and extortion made up the bitter reality. A lineage tainted with accomplishment, making mediocrity an unacceptable facet of life among its men. A family whose sons and sons-in-law aimed to rule and conquer while the daughters and daughters-in-law supported them, pushed them, worked hard for them. A family in which women were encouraged to increase their marriageability by shrinking their educational and professional aspirations. Her husband's voice, hollow and quivering, was his father's voice, the family's voice. And this family she had now become a part of, where her Oxford degree was an awe-inspiring pink lipstick—shocking and something that should adorn no woman in the great dynasty—in which the pearls that bejeweled her neck were more important than the diplomas on her wall, in which her opinions mattered only until the opinion of an older male took over. Her grand-mother would have obliterated them—the old lady would have eviscerated everyone in this family into which she had so proudly married her granddaughter.

Manasa was temporarily parting ways with the fam-ily to see this grandmother. Himal and Bua would fly to Kathmandu from Delhi while she took a domestic flight to Bagdogra. At least fleetingly she wouldn't be a factotum to a father who wasn't her own, a companion to a husband who wasn't of her choosing, and a rebel in a family she had on so many occasions resisted butting heads with. After promising her father-in-law that she wouldn't talk to the Air India people about how disre-spectfully he had been treated—as if anyone would take his grievance to heart and make amends—Manasa bade good-bye to Bua and Himal, both men she had married.

Dirty Sheet and Burberry Coat

Manasa's journey from Bagdogra to Gangtok culminated with a taxi screeching into the new, much rhapsodized gravel driveway of her grandmother's house and the driver obdurately refusing to remove her suitcases from the trunk. Prasanti's making a dash for the gate to attend to what Manasa was sure was a nonexistent errand the moment the Maruti 800—its every door dented—turned into the compound didn't help soothe Manasa's throbbing temples.

The driver declared he was a driver and not a coolie, Prasanti didn't reply to Manasa's repeated calls, and Aamaa surveyed the scene from the terrace, constantly spitting out orange pips onto the driveway, no doubt amused by her granddaughter's helplessness.

"Where did Prasanti disappear to?" Manasa asked, getting out of the car. "I saw her run away. She's still misbehaving, it seems."

"I sent her to get something," Chitralekha said. "She'll be back in a few minutes."

"And who will help me with my luggage?" Manasa heaved out with great difficulty three suitcases of varying sizes from the trunk while the driver made continual attempts at adjusting a wayward lock of hair that repeatedly fell to his forehead.

"Can you give me some money for tea, madam?" the driver said to Manasa, his attention still on the rogue strand and his eyes on the side-view mirror.

"No money for tea. First think of the number of jolts you gave me. Those bumps just didn't stop."

"What can we do if the roads are bad, madam?" the driver asked.

"Drive more carefully. How many times did I ask you to slow down?"

"Give him twenty *rupiya*!" Chitralekha shouted. "Let him have a cup of tea. I'd ask him to stay for coffee, but Prasanti isn't here."

The driver, now out of the car, gave a grateful look to Chitralekha.

"Let the bags be," Manasa said to the driver, who hadn't made for her luggage in the first place. "You don't help with the bags because you're such a big, important man. No, Aamaa, he doesn't get a *rupiya*. You're exactly the reason these people have such high expectations of us. First of all, they overcharge us. Who charges seventeen hundred rupees from Bagdogra to Gangtok? They think we are all fools."

"But, madam, the airport middlemen keep seven hundred rupees."

"Good, you have a thousand, then. Okay, now, go."

"Such a rich woman's granddaughter being so stingy," the driver muttered under his breath. He closed the trunk with all his might, which made the tiny car shudder, then got into the cab and drove away.

"Bring your luggage up to your old room," Chitralekha said.

"I don't want to sleep there," Manasa replied belligerently. "I am not carrying three suitcases up those stairs. I am sleeping in the guest room."

An argument was guaranteed when Manasa requested that Chitralekha come downstairs, and Manasa wasn't in a mood to quarrel the moment she set foot in the house. She employed reason.

"I am jet-lagged," she said. "I want to lie down as we talk. There's not enough sun to stay outside on the terrace. Come to the room."

"No, no, it's warm here. Come up. I have some oranges."

"Can't you bring the oranges down? And can't you wait at least until November before eating them? Are they even sweet?"

"The sun is good for my bones. Just come up."

"Your bones don't need to be any better than they are at eight-three." Manasa's forehead pleated into a frown. "I want to lie down."

"I have a mattress up here," Chitralekha said, and then improvised, "for you."

Manasa bore her grandmother's lie with gritted teeth and said, before huffing in, "Not coming to the terrace. I have flown all the way from London, and we've begun fighting even before I am inside the house."

The house hadn't changed much since she was there six months before. The four red sofas in the sitting room were thirty-five years old—about as old as Manasa. The carpets covering the sofas, a Himalayan decorative idiosyncrasy that Manasa never quite understood, were snow-lion-patterned and shapeless. A map of Sikkim before it became a part of India adorned one wall. A map of India before Sikkim became a part of it was on another.

Manasa had asked her grandmother to wash the sheets in the guest room for her arrival, but, conscious of Chitralekha's combined disregard for hygiene and for suggestions from others, Manasa was certain that the only difference between the current sheet and the one she had slept on during her last visit was an increase in the number of critters it accommodated.

That was the problem with her grandmother—she had never been big on beauty and décor, which Manasa could forgive as long as hygiene, too, wasn't somehow withdrawn from her list of priorities. The one building Aamaa lavished architects, designers, and redesigns on was not the house where she lived but the factory in Kalimpong where she claimed to have started her career as a businesswoman. Aamaa wasn't going to do anything about her home. When Agastaya once teased his grandmother about being the least house-proud woman he knew, the old woman had casually remarked that she could have wasted her time beautifying the house while pushing the family to penury or invested her efforts making good money, the fruits of which her grandchildren enjoyed blowing on their exorbitant education. Agastaya had never questioned his grandmother's lack of aesthetic expertise since then.

Writhing at the animal patterns on the dusty brown sheet, Manasa took out her phone from her purse, hoping there would be no message from her husband. There wasn't. She looked further.

Yes, there, in a folder marked SAVED IMAGES on her phone, was a photo from April. In it, she smiled through her buckteeth, sitting on the same bed. The same sheet shrouded the bed. Were it some other house, Manasa would have understood that the sheet had been washed between then and now, but this was her grandmother's home, where Aamaa lived with an indulged servant whose workload rivaled a queen's. Manasa wasn't going to sleep on the sheet. An arthropod, almost frozen with fear, dashed to safety when she dusted the bed.

"Aamaa!" Manasa shouted, her voice loud enough to travel to the terrace. "Why is the sheet dirty?"

Chitralekha didn't answer.

"Aamaa, I know you can hear me. Why is it dirty?"

"It's not dirty. Prasanti washed it last week."

"Sure, your pet has begun washing sheets, too?" Manasa stripped the bed. "I am glad she does more than paint her nails all day. This sheet is old and revolting."

"It isn't old. We bought it three months ago for your arrival."

"How can you lie? I took a picture on the bed when I was here last. It's on my phone. These stupid horse patterns on the sheet are the same."

"Stop playing tricks on me. Show me the picture."

Manasa stormed up the staircase, registering that the action as well as the stairs were a poor imitation of what she saw on Star Plus family soaps.

"Here." She shoved her BlackBerry in front of Aamaa's face. "Look at it."

"Well, at least you're upstairs." Chitralekha smiled. "At least I didn't have to force my dying feet down the stairs."

"So, you didn't want to see the picture at all? It was just a ruse to get me up here?"

"Come sit." Chitralekha pointed to a stool. "Eat an orange."

"I don't feel like eating. First get the room in order."

"Wait for Prasanti to come, and please treat her well. Where's *jwaai*?"

"He's in Kathmandu with your other son-in-law—the one who's a hundred and fifty years old. I told them not to come. Matter finished. No more questions."

Chitralekha meticulously removed the fiber from an orange slice and handed it to her granddaughter.

"Here, eat this," she said.

"You're so manipulative. I don't want a disgusting October orange."

"I shouldn't have been. I am sure we'd have come to enjoy these riches had I not been manipulative."

"What's the point of all these riches when you make your grandchildren sleep on dirty sheets? Where's Prasanti?"

"On my head." Chitralekha let out a cackle.

"No, where is she? I'm serious. I'm going to make that one work today."

"She's pregnant." Chitralekha giggled hysterically.

"Okay, where is she?"

"She's dead." Chitralekha laughed so hard that she spat out her half-eaten slice of orange.

"I'm happy you're having so much fun. Come downstairs if you want to talk to me."

Manasa had to admit that the bond she shared with Chitralekha had evolved differently over the years from her grandmother's relationship with the other siblings. After Bhagwati ran off with a Damaai, a Bhutanese refugee whose economic instability perfectly complemented his low caste, the pressure to have an arranged marriage with a Brahmin—an Upadhyay, a Category One Baahun, at that—fell on Manasa. When a wealthy Kathmandu family asked for her hand for their Cambridge-educated son in London, Manasa dutifully complied.

She had saved her family, rescued it from the swamp that her sister's elopement had dragged it into, and yet her grandmother had looked upon this martyrdom as if it was simply a responsibility Manasa was expected to fulfill. Far from giving credit, Chitralekha continued insinuating that Manasa could have dissuaded Bhagwati from running away after all.

In no time, Manasa's marital responsibilities had increased, and the realization hit her—as she wiped off for the fifth time in twenty minutes a stream of *daal* coming down Bua's face—that she was nothing more than a glorified caretaker of her corroding father-in-law. Had Aamaa not taken it upon herself to search for her a suitable groom from a suitable caste, of a suitable class and belonging to a suitable region, Manasa's life wouldn't have come down to this. In between giving up her career and looking after her father-in-law, Manasa had decided that every wrinkle in her cheeks and every line on her forehead was a direct result of Aamaa. And, in words and actions, the granddaughter didn't let go of a single opportunity to remind her grandmother of that.

"I have gossip!" Aamaa shouted from behind her. "It will make you laugh harder than I did when I saw your silly face."

"Gossip with Prasanti—your only grandchild," Manasa answered, wishing, for the first time, that Himal were here; it would have been a lot easier to drum some sense into Aamaa's head had he been around.

"Yes, do what you did during that *Dashain*," Chitralekha said in resignation. "Run away from everything. Sulk. Cry. Make my birthday a rotten affair."

Chitralekha had a point. Manasa had made a total nuisance of herself the first festival after her marriage. Her husband to this day brought up her inconsiderate behavior toward her grandmother when he needed ammunition in an argument that was hopelessly going her way. When Himal was in Gangtok, Chitralekha was forced to morph into a docile deer and become cordial, even agreeable. Twisted as this reverence for one's son-in-law and grandson-in-law (it, of course, didn't extend to the daughters-in-law) in their community was, it had worked in Manasa's favor on her first visit home as a married woman.

Part of Chitralekha's metamorphosis could be attributed to her desperate desire to be seen as classy by someone from a clan as old as her son-in-law's. Without Himal's presence, it would be impossible to repeat what Manasa had done that *Dashain*. On the day of *Tika*—the holiest of holy days, which her grandmother had been eagerly looking forward to because it was the first *Dashain* during which she'd apply on her beloved grandson-in-law's forehead grains of uncooked rice blended with a yogurt-based pink paste, blessing him and being blessed in return—Manasa proudly declared to Chitralekha that she was on her period.

"So, you can't participate in any of the functions," Chitralekha had sadly said. "No *tika* for you, and it's your first *Dashain* after marriage."

"No, you will put *tika* on me," Manasa said. "I am married into a different family now. No longer a Neupaney."

"But the period—no, I can't do that. You're impure."

Her ancestors banished their suffering women to the cowsheds so they wouldn't desecrate the house with their vile touch. A version—less draconian but seemingly more rigid, given the day and age—of this practice still existed in her grandmother's house, with the "sick" woman keeping to circumscribed areas, which excluded the kitchen and the altar. Supporters of the quasi-quarantine claimed that abstaining from kitchen duties, from religious rites, and from life itself was practiced to allow the women to rest, to recuperate. As teenagers, Manasa and Bhagwati had whined about the rules they were forced to adhere to during their periods. Sitting separately from everyone at dinner was humiliating—as though the cramps were not painful enough.

"In my new family, a woman having her menses is considered even purer than a woman who's not," Manasa lied. "How often have I told you that I am especially hygienic when I am down? My family thinks the same way."

In this lack of purity and absence of godliness lay the answer to inflicting torture on her grandmother.

"No, that's your family," Aamaa said. "This is mine. I'll only offer *tika* to *jwaai*."

This was the best part. Aamaa wouldn't forgo an opportunity to apply *tika* on Himal.

"Who says you'll put *tika* on him?" Manasa asked. "Who says you get to do that? You either apply *tika* on both of us or on neither of us."

"I understand you live abroad, but not during *Tika*, please," Chitralekha pleaded. "It's my first time offering *tika* to a son-in-law. I may not even be alive next year."

"Not your son-in-law but your grandson-in-law." Manasa felt doubly evil for pointing out the difference in relationship.

"It's the same—all of you are my children as well as grandchildren," Chitralekha had feebly said.

But Manasa was unrelenting. She threatened she would slap her husband for no reason in full view of everybody if Chitralekha didn't concede. Her grandmother, horrified as she may have been about having her beliefs toyed with and her festival desanctified, was forced to give in. The day Manasa left, she disclosed to Chitralekha that she had lied to her about the period.

"It was just to give you a heart attack, to cause you the pain that you caused us girls when we were growing up," Manasa said. "Now you know how we felt."

Yes, she had gone far, and she felt guilty about having done what she did to a barely educated old woman, more so when she saw the repulsion on Himal's face as she narrated her victorious story to him on their way home. She had forced her grandmother, so set in her ways, to do what she had always been opposed to. It was a great triumph—one that she hoped to repeat but couldn't because of Himal's absence. When she had no person from whom to mask her monstrosity, Aamaa was a tough opponent.

"See? I walked downstairs," Chitralekha said as she sat on the bed whose sheet had been the object of so much rancor. "My bones feel like they will melt."

"You're so generous—you're Mother Teresa," Manasa said as she unpacked.

"What did you get for me?"

"New sheets," said Manasa.

"Like this one," Chitralekha added, patting the sheet that now lay in a heap at the bottom of the bed. "This is new."

"And you're a good human being."

"I am better than Mother Teresa. At least I don't convert my charitable cases into my religion."

"Is the driver home?" Manasa asked, wiping away the dust that had accumulated in the rickety closet.

"One of the factory staffers has given birth," Chitralekha said. "I think I should send some sweets to her family."

"Good. What a nice way for you to make up for not having bought your grandchildren any when they were growing up."

"So, will *jwaai* not make it to my *Chaurasi*?" Chitralekha said.

"You'd better treat Bhagwati well." Manasa and her grandmother had both become experts at non sequiturs. "She's coming after so long. Not a word about castes. Where are the clean sheets? Is there anything in the house that's not this filthy?"

"Use the ones you brought for me." Chitralekha laughed. "I am not the only one who lies. No sheets for me? No gift for me? Okay. I hope you brought something for Prasanti."

"Yes, a slap. In fact, I'll give it to her now rather than later for running away when she was supposed to be helping with the luggage. And now I have to clean the closet myself."

"Look at you. You gave no trouble—not even as a teenager," Chitralekha said, somewhat wistfully. "And now you've become a rebel. Marriage has turned you into an adolescent."

•

The original plan was for Agastaya to meet Bhagwati at the Chicago airport and for them to take a flight together to Delhi. This solved many problems. Chicago was almost equidistant from New York and Denver. The

direct-flight tickets from there were surprisingly cheaper
than those from New York; a $150 difference didn't
mean much to Agastaya, but he was positive that Bhagwati wasn't comfortable spending the extra amount. In
addition, the savings were sufficient to deflect Bhagwati's
trip to his city. Her coming to New York would mean
that Agastaya would have to change his entire life. Asking Nicky to spend a few nights at a friend's place would
give rise to a Mount Everest-size problem.

Before long, the reality of spending eighteen hours on
flights to Delhi and then to Bagdogra with a person he
hadn't seen for nearly two decades sank in, and a day prior
to their scheduled departure, Agastaya, using a barely
believable excuse of a work-related detour to Paris, hastily
chalked up for himself a new itinerary. This ensured that
he'd reach Bagdogra just an hour after Bhagwati, upon
which they'd take a taxi to Gangtok together.

Agastaya had talked with Nicky about paying for
Bhagwati's ticket to India. Nicky, as clueless about the
functioning of his boyfriend's family as he was about all
things pragmatic, opined that Bhagwati might find the
offer insulting. After discussing with Manasa the logis-
tics of payment, it was decided that Agastaya would buy
Bhagwati's ticket online and not make a mention of
the money. A few days after the purchase, he received a
check in the mail from Bhagwati for $870.36, the receipt
of which he never acknowledged to his sister and which
he didn't cash. Manasa later disclosed that Bhagwati had
forced her to divulge the amount Agastaya had spent on
her ticket. Bhagwati hadn't yet brought up the issue of
the check that didn't get cashed.

Agastaya had last seen Bhagwati eighteen years back.
He should have met up with her at least a few times since

she and the other Bhutanese refugees had been relocated to America two years before, but life had always intervened. When life came with a package called Nicky, it complicated meetings and reunions. Bhagwati had eloped at nineteen, and a fifteen-year-old Agastaya—acrimonious about his adolescence becoming even more tangled, now that Aamaa had one fewer person on whom to lavish her idea of affection/authority—decided he would have nothing to do with his sister for the rest of his life. Aamaa's infuriation at his sister's running away manifested itself in strange ways: phone calls to the grandchildren from the opposite sex found themselves mysteriously interrupted with coughs on the extension, a permanent embargo was placed on Bollywood movies, and tirades against lower castes increased in frequency as well as vehemence. Agastaya's teenage self understood his sister's fleeing as a betrayal of the family, a deed that changed everything in his life. He promised he'd never forgive Bhagwati.

How different a teenager's understanding of issues is from an adult's. How quick and callous he had been to judge his sister. How easy it was to forgive her in light of the relationship of which he was now a part. The idea that an entire family should be so united in the denouncement of Bhagwati's action—a scandal over one of its members being married to an untouchable—made him wonder just how much less palatable the notion of the son of the family putting off marriage plans with his *boyfriend* would be.

He had tried to make amends with his sister, but long-distance phone calls and MSN Messenger chats couldn't fairly convey the sentiments behind these apologies. Call-waiting beeps and smiley faces trivialized his repeated expressions of contrition, so much so that he was afraid that Bhagwati had begun doubting the sincerity behind them. Perhaps she suspected that he, too, had indiscretions now. Or maybe she just didn't care—this was Bhagwati, after all. Only a certain kind of person, unmoored by repercussion, would stand up to a grandmother, a family, and a community like theirs.

He often wondered how Bhagwati looked upon her natal family, whether she took responsibility for having caused all those years of irreversible pain. Did she feel remorseful? Was it possible to focus on the bigger picture and dismiss other matters as inconsequential? Is that what Bhagwati had done to make life work for her? Could he do that? Would compartmentalizing his two lives—one with his family and the other with Nicky—continue uneasily working and work forever?

How was he to greet the older sister he hadn't seen in almost two decades? Hugging was too Western, a handshake too forced. They'd just awkwardly stare at each other and smile. That's what all his family members did. No one touched—just as no one shared bad news. That was for other families. His only cared about successes and victories and joys. Sorrows, you dealt with yourself. Touching, you kept to yourself.

He was determined that things would be different with Bhagwati this time around. He'd ask her questions and try to understand her decision—he owed at least that to her. He had missed out on eighteen years, eighteen long years, and he would catch up. He wanted to know about the camps, about her slide from the uppermost to the lowermost caste. She had lived through a lot, his sister, and he may not have been there when the actual living was taking place, but he hoped to make up for it now.

Agastaya removed his coat because Bagdogra was hot even in October. He should have called Nicky to let him know that he was almost home, but instead he texted "wish me luck with the sister. hope it's not awkward." A response arrived in a few minutes: "give her my kisses." Agastaya always read and reread between the lines of all Nicky's messages. He hoped this one wouldn't have a qualifier similar to "if I exist for her, that is." When no such viciousness came, he decided that Nicky had probably satisfied his malice quotient for the week.

They were bound to be ill-at-ease with each other. When Bhagwati headed toward him, looking at least a decade younger than her thirty-seven years—her skin radiant, her gait energetic, eyes luminous, and her hair in a bun with not a strand out of place—it was difficult to connect this person with the pitiful woman who had been the subject of his ruminations for much of his flight. She looked cherubic. He didn't remember his sister being so youthful, but you didn't look for signs of aging in a nineteen-year-old when you were fifteen.

"Hi," Bhagwati said, bridging eighteen years with a simple word. "You've lost more hair than your Facebook pictures depict."

"And you're prettier than your profile picture."

"It feels like we're on a blind date, does it not?"

They proceeded to the taxi stand, Agastaya mindful of his sister's gaze on him. He suddenly became conscious of the Burberry coat he was holding. Would Bhagwati, who had spent half her life at a camp, even if she looked as if she had luxuriated in a spa for the last eighteen years, know of the brand and how expensive his coat was? He was nervous she'd get offended; she could have put the money to far better use.

"How do you like my coat?" he blurted, and then he silently berated himself. He was such an idiot at times.

"It's nice," Bhagwati said. "Burberry?"

"How do you know?" Agastaya asked, curious.

"Your sister's worked retail since moving to America," Bhagwati nonchalantly said. "Retail and restaurants— I'm quite an expert. I don't think the Americans themselves know of as many styles of eggs as I do."

She spoke more in English than in Nepali, as she did on the phone, but her accent was distinctly un-American. Possibly a lack of assimilation. "Macy's, right?" He jogged his memory.

"No, Nordstrom's, and I couldn't deal with having to show my teeth all day," Bhagwati said, not returning the smile of the obsequious Hyundai Santro driver who rushed to help with their luggage.

Her bags didn't look very different from his. In fact, she looked richer than he did, so what if his god-forsaken coat probably cost more than all her clothes in all her bags? That was the beauty of America: in a strange way, it brought everyone to the same level. Rich or poor—with the occasional exception— everyone looked the same. A millionaire in India would stand out in a crowd even if he tried fitting in—sort of the way they, an America-returned doc-tor and an America-returned refugee, did right now. In America, with its jeans-and-T-shirt egalitarianism, everyone was uniform.

"How's Venaju?" he asked about his brother-in-law, whom he had never met and with whom he hadn't even had a phone conversation.

"Fine. Started a new job." Short answers were Bhagwati's forte when queries involved her husband.

Agastaya wanted to ask where but thought it impolite. "And the children?"

"Totally American. Complain about the smell when I stew *gundruk*. Don't reply when spoken to in Nepali. It infuriates their father."

She had already told him on several occasions about the imperceptible absorption of her children by America.

Agastaya started to suggest that they grab a drink before they went up the hills. Then he contained his proposal because he didn't know if Bhagwati drank. How little he knew of his sister! Two years of unfailingly talking to her on the phone at least once a week should have increased their comfort level, but it didn't. Was it because they always made efforts to conceal certain aspects of their lives and the other was respectful of that? Was that why their talks veered nowhere beyond gossiping about others in their family? Agastaya, just moments before so assertive to himself about getting Bhagwati to talk of matters outside the superficial, hadn't taken into account that awkward silences would compound now that they were not talking on the phone.

"How nervous are you about seeing everyone?" he asked, deliberately ambling into the familiar.

"I don't know. I can't help thinking this trip is a big mistake."

"Why?" At least this would keep them going until the pleasures of vomiting, triggered by vertiginous roads, kept his mouth busy once they left the plains.

"What's my last name?"

"Neupaney," he said without thinking or understanding where she was going with the question.

"No, after my marriage."

"Damaai," he said.

He hadn't known she had appended her husband's last name to her maiden name until she explicitly told him to book her ticket under *Bhagwati Neupaney Damaai*—"devoid of hyphen," she had warned several times.

"Yes, I am Bhagwati Neupaney Damaai."

"Uh." He didn't know what to say.

"And what are we going to?"

"Aamaa's *Chaurasi*."

"Which is, let's face it, a religious function."

"So?"

"A Damaai in the Neupaney house for a religious function—ooooh, the horror."

"Do you think that will create problems?"

"It's Aamaa, you know. Aamaa and a group of pundits. They will have a field day with a Damaai in their house."

"But you and Aamaa have rekindled your love story."

"If talking about the weather and discussing Prasanti is romance."

"At least there's talk—that's progress."

"There's a lot of unresolved anger from her side—I'll tell you. She will not let go of the Damaai issue. It's been simmering for a long time."

"You can always argue that you weren't born one."

"It will make for compelling argument."

"You don't speak like a person who works retail at all."

"Tell that to all the hiring Americans. Fools—they look at my face and assume I can't speak."

The dusty plains of Siliguri gradually gave way to hills with serpentine roads. Lighter-skinned people—their eyes and frames tinier—replaced their darker cousins, and the air became colder as they climbed higher. A drink would have helped alleviate his dizziness, but Agastaya popped a Tylenol, which invited a comment about his Americanization from Bhagwati. How long had it been since he was last in Gangtok? Six years? Almost seven years. As a child, he had always added half an hour to every journey between Gangtok and Kalimpong, much to the annoyance of his siblings because he needed to throw up at regular intervals. That's what these winding roads did to him—right now, he could sense the hills moving while the car felt stationary.

Past Chitrey, where monkeys plucked ticks off one another's backsides alongside copulating dogs, a big group of young women, dressed in their traditional *gunyu-cholo* and shouting anti-West Bengal slogans, encircled their car.

"We are the *Gorkha Jana-shakti Morcha*," one of them said. "And we recommend that everyone in Gorkhaland wear traditional clothes during *Dashain* and *Tihaar*."

"We are from Sikkim," Agastaya gently said.

"You're in a West Bengal car," the woman replied.

"It's a taxi," Agastaya countered.

"You people from Sikkim have so much money," said the woman's friend as she signaled the group to move to another car. "You should be traveling in your own cars."

"The Gorkhaland movement is gaining traction," Agastaya said, in Nepali.

On hearing the G-word, the driver quickly added, "Yes, sir, the chief minister of Sikkim has given his support to the revolution, as have several big people."

"A lot of men are wearing *daura-suruwal*," Agastaya said, unnerved by the absence of men in Western clothes.

"Yes, sir, it is mandatory to wear it today. Even I am wearing the *daura* but not the pants."

Agastaya hadn't seen the man's top before—the jacket must have hidden it. He only now noticed that the driver even had on a black Nepali hat whose front was adorned with two miniature knives.

"It must be uncomfortable," Agastaya said.

"A little discomfort for Gorkhaland, sir," the driver replied. "Moktan will make it happen."

"Just as the leaders before him did," Agastaya said with an undercurrent of sarcasm. "Forcing people to wear traditional outfits isn't the way to go."

"I had some Nepali woman stitch a set of *daura-suruwals* for my sons," Bhagwati said. "They haven't taken to the costume. They say it makes them stand out. I told them to wear them for Halloween."

"Do you love both of them equally?"

"Yes," Bhagwati said. Then with some uncertainty she added, "Yes, I think so."

"Your almost-American children."

Bhagwati repeated the sentence with the requisite change in pronoun.

For childhood memories' sake, they got out at Rangpo, on the border between West Bengal and Sikkim, to eat *momos* at Mid-Point Restaurant.

"I wonder what it will be like," Agastaya said. He detected a pattern—where silence became uncomfortable, it was always wise to go back to the *Chaurasi*.

"What do you mean?"

"You know, all of us—except Ruthwa—together after this long."

"And the best part is, none of the spouses will be there," Bhagwati said. "We can be ourselves, I hope."

"Yes, Manasa says her husband won't be there."

"It was a last-minute decision, wasn't it?"

"Yes, there's more trouble there than we think," Agastaya said.

"What do you think will happen?"

"She's headstrong."

"What, exactly, is wrong with him again?" Bhagwati asked.

"Apparently, he tries too hard." Agastaya gave her a quizzical look. They both shook their heads and laughed. "It's not because he's abusive or a cheater. It's because he tries too hard."

"There may be other reasons."

"It's not because he's selfish and neglects her," he said in between peals of laughter. "It's because he tries too hard."

"Oh, shh," Bhagwati said.

Her convulsions egged him on. "Not because of caste or money problems . . ." Then he stopped. "Sorry," he said.

"That's fine—we don't have money problems. And Ram's caste is now my caste, so it's something I have to live with. If that prohibits me from taking part in the *Chaurasi,* so be it."

"I am sure they won't be that discriminatory."

"They will."

"And you say you have no money problems. How do you expect me to believe that? I know Venaju hasn't had a proper job in a long time, and I know you don't make enough. You should be able to get a well-paid job. At least, unlike most other refugees, you can speak English."

"I doubt that many in America think that."

"You speak better than most immigrants."

"You think so, but I still have a difficult time understanding the accent. It takes me five seconds to get what you'd comprehend in two."

They polished off the dumplings before them while swatting flies away.

"You'd think there'd be no flies in October in Sikkim," Agastaya said.

"You forget you're in Rangpo," Bhagwati said offhandedly. "The *momos* aren't as good as I remember them."

Agastaya had an epiphany. "Why don't you start one?"

"Start what?"

"A dumpling business in Boulder." He was excited. "Think of it."

"I don't have Aamaa's business acumen or your intelligence."

"You don't need any intelligence for a *momo* stall. And the acumen, you will pick up. I think we all have some business sense ingrained in us."

"It's too much of a hassle." Bhagwati sighed. "There's just so much work. And with the children, the absence of capital, and everything else, it's difficult."

"Capital can be raised. We others could be silent partners."

"And then I become indebted to you forever?"

"You don't have to be—it's an investment." Agastaya touched her arm to wipe the spot of spit that had projected from his mouth and landed there. "You have the papers. All you have to do is come up with the capital. Maybe you could sell something to CU Boulder students. Think of the kind of lines that would set off."

"Should we take *momos* for the others?" Bhagwati said.

"Yes, let's."

Agastaya asked the shopkeeper to pack ten plates of
momos. After a quick argument about who would pay—
Bhagwati wouldn't allow him to foot the entire bill, so
they split it—they exited Mid-Point for the last leg of
their journey.

•

Bhagwati was at first dismissive of Agastaya's suggestion
and thought of it with the lack of seriousness she devoted
to most of her younger brother's ideas. Agastaya, whom
success had never eluded, was quick to get excited about
everything without thinking it through. Just a couple
of weeks before, he had called her about the profit mar-
gins gas stations yielded. Experience had played havoc
with Bhagwati's optimism. Still, she knew that not to be
animated about Agastaya's grandiose plans was to invite
scorn and derision, so she played along until his enthusiasm fizzled and some other business plans caught his
attention.

But a dumpling stall—not a proper restaurant—
definitely made more sense than other ideas. Preparing
momos was a labor-intensive process, so perhaps she could
do without the huge capital. The overhead costs would
be negligible because she and Ram would do all the work
in their kitchen. Ram would knead the dough, she'd roll
out the wrappings, he would stuff the wrappings with
meat or cabbage, and she'd steam the dumplings. The
boys would help, too. She wondered if she could use one
of the credit cards to establish capital. With all their cards
close to maxing out, that could be impossible. Because
she had no job to go back to, she could maybe take
risks and experiment a little. For the first time in years,

she felt somewhat optimistic. Weary as she was of Agastaya's fleeting fervor, she had to admit, he had outdone himself this time.

"More and more buildings!" Agastaya exclaimed as they approached Singtam.

"Probably more landslides, too," Bhagwati said.

The driver once again tried sharing with them stories of political goings-on. "And they thought Congress would win, but, no, no one can beat Subba. Subba is a tiger, a lion."

"A benevolent dictator," Agastaya said to Bhagwati in English. "He's all-powerful."

The driver asked them which family in Gangtok they came from. Both, preferring obscurity, were reluctant to disclose their grandmother's identity. Having this man know of their family would require them to censor themselves, so they rebuffed most of his attempts at talk and spoke to each other in English.

"Ah, remember how these hairpin curves gave you motion sickness?" Bhagwati remarked after an especially treacherous bend. "You were such a vomiter."

"I still am," Agastaya said.

"And look how brown the Teesta looks," Bhagwati remarked. "October and still so murky."

"See? That's what I mean when I say you have good English. You use such surprisingly good words."

"You mean 'vomiter?'" Bhagwati asked.

"No, 'hairpin.' 'Murky' to describe the river. Those are words even I wouldn't use—so apt and expressive. I'd have probably used 'muddy.'"

"Whatever. If only I didn't have to strain my ears to understand the Americans, my life would be so much easier."

"Perhaps if you had watched *Small Wonder* as a child, you'd have a better understanding of accents."

"Whatever again. Those TV shows were dubbed in Hindi."

Brother and sister marveled at how much they remembered and how much they had pushed to the dark recesses of their brains.

"What do you think the highlight of this trip will be?" Agastaya asked.

"The fact that I'm going to my own house after eighteen years?" Bhagwati answered unsurely.

"Think of it. All of us—well, the three of us—together after so long. We have all become different people."

"I am a little nervous about the tension between Manasa and Aamaa. I want to see what it looks like when someone stands up to Aamaa. Prasanti told me on the phone that it was a sight."

"Yes, she exaggerates a lot," Agastaya said. "Better not believe it."

"I'm sure not everything she says is exaggerated. Marriage has made Manasa the gutsiest person in the world."

Agastaya claimed he felt much better after the *momos*.

"The trees outside aren't running anymore," he said. "You'd think with age, it'd get better, but it seems to only worsen. Why am I the only one of us who gets motion sickness? I seem to have gotten the bad hair, the bad skin, and the vomiting gene."

"And the money-making ability," Bhagwati countered.

"No, that's Manasa."

"You and Manasa."

"More like her husband now," Agastaya offered. "Her marriage seems to be the one with the most compromises."

This was where Bhagwati would have to bring it up.

"Not all marriages are like that," she said. "Sometimes they bring out the best in you. Haven't you thought of marriage at all? Isn't it time?"

"Not for me," Agastaya said. "No children, no marriage. I hope I don't have to deal with too many marriage questions once I get home."

"Why are you so against it?"

"Have you seen a happy marriage?"

"Yes, mine," Bhagwati said.

"That's why you talk so much about it. Are you sure it's entirely happy?"

That put a stop to what Bhagwati hoped would progress into marriage chat.

Years after she had eloped, years after beginning life at the camps in Khudunabari, years after her first son was born, years after her second one was born, about half a year after moving to America, Bhagwati had reopened lines of communication with her grandmother. She had tried making up in the past—when she phoned from Phuntsholing, her call had been hung up on, once by Agastaya and on another occasion by Aamaa herself. The desire to correspond with her family had dwindled greatly after she was moved into the camps. She was stupid about not wanting Aamaa's help—so many wrinkles would have been ironed out, so much of the limbo that was to characterize their stateless existence avoided.

With moving to America, and life seemingly prosperous, a new kind of confidence had sprouted in Bhagwati. Now that she was in the golden land, her grandmother wouldn't question if any of her calls were motivated by financial difficulties. So, one spring day, sixteen years after being dead to her grandmother, Bhagwati took matters into her own hands. Facebook and its intrusive self had already helped heal her relationship with her siblings. Aamaa was the only person with whom things had yet to be mended, and Bhagwati would feel so much more at peace with herself if the repairing of this relationship—the most fractured of them all—happened before her octogenarian grandmother inevitably lost control of her faculties. The encouragement coming from Agastaya trumped the repeated discouragement from Manasa, so Bhagwati called home.

Aamaa picked up.

"Hello, it is Bhagwati," she said, not at all nervous for a person who was greeting another whose life she had ruined.

Silence.

"Aamaa, I am in America," she said. "We have to talk. How long will we continue this way?"

Silence.

At least Aamaa hadn't disconnected the line.

"You have two great-grandsons. I am the only one among all your grandchildren who has given you great-grandchildren."

To this Chitralekha calmly answered: "Those low-caste Damaai grandchildren? I don't need them."

"Say of them what you will, but they are your blood," Bhagwati said.

"Polluted blood."

"How long has it been?"

"It doesn't matter," Chitralekha said. "The damage has already been done."

"And it can never be repaired?"

"No, it can't. So, why did you call? Do you need money?"

"I am in America. The government takes very good care of us here."

"Do they have quotas for Damaais there, too?"

Bhagwati bit her lower lip. "No, we are here as Bhutanese refugees."

"Serves you right for not calling home when in need."

"I did call you, but you hung up. You taught Agastaya to hang up, too."

"Yes, that was before the trouble began."

"It doesn't matter. We are talking now."

"Don't you dream of bringing your half-caste children close to me."

Still, it was a start. Bhagwati recognized that as long as she could endure the stings that came from Aamaa more regularly than pleasantries, reconnecting with her grandmother wasn't as difficult as she'd thought it would be. The digs decreased when Bhagwati said nothing in retaliation. Aamaa thrived on confrontation, but there was no excitement in confronting when her granddaughter accepted every one of her allegations.

Bhagwati tried hard to get her grandmother interested in her children. To an allusion that one of them was just like her in temperament, Chitralekha remarked, "Yes, I don't want to meet another me. One of us is enough for the world." To an anecdote about the younger one chewing on his meat bones more enthusiastically than a dog did, Aamaa quickly added, "So, they eat cows? Oh, I forget they aren't Baahuns." To a reference about their diminishing Nepali skills, Aamaa remarked, "Caste-less, language-less—all the same."

Bhagwati had been castigated enough; eighteen years of isolation was sufficient. She would willingly take this grudging acceptance and the frequent digs about her children. Aamaa wanted her to talk marriage sense into Agastaya, which she was determined to do on this trip. Her grandmother may not have forgiven her, but she had at least started talking to her, and Bhagwati took it upon herself to somehow repay the favor. She was thankful that the anger had waned, even if it showed itself more frequently than she'd have liked. She was grateful her grandmother at least knew that her great-grandchildren existed.

She had told Aamaa that she didn't want to brew any tension by bringing Ram to the *Chaurasi*. When relatives gathered, where *pujas* took place, when God was involved, a non-Brahmin was discriminated against no matter how accommodating the family pretended to be, no matter how liberal it was. What made it doubly hard was that this was *her* family. Aamaa had offered no suggestion to Bhagwati's idea of excluding her husband and children from the celebrations, which in Aamaa-speak (or no-speak) was approval for her granddaughter to leave her family behind in America.

The real reason for Ram not accompanying Bhagwati, though, was financial. They were bankrupt— five-figure-debt-on-credit-cards broke. During their orientation to life in America, the International Organization for Migration had warned them about the vagaries of debt. What had started as a sincere attempt at establishing a credit history, which they built by militantly paying off every last cent of their credit cards by the month's end, quickly graduated into their barely being able make their minimum payments, thus making all their accounts delinquent. Ram had language issues— with understanding and being understood—at every job, and that didn't help smooth their financial troubles.

Rice plants glistened on the terraced farms to her right. The crop hadn't ripened enough for the panicles to turn yellow. To the left, their taxi zipped by familiar messages written on rocks: IF MARRIED, DIVORCE SPEED; BE GENTLE ON MY CURVES; ALWAYS ALERT, ACCIDENTS AVERT. Bhagwati looked at Agastaya, who was forcing himself to sleep so he wouldn't throw up, and wondered what he'd say if he knew that she had been asked not to return to her job or if she disclosed that she had just been fired from the very prestigious position of a dishwasher. "Restaurants and retail" were such great euphemisms for "dishwasher" and "salesgirl."

Ram may have wanted to come. A furtive reunion could have been planned with his still-Bhutanese brothers in Gangtok. His siblings had distanced themselves from any anti-monarchy demonstrations and had been proud, if scared, residents of Bhutan, but when they found out about Ram's move to Denver and then to Boulder, they begged him to figure out a way for them to get out of the country. They were like others in that way—people who assumed that with a quick flight to the West, your troubles stayed behind in the East. The East was poverty. The West, riches. The East was disparity. The West was equality. The East was problems. The West, the solution to these problems.

When they reached the spot for which she was waiting, Bhagwati called out her brother's name. He probably would want to see it, too.

"It's still here," she said.

They both looked out. Yes, the structure stood where Bhagwati remembered it. The rest stop with its pair of cement benches and tin roof was meant to immortalize their parents, whose jeep had lost control after a collision at this bend and fallen into the river some thirty years before. All the passengers were declared dead. No bodies were found.

"Do any emotions come up?" Bhagwati asked.

"No. I don't have any memory of them."

"I hope our children don't forget us the way we've forgotten our parents."

"I was three when they died. You were seven. We should be forgiven for not remembering very much of them."

Agastaya asked why she hadn't brought her children, especially as this could possibly be the only time they'd get to see their aging great-grandmother. Bhagwati replied that they'd wanted to stay behind. Of course, that wasn't the truth. It all boiled down to money.

"It would have been nice to show them off, wouldn't it?" she said.

Their burgeoning Americanization would at least divert the attention from their caste.

"Pretend you're appalled at how American they are." Agastaya laughed. "And secretly gloat."

Bhagwati was worried about her children's rapid Americanization. The IOM people had told her to embrace it, to wish for it because it made life easier, but the rapidity with which her children had forgotten about life at the camps scared her and sometimes made her envy them. She was afraid that they, too, like white children, would move out once they were eighteen and only rarely visit their parents.

Gangtok had grown, expanded vertically and horizontally and recklessly. What Bhagwati remembered as rural was now covered with buildings elbowing one another—shops, hospitals, colleges. The number of new constructions was countered by the number of new cars, all of which whooshed by dangerously close to their taxi. She had left behind a sleepy town and returned to find a place she barely recognized. So much had changed in two decades. She had left when Basnett was in power and was now in an era in which he was totally powerless. Of course, she, too, had changed and grown. She would soon become an American. She was married. She had two children. She had just lost her job as a dishwasher. She had left town a nervous Brahmin and was back here a nervous Damaai.

•

To watch Mount Kanchendzonga weaving its magic on the world was one of Chitralekha's favorite solitary activities. She walked to the rooftop, relishing the slight chill in the air that would grow severe in the next few weeks and saw Manasa observing the mountain, a striped Naga shawl wrapped around her upper body. Her granddaughter looked serene, as though she wasn't the same person who had just yesterday created a ruckus for want of a clean sheet. Chitralekha lit a *beedi* with a match, stretched herself, and let Manasa be. Chitraleka was finally bored because what in the beginning had appeared to be her granddaughter's tranquil face now had transformed into a vapid look, conveying no depth, nothing, Chitralekha coughed and asked Manasa what she was doing.

"Slept all morning. Just woke up. I was jet-lagged," Manasa replied. "The weather is beautiful."

"When will the others be here?"

"Tonight. Be nice to Bhagwati."

"Don't spoil such a beautiful day by picking a fight."

"I like how I haven't seen your favorite granddaughter yet. Is Prasanti avoiding me?"

"No, I don't think she is," said Chitralekha, trying to ignore the howling street dogs that would soon participate in a riotous orgy right outside her gate. "You're so pleasant to her."

"I'll make her work today. I have so many dirty clothes."

"Don't you have washing machines in England? You could have washed them there."

"They never come out as clean as when Prasanti wrings them with a man's might and irons them with a woman's fastidiousness. I forbid her to use the washer."

"That's just creating more work for her," Chitralekha said. "She's already overworked."

"Yes, I know. She has to provide you with the entire neighborhood's gossip. She has a difficult life."

"Look at the dark circles under your eyes," Chitralekha said. "You look old."

"Perhaps that's because I feel old. All I do is take care of Bua."

"Here, come closer. Let me look at the dandruff collecting around your eyes." Chitralekha moved toward her granddaughter and blew a mouthful of beedi smoke into her face. "That's for being mean to me," she said, and she laughed loudly enough to muffle the racket the dogs created.

"Why do you smoke that disgusting thing?" Manasa shouted. "Are you losing your mind?"

"Would you rather I chew tobacco?" Chitralekha stubbed out her cigarette. "Chew it and spit it out everywhere like your grandfather used to?"

"At least that's better than blowing smoke into people's faces. And who said you'd have to give up one vice to take up another? Don't smoke. Don't chew tobacco. They are nasty habits."

"Do you think a person can change at a hundred?"

"You're still not eighty-four, Aamaa. Stop exaggerating."

"Eighty-four. Ninety. A hundred—all the same. There is no way any of you children will live up to that age. You barely eat anything. You may live up to fifty."

Prasanti—full of chirpiness, face well-scrubbed, Adam's apple hidden with *chunni*, nose studded, hair in ponytail, red *kurta* as glossy as her makeup—broadcast her arrival with the declaration that it was Diwali and that there should be no quarreling during the festival. "We are celebrating the victory of good over evil," she said, looking sheepishly at Manasa while handing a cup of tea to Chitralekha. "We know who the good one here is."

"Silly girl, *Dashain* is the celebration of good over evil—we just finished it." Chitralekha couldn't help laughing. "This is *Tihaar*, and Manasa isn't as evil as you think she is."

"Yes, have fun with this nonsense, Aamaa," Manasa said. "And, Prasanti, where have you been all this while? You don't show your face. You run away when you need to help me with my luggage. Oh, and then don't get me tea when you know I am here."

"No tea for the evil," Prasanti pronounced in a lilt, which Chitralekha endorsed in a screech.

Her granddaughter glared at Chitralekha, who stopped once she saw that those murderous eyes wouldn't soften.

"Maybe coffee but no tea," half sang Prasanti before slinking off. "Tea only for the good. Coffee, perhaps, for the evil."

"Why do you encourage her?" Manasa asked.

"She's funny. She brightens my day."

"With such juvenile jokes? How can you find them funny?"

"You're so harsh on her."

"You have a bizarre sense of humor. Blowing smoke into my face, Prasanti's silly antics—how can they amuse you so?"

"I should have told her about the smoke."

"You do that, and I'll double her workload."

"Don't, please. I need her to do some real work this evening."

Gangtok was a city of stairs. It also had streets with crater-size potholes, dirt trails, and a slowly widening two-lane highway, but the city was infested with stairs. People preferred stairs to roads. Stairs often took you to the same places roads did. Stairs created short cuts. Stairs saved time. Stairs saved you from traffic. Stairs could easily be built. Stairs were often makeshift. Stairs were economical. Stairs could cut through terrain where laying roads proved challenging because of widths and slopes. Stairs were ideal for a city situated on a hilltop with so many inclines and declines. Stairs were perpetually wet, perhaps because a maze of leaking water pipes often substituted for banisters. Stairs flourished.

Chitralekha had never liked stairs. As she became more advanced in years, she dreamed of getting rid of every step in the city. Just a few months before, she had succeeded in reducing the number of these city stairs by converting the flight that led to her house into a proper road, which would increase the value of her property and make certain she didn't have to walk up and down flights in her old age. She had fought and bribed many an officer, alienated and threatened numerous department heads, and disregarded plenty of city ordinances to get the job done, the worth of which was reinforced every time her car rattled uphill on gravel. Ascending in a car on what felt like her personal driveway still brought a smile to her face—the construction of the road was one of her proudest achievements.

The beauty of the location of Chitralekha's home, overlooking the Presbyterian Church, was the easy access to the town square—it was just some stairs and a bridge away. Yet her house was far away from the bustle of city life. Because the cottage was at least five minutes from the main road, no honking cars passed by in their hundreds, a problem that irritated her street-level neighbors. Chitralekha's was the only cottage in the midst of a jungle of midrise buildings and the only house whose outdoor space rivaled the square footage of its indoors. Ruthwa, her now-forgotten writer grandson, had named it the Neupaney Oasis. It was an oasis, no doubt, with unobstructed views of Mount Kanchendzonga, Sikkim's guardian deity, which she would soon be robbed of if she didn't act fast.

Chitralekha had some serious confrontational work to do today. It wasn't going to reap her any financial rewards, but she had to accomplish it before the rest of the family arrived. One of her neighbors, a minister, was constructing a building so massive in its scope that it threatened to block the view of the mountain from Chitralekha's terrace.

Gangtok was becoming a strange place—everywhere she looked, buildings mushroomed, precariously balanced on small surface areas while their breadth and height swelled frenziedly. Rumor had it that, close by, on the steep, hilly patch that flanked the path to the Palzor Stadium, the land was *manpari*—inhabited as you pleased. Tiny two- and three-story buildings, therefore, had sprung up to occupy every free square inch of the lot. To an onlooker, a person from the plains, it looked as if a force of nature, maybe a landslide or an earthquake, could uproot the tiny buildings and send them crashing down. Staring back at the construction site in front of her, Chitralekha was thankful that she had her little green space, but what use was a garden when the ugly monolith in front of her was all set to get in the way of her and her mountain?

She needed to persuade the politician to scrap his plans of a seven-story construction and stick to just six floors. The scoundrel had told her that his building would be a hotel, which explained the rows of blue-tiled bathrooms that faced her garden. Already, the lower floors had begun putting up customers. On the terrace, the politician-cum-hotelier said with a flourish, patrons could enjoy a continental breakfast while watching the Kanchendzonga. Chitralekha had no objection to the hotel plan in theory. She may have had an issue with noisy Bengali tourists, but Prasanti and her foul mouth would take good care of them. What she needed was a rectification to the blueprint obstructing her view of the mountain—and that meant cutting the building plans to a smaller size.

Manasa had gone back to bed, mumbling in one sentence something about jet lag, an aching head, and dizziness. She had, true to her word, assigned to Prasanti a laundry list of chores to finish by the end of the day. As peacemaker, Chitralekha had let Manasa know that she'd keep Prasanti busy the entire evening, and it hadn't been a lie. Employing her servant to stop the politician from going beyond six stories was the last resort. When she had complained to the chief minister about his sycophant subordinate's insolence, Subba firmly told Chitralekha that it was too small a tiff for him to get involved in. She'd have to fight some of her own battles, he said.

Just a few days before, Agastaya had laughed at Chitralekha when she complained on the phone about the grotesque new construction. He said that she, who wasn't big on beauty, wanted to create trouble because she had nothing better to do. Yes, she didn't care for vases with flowers, Buddha paraphernalia on the walls, trophies in the living-room showcase, and paneling the walls with wood, but this mountain, the Kanchendzonga, was her god. It wasn't something she had picked up from the Buddhists of Sikkim. She just felt more at peace with the mountain than she did at temples or *pujas*. She had spent so many mornings eating oranges on the terrace and puffing on her *beedi*, watching the mountain change hue, so many evenings watching the sun disappear behind it. To have a politician encroach on this sacrament just because he wanted a hotel to house the very tourists who wouldn't let go of Gorkhaland, her natal home, and on account of whom her people in Kalimpong and Darjeeling were suffering, was preposterous. She had no intention of forgoing her morning ritual of praying to the mountain and replacing it with scenes of half-clothed Bengali tourists doing their ablutions.

"Go do your thing." Chitralekha muttered encouragement to Prasanti. "Go show them what you do when you're unhappy."

People from the plains would know better than to invite the curse of a eunuch. Prasanti had already dressed up in a loud yellow sari, anointed herself with red lipstick, dabbed red makeup on her cheeks, and even acquired a red drum. She'd knock at every door in the hotel, sing, clap, dance, create a rumpus, undress herself if need be, try undressing those men who refused to oblige, but she wouldn't come back until the patrons had parted with satisfactory amounts of cash.

Chitralekha wished she could witness the scene. She wished she could see the terror unleashed by her half-sex servant on the people whose money would finance the seventh floor of the hotel. How she wished she, too, could join Prasanti in the extortion. Prasanti wouldn't disappoint. She was a great bully.

Chitralekha knew she had vanquished her opponent when her servant returned with Rs. 1,051. Soon the phone would ring, and the politician would offer a compromise: he'd give up the idea of the seventh floor if Prasanti stayed away from his hotel for life. Chitralekha would dither a little before finally agreeing.

Questions and Answers

Agastaya maintained that no time in Gangtok was quite as beautiful as October. The skies cleared, the rains retreated, and the clouds were too scant for the mountain range to disappear behind after a few hours of visibility. The sun shone with all its might, as if knowing that it would be frail and sickly once November set in. The temperature was just right—warm with a hint of chill in the evenings. October was festival time. When the Nepali and Gregorian calendars decided to cooperate, *Dashain* mostly took place in the month. Every so often, *Dashain* and *Tihaar* both occurred in October. This was one such year. *Dashain* had gone, but it was Day One of *Tihaar*, the Nepali Diwali, which shared some of its characteristics with the Indian festival of lights, while various features, such as the worship of crows and dogs, were unique to the Nepali-speaking Hindu world. Today was Kaag *Puja*, to celebrate which offerings were set aside in the sun for crows to feast on. Pigeons, pheasants, and sparrows, too, basked in reflected reverence and found easy morsels of food on building terraces. The Kaag *Puja* wasn't as resplendent as the Kukkur *Puja* following it, during which such affection was showered on dogs. Even stray dogs, much maligned and an absolute menace to Gangtok, were garlanded and their foreheads smeared with *tika*.

When his cab approached the vicinity of Gangtok town, Agastaya didn't spot any gargantuan display of festivity—no marigold-garlanded windows, no colorful lights, and no fireworks. He asked Bhagwati if she remembered past *Tihaar* celebrations being this muted. Bhagwati muttered that everything seemed subdued probably because it wasn't dark yet. The driver, whose interjections every time he gathered what his English-speaking passengers were talking about Agastaya was now used to, explained that the more ostentatious celebrations would begin the next day.

For now, Gangtok was trapped at a crossroads—convalescing from *Dashain* and fastening its seatbelt for *Tihaar.*

Agastaya wondered aloud if the driver would help them with the luggage up the hundreds of stairs they'd have to tackle to reach the house. The driver responded by making a turn where the stairs used to be and slowly going uphill.

"Didn't you know about this?" he asked, looking back at Agastaya, who was nervous about the vehicle skidding. Neither Bhagwati nor Agastaya had seen the new driveway leading to the house.

"Aamaa did tell me about it," Agastaya said, bowled over by the narrow path and the genius with which his grandmother had engineered both the design and execution. "She mentioned it a million times, and yet I forgot."

"It's one of her big stories, isn't it?" Bhagwati said. "It's her favorite topic when we make awkward conversation on the phone."

"How she managed to do it, I am still to understand. I am impressed. Do you remember those stairs?"

"Yes, I first talked to Ram on them. Eighteen years later, I am in a different Gangtok and belong to a house that has its own driveway."

"The legality of which is questionable."

"As with everything else on Aamaa's list of accomplishments," Bhagwati said, following Agastaya out of the car.

Prasanti was toweling her hair when they entered the house.

"Not a day older than when you left," she said to Bhagwati. "A lot older than I remember you," she said to Agastaya.

"I can't believe I'm actually seeing you again," Bhagwati said. "Are the others here?"

"Yes." Prasanti giggled. "Yes and no."

"What do you mean?" Agastaya towed the bags in.

"Only Manasa came." Prasanti laughed. She didn't help Agastaya with the luggage. "The oldest-looking of the bunch came without her husband. Come sit. Aamaa has gone for a meeting."

"She can still work in her old age?" Agastaya said.

"The meeting is with a minister," Prasanti proudly informed them.

"Have you put on weight, Prasanti?" Bhagwati asked.

"Yes, I look better," Prasanti replied.

Manasa's entrance lent wings to the servant's feet, and she vanished into the kitchen.

"What was that?" Agastaya asked, amused.

"She's been given a lot to do—only half of her chores are complete," said Manasa. "Aamaa is out for a meeting."

"I'd be lying if I said I expected her to stay home to welcome us," Agastaya said. "We heard it was with a minister."

"I don't think so." Manasa sat down on one of the sofas around the coffee table. "Whom did you hear it from?"

He pointed toward the kitchen and laughed.

"You should know better than to believe her. She's become even more disrespectful and still does nothing around the house."

"We could sense that," Bhagwati said. "She didn't help us with the luggage at all."

"At least she was here when you arrived. She ran away when I came. Perhaps a good thing because I'd have lost my temper at her incompetence. How was your flight?"

"Average," Agastaya said. "The way flights are."

Comments on weight gained and receded hairlines should have been bandied around with gusto, but they weren't. Agastaya wished someone would remark on his balding pate. That would clear the path to talking about Manasa's appearance. The abundance of lines on her face was everything graceful aging was not.

Manasa punctured an uncomfortable silence with a call to Prasanti. "Prasanti, where's the tea?"

"I have two hands, not seven, *condo*," Prasanti replied. "And of the two, one is swollen because of all the work you made me do."

Manasa and Bhagwati chuckled.

"See? I make you laugh even when I work!" Prasanti shouted.

"Don't force me to throw some more clothes at you to wash," Manasa said, and then she narrated the story of the bed sheet to her siblings. "Aamaa is like a stubborn child. I find it absurd that she treats the stupid factory in Kalimpong like it's a palace when she doesn't even live in it. This house is filthy."

"It's always her way of doing things—what's new there?" Agastaya said. "If she didn't like it, she'd let us all know."

"You shouldn't tolerate that," Manasa said. "She needs to be put in her place."

"Too much drama," Bhagwati said.

Prasanti sashayed in, bearing three cups of tea.

"I don't take any sugar," Agastaya grunted.

"I can't make another cup," Prasanti replied, matching him in gruffness.

"Prasanti, go make another one," Manasa said. "And learn some manners."

"She's become even more terrible," Bhagwati observed.

"Somebody needs to beat her until she cries," Manasa said. "Since when did you become so foreigner-like, Agastaya? No sugar in the tea, huh?"

"It's been a number of years. No sugar for me."

Yet another awkward silence was brewing. It was Agastaya's turn to terminate it. "I am still jet-lagged, so I'll sleep," he said.

Agastaya had escaped to his old room from the first major meeting without having to skirt around any talk of marriage. Bhagwati had made an attempt in the car, but, to give her credit, she'd stopped immediately after he made it known that he wasn't keen on discussing the topic. His sister had clearly come with a desire to make him bare his soul. She hadn't succeeded, just as he had been a failure at getting her to talk. How complicated adulthood was. It had so many dangerous curves, so many restricted areas that, if trespassed, the adults could find themselves squashed in. Had they been children, they'd have probably called each other names, fought and made up a dozen times throughout their journey to Gangtok. As adults, they could barely muster enough courage to ask questions that mattered.

What would it be like to bring Nicky into the middle of all this? People, especially women, loved the man. Would he become as big a hit with his grandmother and sisters as he was with the ladies of New York? Were Nicky to be here, would people suspect something was going on between the two of them? Agastaya was erudite, intelligent-looking, humorless—a man who would look like a doctor even if he decided to wear a jumpsuit and carry a purse. The glasses, the hairline, the graying around the temples of the hair that still remained lent to his persona a kind of sexlessness—guardian-like, avuncular. It surprised strangers when Agastaya, just to see their reaction, declared that he liked men—not because he was the last thing a stereotypical homosexual looked and acted like, but because he was one of those people about whom no one thought sexually. Nicky often said that he felt as if he was dating an older brother. Chances were that if Nicky, who was good-looking in a rugged, manly way, did accompany Agastaya here, no one would guess they were lovers—they were just too odd a couple to arouse people's suspicions.

How brave the eunuch servant was to live life on her terms. She *was* her sexuality, reveled in her in-betweenness, lusted openly, lived unapologetically. Gender, sex, sexuality—they meant nothing to her. How fortunate she was to be so transparently, so blatantly, unmistakably gay. Would he have had it easier were he more like her and less like himself? Would a lisp have helped? A prettier face? Fuller lips? Longer hair? Had he deliberately toned down any flamboyance? Was he ever loud? How many aspects of his personality were repressed? Did the repression double up now that he was home? Was Hanuman, the Brahmacharya god, like him a homosexual? Did the god, too, try his best to stir longings in himself for women? Was Dr. Agastaya Neupaney a hypocrite? Did his homosexuality have something to do with the unisexual nature of his name? If the fourth *a* in *Agastaya*—seldom gender neutral, almost always feminine—didn't trail him, would he have become a different person?

He was a successful doctor who lectured at NYU while Prasanti was an uneducated servant with nothing to her name. He had traveled the world while Prasanti had never been on a plane. He was super-specialized while Prasanti could barely do the dishes right. He was annihilating tumors while Prasanti had no role to play outside her employer's house. Yet Prasanti was a superior human being. She loved who she was, wouldn't change how she had been made, didn't care about how she was perceived. When he became like this eunuch servant—as sure of himself as she was of herself, as impenitent, as devoid of hangups—he'd consider himself a human her equal. Until then, he'd live the way he had always done—cautiously masked, afraid of being discovered, detached from reflections that would keep him up at nights. At least the jet lag quieted his thoughts and was quickly putting him to sleep. If only every night were as simple.

•

Bhagwati had a story to set straight. The claustrophobia that she had experienced in the house as a teenager now returned in waves. She felt suffocated the minute she stepped into the sitting room, bright and airy as it was. She guaranteed herself, as she tried swallowing the nausea building in her, that this feeling of incarceration would only increase once Aamaa came into the picture.

This room was where it had all started. Here was where, on a rainy May afternoon, after a hailstorm had cloaked Gangtok in white, Bhagwati first cast eyes on Ram Bahadur Damaai, the man who would later be her husband. He had come to talk to Aamaa on an assignment for some obscure Nepali newspaper in Bhutan. It had a devoted underground readership, he said to Chitralekha.

Ram asked Aamaa pointed questions about her wealth, of which Chitralekha was reticent to talk; about her social obligations, of which she coined apocryphal details; of her education, the lack of which she proudly proclaimed and the importance of which she dismissed; and about Nepalis in Bhutan, the indifference to whose plight she could barely mask. At that point, Bhagwati would have never guessed that she'd spend the rest of her life with this sanctimonious journalist.

Once the interview was over, and he had sufficiently impressed Aamaa for her to deign to ask his name, he replied, "Ram Bahadur."

Bhagwati, who didn't understand why she chose to linger, tried hard not to laugh at the antiquated name.

It was a name that belonged to her parents' days. Her generation was full of lesser-known variations of well-known gods—names like Bhagwati, Manasa, Agastaya, and Ruthwa. Ram, Lakshman, Sita, and Shiva were too ancient to belong in her age group.

"Ram Bahadur what?" Aamaa had asked.

"Ram Bahadur Damaai." He was unflappable.

"Such a nice, long, pointed nose on such a fair face—you look as good as a Brahmin," said Aamaa. It was a remark that only Aamaa could get away with. Aamaa also needed a lesson that her idea of beauty—the long, pointed, aquiline nose and a forehead the size of Palzor Stadium that she spoke of so gushingly—had lost favor among Bhagwati's generation. No one wanted a nose too prominent these days.

"What difference does it make?" Ram had defensively asked.

"None in this day and age," Chitralekha said, but she rose without waiting for the tea that Prasanti had been asked to serve.

Ram showed himself out after informing Chitralekha that the piece on her would be out in the next issue and that he had various other important people to interview. He added with an acerbic smile that he was sorry he couldn't stay for tea.

Once her grandmother withdrew to her office, Bhagwati ran out of the house, out the gate, and to the stairs that led to the main road. She slipped twice on the melting hailstones.

"Wait, wait!" she shouted.

Ram turned.

"I am sorry she behaved that way," Bhagwati said, out of breath.

Ram looked taken aback. "Who?"

"My grandmother—what she said about you looking like my caste."

"You don't have any reason to be sorry for that," Ram said. "A lot of people mistake me for a Brahmin."

"It must make you angry. Brahmins are ugly."

"You aren't." His candor surprised her less than hers did.

"I know. That's because I don't look like a Brahmin."

"And what do you look like?"

"I don't know—a Punjabi?"

"Punjabis are hairy."

"And tall."

"Are you?"

"What?" Bhagwati said. "Hairy or tall?"

"You're just tall."

By the time they parted ways, she had offered to take him to the monasteries around town. It had been over two months since she completed her Class 12 board exams, and she was at that beautiful juncture in life where lazy day after lazy day stretched out in front of her. A number of her friends were preparing for entrance tests to engineering and medical schools, but Bhagwati had faith that the Sikkim quota and her grandmother's connections would get her a good seat in a reputed college. She had been waking up the last few mornings not knowing what would occupy her day. The least she could do for this stranger Aamaa had humiliated was show him her town.

Ram declared that the Rumtek monastery, the pride of her state, was unkempt. The Ranka Monastery was better, but he didn't feel as spiritual there as he did at the Paro *Taktsang* in his own country, he confided. The Enchey monastery wasn't anything too special. To Bhagwati, all this was new. She had played tour guide to her mother's family from Kathmandu, her grandmother's clients from Kolkata, and a missionary couple from Belgium, and no one had belittled Gangtok's beauty the way Ram had.

"Gangtok is nice, but it's too unplanned," Ram said, once they were on MG Marg. "You should see Thimpu and Paro."

"I don't want to." Bhagwati was combative. "There's beauty in the chaos of Gangtok. From what I hear about your capital, every house looks the same. Every street is a clone of another."

"And that's a bad thing?"

"Yes, it is. I like that the building up there looks like a matchbox, that another looks like a biscuit house from a Blyton book."

"Never heard of those books," Ram said.

"That's because we in Sikkim read, unlike people in Bhutan." Ram probably hadn't read Enid Blyton because he hadn't gone to a posh school as she had.

"Sorry if I offended you," Ram said. "It's just that I don't care about monasteries. Take me to a temple."

"Why? So you can compare our temples to yours and find ours lacking?"

"No, because our temples aren't anything like yours. Ours are a bit of a joke."

"Really?"

"Yes, so many Hindus and no temple anywhere as well funded as the poorest Buddhist monasteries," Ram said, before informing her of the plight of her fellow Nepali-speaking people in the neighboring country. Bhagwati had never felt more ignorant in her life; she had never been guiltier of her charmed, apolitical existence.

For the temple visit, she'd wear a yellow *kurta*—it behooved her to look traditional. She'd perhaps even cover her head with the red *chunni* when she did her obeisance. For a millisecond, the idea of a sari was appealing, but it would be difficult to deal with the stairs to the Thakurbari temple. Also, wearing a sari would attract too much attention, and she needed to be discreet. Her grandmother assumed she'd be at the Community Library all day.

"You look like an actress," Ram said with a laugh. He had been waiting for her outside the gate to the temple. Bhagwati knew she looked great. The whistles of passersby—louder, more aggressive, and more frequent today than any other day—were testament enough. Some lottery seller serenaded her with a new Bollywood song doing its rounds with the censor board.

"And you're wearing what you wore yesterday," Bhagwati said.

"Should I've worn the *daura-suruwal*?"

"Why not? I wore a *kurta*."

"It's frowned upon in Bhutan—remember?"

"Is anything not frowned upon in your country?"

"Almost everything—for us Nepalis. To live in a house as big as you do would only be a dream for the Nepalis of Bhutan."

"Our house is old and disgusting." Bhagwati wished she could show off the factory in Kalimpong to Ram. If the house in Gangtok impressed the poor man, the Kalimpong factory would reduce him to speechlessness.

"No, it's not. It's big."

"Aamaa doesn't care too much about living in a beautiful home. She doesn't like spending time or money on the house."

"My house in my country may be even smaller than your sitting room."

"Do you even think of it as your country?"

"Of course, it's mine."

"Stupid country. Stupid you."

"And you? A heroine? Because everybody's staring at you?"

They rang every temple bell they could find. Some clappers swayed too high for her to reach, so he lifted her to them. She'd hang on to the bell while trying to wriggle out of his arms. Both laughed.

"This one seems to have been made for giants," Ram said, as he jumped to strike a bell's clapper. It was too high even for him.

"Let me carry you," Bhagwati said.

"Can you?"

She crouched and asked him to hop onto her back. Straining her shoulders, she lifted him to the bell, which he rang once, twice, three times.

"I rang all the bells—that's a first," Ram cried.

"Tomorrow we should go to a church."

"I think some unhappy girl is walking toward you," said Ram.

It was Manasa—frantic, panting, in her pajamas.

"Where were you?" Manasa asked. "I looked everywhere for you."

"We had come to the temple."

"Aamaa is searching for you."

"This is Ram," Bhagwati said. "Aamaa knows him."

"Aamaa is furious."

"She thinks I was at the library—why should she be furious?"

"Your results are out."

Bhagwati hadn't passed her boards. At Tashi Namgyal Academy, patronized by the elite of Gangtok and inarguably the most glamorous school in the state, failure in board exams wasn't a regular phenomenon. Maybe one or two unsuccessful students blotched the school's perfect records every few years, hurling themselves to infamy while the toppers graced front pages in the *Sikkim Express*. This obsession with examination grades, a very South Asian malaise that had now permeated Sikkim, lasted for weeks and months. The failure's family would be pitied and the failure stared at. *She wasn't a great student but not failure material*, friends and neighbors would titter about some unfortunate girl.

And that had been true for Bhagwati. She was no budding genius such as Manasa or Agastaya, but she wasn't as academically disinclined as Ruthwa either. No one would think of her as the type who failed. In fact, she herself couldn't believe it. The granddaughter of the great Chitralekha Neupaney had failed an examination.

"She's going to kill me," Bhagwati said. "A failure in her family—she'll hate me for the rest of my life."

"She will," Manasa said. "Don't go home now, please. Don't."

"What if there's an error in the result?" Bhagwati asked.

"Yes, the principal called Aamaa to let her know that he has requested a reevaluation."

"But that could take weeks," Bhagwati argued.

That's how Bhagwati ran away. It was going to be temporary—a quick disappearance until Aamaa's wrath subsided. Ram became the person with whom she escaped because it was convenient.

She had no intention of eloping, of getting married. She just wanted to escape the humiliation of failing an examination.

She ran away because she knew not running away would destroy her. She was up against Gangtok's gossip mill. Her getting inadequate grades in an exam would be entangled with tales of affairs, alcohol, drugs, pregnancy, and depression. She'd forever be the girl who failed.

Ram and she first went to the Green Hotel, where Ram was putting up, grabbed his bag, and reserved a taxi to Phuntsholing, in Bhutan. During the journey, Bhagwati frequently looked back, sometimes in fear and sometimes in hope, to check if they were being followed.

Life, as she knew it, was over.

Once on the other side of the border, she called home, praying Manasa would pick up.

"Some people saw you with a man," Manasa whispered. "They told Aamaa you eloped with him. Aamaa is convinced that you ran away with a Damaai."

A month after the entire town of Gangtok pronounced her married, Bhagwati got wedded to Ram. She didn't love him then. The love came much, much later. She got married because she couldn't continue burdening Ram—his relatives were already asking questions.

Two days later, Manasa—the only person in the family with whom Bhagwati corresponded—called to let her know that Bhagwati's reevaluation result was out. A 62 in math, by all means a respectable score, had earlier been mistyped as 26. The 36 in physics was still a 36, but that didn't matter. She could fail one subject and yet pass the boards.

Bhagwati hadn't been a failure, after all. She was married, but she had passed the examination that had pushed her to marriage.

Was her grandmother's absence at home now a deliberate snub? She wouldn't put it past Aamaa. The granddaughter would have to thaw the old woman. Perhaps Bhagwati's attempts would translate better in person than they did on the phone. She wondered if she hankered so much for forgiveness because she knew it would never come. Even if it did, how would Aamaa dispense it? Would she declare her granddaughter exonerated? Would she shower on her an old person's blessing that was so revered around here? All Bhagwati needed was for things to return to normal. What this normal was, Bhagwati couldn't quite tell. Was it her relationship with Aamaa pre-elopement? Was it the bond her grandmother shared with Manasa?

Bhagwati missed Ruthwa. His irreverence would have come in handy here. The youngest of the siblings would make light of the whole situation, call attention to Manasa's graceless aging, and draw comparisons of her face with Bhagwati's. He'd probably ask Bhagwati if the secret of her beauty lay in a healthy sex life. He'd throw in a joke about sex with the untouchables being good for your skin. There'd be a play on the words *touching* and *untouchable* or an analogy only her banished brother could come up with. It would do everyone a lot of good for Ruthwa to be here. She wondered if he was still traveling between one ex-lover and another, perhaps still trying to write.

She found Prasanti flipping through the pages of a glossy magazine in the kitchen. The room looked smaller than when Bhagwati had left it. In fact, everything in India seemed minuscule. The telltale signs of her grandmother's increasing opulence were visible in the sizes of the refrigerator and dishwasher, which sparked memories about the job from which she had just been let go. Even she, who lived in America, didn't have a dishwasher at home.

"What function does it serve here?" she asked Prasanti, who stared at her scrutinizing the machine.

"It's no use," Prasanti answered. "The minute I switch it on, the power goes off. I have to do all the dishes by hand."

"You mean, clean the dishes of two people?" Bhagwati asked. "You're lucky."

"Now, with the arrival of all you people, there's even more work to do. Manasa thinks I am a servant."

"You aren't," Bhagwati quickly added. "You're part of the family."

"Which family member would be so badly treated? You should have seen the number of dishes I washed this morning."

"You did dishes for three people this morning, Prasanti." Bhagwati laughed. "I clean the dishes of so many people."

"How is four people many people? You people are just four. And I hear in America even the husbands help. Is that true?"

"Mine does." Bhagwati wondered where the openness came from. She'd nearly made an admission to her servant that their professions were similar.

"You may think it's easy to wash two people's dishes, but you don't know about your Aamaa's eating habits. She's a true *Maharani*—wants a different bowl for a different vegetable. Sometimes, seven, eight bowls surround her plate."

"Dishwashers are overrated. The dishes don't come out as clean as they do when you use your hands."

"And then the hands look like this." Prasanti demonstrated—each nail was painted a different color.

"Also, you don't have to clean the house every day," Bhagwati said.

"Sure, I don't," Prasanti replied.

"Do you?"

"Not every day but every other day."

"Lying. Aamaa doesn't care about cleanliness here."

"You wouldn't know."

"How's your life?" Bhagwati asked. "You look happy."

"I am fine. Growing old. Looking better. Looking after your grandmother, whose grandchildren don't care about her. She's not the young woman you left when you ran away, you know."

"I know," Bhagwati said. "Does she take good care of you?"

"I am a servant. She treats me better than a servant. I'd say I am like a poor relative to her, which is better than being treated like a servant."

"I am seeing her for the first time since my marriage."

"Yes, I know," Prasanti said. "Your marriage with the untouchable. How are your children? Are they more Brahmin or Damaai?"

"They're humans," Bhagwati said.

"Like I am, *condo*," replied Prasanti. "Second-class humans."

"Who says you're a second-class human?"

"It's in the way people treat us."

"You have a job, a nice home, and a family," Bhag-wati said, feeling sincerely sorry for Prasanti, even though the servant's categorizing her children in the same group as eunuchs unsettled her. "You have nothing to worry about."

"Yes, I have some money and gold," Prasanti said.

"That's more than what I have," Bhagwati confided.

"Won't I need all that when Aamaa dies? She's in her eighties and won't live forever. I've got to think of the future for myself, too, don't I?"

The absurdity of bartering stories with a servant didn't escape Bhagwati. Their shared struggles in their similar professions must have engendered this new level of connection. At least the conversation with Prasanti was free flowing. The eunuch divulged information liberally and asked questions she needed answered. There was no palpable discomfort as was evident in her sister, no guardedness that characterized her brother's conversations with her, and none of the resentful taunts that Bhagwati was sure would start once Aamaa was home.

•

Manasa had already exceeded her sleep quota for the day by the time Agastaya and Bhagwati arrived. Once her brother excused himself, the prospect of making small talk with Bhagwati all by herself was more than she could handle, so she, too, extricated herself from the sitting room. She was back at home, in a familiar setting, with people from her past whom she was reluctant to make a part of her present. Her siblings and she had become painfully proper with one another. She was more herself with her husband's family than she was in her old one.

She had only five more days to go—five never-ending days. She'd then return to being nanny to her father-in-law. The thought of Himal's inability in dealing with

Bua's handicap fueled her with momentary pleasure, but she quickly stopped herself from feeling too smug—her husband was in Kathmandu, and a retinue of female relatives would relieve him of his filial duties. Himal had a comfortable life.

It was easy to forget that she was here to celebrate her grandmother's eighty-fourth birthday—to commemorate eighty-four years of Aamaa wreaking havoc on humanity. It didn't feel festive at all. Bhagwati and Agastaya could hardly be trusted to liven up a drab affair. Manasa understood that Bhagwati's life was too complex for her to celebrate a silly birthday with reckless abandon, but Agastaya should have been the most jovial of them all. He led such an unencumbered, uncomplicated life. He was free to do as he pleased, had no children to look after, and no father-in-law's pee dribble to wipe off the toilet seat.

When Manasa emerged from the guest room for dinner, Agastaya and Aamaa were seated at the dining table. She wasn't going to be spared the brisance that would result from the reunion between her sister and warmongering grandmother, after all.

Manasa chose a seat next to her brother and helped herself to a ladle each of *murai* and *aloo dum*. Hardly had she mixed a spoonful of the puffed rice with the fenugreek-heavy potato curry when Chitralekha said, "And this one doesn't eat at all."

"I am not hungry," Manasa retaliated. "And why, exactly, has your pet made such snacky food for dinner?"

Bhagwati quietly trudged in. "Oh, everyone is here," she said to no one in particular as she took the chair farthest from her grandmother—the one at the opposite end of the table. Manasa felt sorry for Bhagwati. Her sister couldn't muster the courage to greet her grandmother.

"This one will starve herself to death—and that one doesn't want to get married!" Chitralekha shouted. "These are my grandchildren."

"Is that what this is all about?" Manasa asked. "You have a problem with Agastaya, and you just drag me in?"

"He says he has no time for girls. He'll be here a whole month."

"No, I'll be here only for a week," Agastaya said. "I have to go to Delhi, Bombay, and other places after that."

"Only for a week?" Aamaa wrinkled her nose. "What's that? Why did you come at all, then? A week will vanish in no time."

"I know. But it's work."

Aamaa looked at no one and moved her lips with her mouth still shut. "If you're staying only for a week, then we'd better all go to sleep now. We don't have too many hours to spare for our family members."

"Why would we sleep this early?" Agastaya boldly volunteered. "Tonight is talk night."

"I don't know about that." Aamaa got up. "I am going to sleep. I am old and frail."

"Aamaa, nobody sleeps at seven," Manasa said. It hadn't taken Aamaa much time to start her shenanigans. Manasa had warned her grandmother to be nice, and Aamaa, the woman of her word that she was, had kept her end of the bargain by ignoring Bhagwati. How was Manasa to know that her grandmother had a bone to pick with Agastaya, too? Manasa was stupid for not considering that—her grandmother had scores to settle with everybody.

"I will. I am an old woman. My grandchildren visit me after years and will leave as soon as they come. One grandson, and unmarried."

"Shut up, Aamaa," Manasa said. "You have two grandsons."

"Just one," Chitralekha said, starting to get up.

"Stay there, Aamaa." Manasa was aware that she was raising her voice. "Just sit down. Not everything has to revolve around you. I am sure Agastaya has reasons for not staying too long. It may have something to do with how overbearing you are."

She saw Bhagwati and Agastaya exchange anxious glances.

"Look at that." Aamaa jumped at the opportunity. "Look at that. That's how she treats me. That's how she's been talking to me since she got here. I feel no better than a servant."

Manasa was about to speak, when Agastaya kicked her under the table.

"She doesn't mean it," Bhagwati said in a quiet, trembling voice. "Let's all be happy. We are together after so long. This is a proper reunion."

"How can I be happy when my granddaughter is a Damaai?" Aamaa replied. "I need to go. All this wealth I've earned, but for what? A grandson who's unmarried, God only knows why, a granddaughter who's married to a Damaai, and another granddaughter who treats me worse than she treats Prasanti. Why did I even work hard after your parents died?"

Aamaa picked on Bhagwati because she was the weakest; she could never strike back. "It was a fight between you and me, Aamaa!" Manasa shouted. "Why bring Bhagwati in? Stop finding fault with her for what she did so many years ago. Are you jealous that she has a live husband, whereas you don't?"

Prasanti, never one to miss any commotion, made an appearance. She stood protectively by Aamaa.

"Take me away, Prasanti." Aamaa held the servant's hand. "Take me away to my room so I can sleep and wonder where I went wrong in rearing my children."

"Prasanti, you've become prettier," said Agastaya, in what Manasa understood was a sad attempt to make light of a situation that wasn't going to get any better.

Prasanti glowered at him. "And you have less hair on your head than I have on my chin."

"Where does she get her mouth from?" Agastaya said, and then added in English so the servant wouldn't understand, "Somebody needs to wash it out with soap and water. I'd gladly volunteer."

"Yes, talk in English," Prasanti said. "Come, Aamaa, let's go."

"Prasanti, you can clear all the dishes from the table," Manasa said. "Just make sure the *daal* stains are properly wiped out so I don't have to spend hours scratching them out from the bowls."

"Will you make me work until midnight?" Prasanti thundered out of the room. "I've been working all day because of you."

"Look what you all have done," Aamaa said. "Look at how difficult you make my life. If you treat her that way, she will leave, and no one will take care of me. As it is, all you people have left and can't even spend a month here. At least let the servants be."

Aamaa was now blaming them all—she was seeking refuge in the plural. Manasa knew she did that because her grandmother was afraid of singling her out. "Stop channeling on Prasanti all the affection that should have been given to us," Manasa said, getting up from her chair and roughly pushing the table. "Stop fighting for her."

She walked out, too, with Aamaa close at her heels. They both retreated to their rooms.

"Where are we sleeping?" Manasa heard Bhagwati ask. "Prasanti, Prasanti, are we sleeping in our old rooms?"

"Why do you need to sleep at seven in the evening?" Prasanti snapped.

"Because I am tired," Bhagwati said. "Where do I sleep?"

"Go sleep with Manasa, but she has just locked her door, so I guess you will be sleeping with the driver."

The reply needled Manasa more than anything else that had happened the entire day. She dashed out of her room and. grabbing a broom, went looking for Prasanti, who, perhaps sensing more trouble in store for her, had vanished into the streets, returning only when the garrulous gossip of coolies around an improvised fire, a tad premature for October, outside the Neupaney Oasis had started.

•

Slouched on her king-size bed with pachyderm patterns that dwarfed her tiny frame, Chitralekha turned to the wall when Prasanti timidly walked in later that night.

"You didn't defend me when all of them butchered me," Chitralekha complained.

Prasanti stayed quiet.

"They've begun treating me like I am a toddler. What did I do wrong? All I think about is their well-being. Is it wrong if I ask my grandson to get married? Is it wrong if I ask my granddaughter to pay attention to her marriage?"

Prasanti nodded.

"Are you agreeing or disagreeing with me, you stupid girl? Or have you become like the rest of them? Will you go off elsewhere?"

"Talking about people going elsewhere, did you hear about Mr. Bhattarai getting Bride Number Two for himself? Apparently, he couldn't look after his retarded wife on his own."

Chitralekha clucked exaggeratedly, encouraging Prasanti to continue with the gory details.

"Yes, all these years of marriage gone down the drain. Just like that—like the sun in the evening. He has taken up with a woman thirty-five years younger."

"How do you know?" Chitralekha nudged, ignoring yet another of her servant's similes that made no sense. "Last month you were talking about his affair with Rakesh's mother."

"Oh, I know everything," Prasanti said. "What will she do now? His maid told me that he painted pictures of Rakesh's mother. But now she's back with her husband, while he runs around trees with his child bride."

"Yes, men these days—they have no respect for anyone," Chitralekha said and then loudly added, "But it's not just men. No matter men or women, sons or daughters, grandsons or granddaughters—they are all the same. No one pays attention to their parents' needs. When the grandmother is a poor widow, people care even less."

Prasanti squatted on the tiled floor with a sigh. "And then, Bhola says the child bride might even be pregnant. The poor girl is barely developed. How can she be pregnant? What will she feed her child? The mad wife's milk?"

Chitralekha, in splits now, asked Prasanti to shut up.

"And, yes, I am more developed than the child bride."
Prasanti looked down at her chest. "Maybe I could feed
her poor child. Would a child fed with a *hijra*'s breast
milk be a *hijra*?"

Then, with a twirl of her *chunni*, the scarf she used
to cover her insufficient cleavage, Prasanti leapt up. She
oscillated from one foot to the other. Rhythmically,
she shook her entire body and gyrated. She jumped
up and down, pulled her pants up so it looked as if she
was wearing nothing under her *kurta*, spun around the
room, fluttered her eyelashes, cocked her eyebrow sug-
gestively, clapped, let go of the rubber band that held her
hair together, threw it at a hysterical Chitralekha, smiled
coquettishly, wriggled her entire body, and pranced
around the room with enough intensity to bring a bewil-
dered Agastaya into it.

"What's the celebration about?" Agastaya peeped in.
"I thought it was an earthquake."

"No, it was a volcano," Prasanti replied. Chitralekha
was still laughing.

"We have a lot to do," Agastaya said. "The *Chaurasi*
is only a few days away. Don't you have work to do,
Prasanti?"

"I don't want a *Chaurasi*," Chitralekha said as she
swaddled herself in a quilt and reclined again. "I don't
want a *puja* when no one cares. The only person who'd
cry at my funeral would be this *hijra*. No one else brings
me happiness."

"Prasanti, can you see if Manasa wants anything?"
Agastaya said. "You need to get things ready for the
Kukkur *Puja* tomorrow."

"I am not going to look around for dogs to worship
when there are so many dogs in this house," Prasanti

said. "I am staying here because you'll make Aamaa cry
again. I know all you people."

Chitralekha had made an effort. She had tried behaving
herself. She couldn't be faulted for not trying, but
it had all gone wrong. She had rehearsed so many times
the meeting that would take place with Bhagwati. In
front of the bathroom mirror, in front of her *Godrej* mirror
in the bedroom, even before the windowpane of her
office, she had acted and re-acted the scene that would
play out once her granddaughter showed up. Sometimes,
Chitralekha was unforgiving. At other times, she was
cold. Yet, on a few occasions, she announced that the
past should remain in the past. She was always the most
at peace after the last performance.

Her cowardly granddaughter had finally come. Eighteen
years after doing what she did to the family, Bhagwati,
the girl who ran away, who threw away everything
for the Damaai, had the courage to face her grandmother.
Sadly—and it was always the parents who were
at a disadvantage—it was the grandmother who couldn't
face her granddaughter. Chitralekha could barely look
at Bhagwati, and there she was—her granddaughter—
stuffing her face with mouthfuls of *murai* as if nothing
had happened. In another era—perhaps in some other
place in the same era—Bhagwati's mere presence at the
table would have driven everyone else away.

At dinner, Chitralekha developed a renewed sense of
alertness with regard to Bhagwati and hadn't been able to
eat. She heard her granddaughter chomping. She could
hear Bhagwati's spoon scraping the plate. She heard the
thud with which Bhagwati placed the glass on the table.

She could feel her *naatini* shaking her legs. Chitralekha
saw Bhagwati's head turn. Yet, grandmother couldn't
look granddaughter in the face. After all these years, she
couldn't bring herself to do it. Bhagwati and she had a
few days under the same roof—she'd have to face her
granddaughter sooner or later. What would she do then?
Cry with her? Wail for her granddaughter? Weep for
herself? Sob for the unborn offspring of her granddaughter's children?

Chitralekha was born during the First World War,
well before India attained independence, well before
the Indo-China war, well before Sikkim was swallowed
by India in what historians referred to as a smash-and-
grab annexation, before the Sikkim kings were rendered
impotent, well before the American queen of Sikkim
left the king, well before Basnett's downfall. She was a
relic. How could someone as ancient as she be expected
to understand love—that convoluted love Bhagwati
immersed herself in? Chitralekha, too, had loved her
husband. She had loved her son. She had even loved
her daughter-in-law. Yes, she couldn't be accused of
not having loved. It was just that she loved within limits,
loved where it was wise. How could this woman, who
embraced, propagated, and preached pragmatism, have
brought up a child who had chosen to disregard all rules
of life for love? Chitralekha had been a failure. She may
have built an empire, but she was a failure. Her granddaughter was a fool in love.

Chitralekha asked her servant to massage her head,
and, punctuating her acridity with giggles and squawking,
carried on about half-caste grandchildren, a grandson-
in-law she couldn't even allow inside the house, and two

unmarried grandsons, one of whom she would never see again. After running her fingers through Chitralekha's white hair, Prasanti quietly sewed marigolds into a garland while she listened. Chitralekha could sense that even her servant didn't agree with her.

"So, are the neighbors in good health?" It was their code for *Give me a report on the rest of the world.*

"Gurung Aamaa says all her children are equal to her. I said she was lying."

"No, she's lying," Chitralekha said. "You cannot love all your children, or your grandchildren, equally."

"That's what I said to her fat, ugly face. She called me names."

"Everyone calls you names. What's new there?"

"She called out to Keepu, who supported her. Even Keepu said she loves all her children equally."

"You believe everything these stupid women say. They are both housewives and haven't stepped out of the comfort of their homes in decades. What do they know about the world?"

"But shouldn't they know what they are talking about when it comes to loving their children?" Prasanti asked. "Wouldn't they know better about loving their children because they stay at home rather than work?"

"If it suits you to think like a moron, think that way. Parents do not love their children equally."

"That means you don't like them all equally?"

"Yes, it depends on who the weakest is. You have the most affection for the weakest, for the one you're afraid will be destroyed by life."

"Among your children, that would be Bhagwati, right?"

Chitralekha stared hard. "But she's different."

"Why don't you like her? She is the weakest. You just contradicted yourself."

"You know nothing about castes, Prasanti," Chitralekha said. "It's time for you to shut up."

"She's the only one who has said nothing to you. The others treat you so badly. She doesn't say a word. I know I am only a servant, but I think you should make amends with her. She's a good person, and I think she's really hurting."

"Yes, you are only a servant," Chitralekha said. "And it would serve you well to behave like one. Don't tell me what to do."

"I saw her crying in the kitchen this morning."

"She's crying for the trouble she has brought on herself and the family. She deserves to cry."

"I felt really bad."

"Go away, Prasanti." Chitralekha sighed. "Get lost before I kick you out, you *badarnee.*"

No one could fault her for lack of effort. She had in her almost eighty-four years of rigidity, eighty-four years of life. She was a product of her time. Those phone conversations with her granddaughter had been so much easier than seeing her, but Chitralekha would continue trying. It'd take her longer than she thought, yes, but she'd give it her all.

Where was sleep when she needed it? She would turn eighty-four in a few days. She felt eighty-four today—more ancient than she usually did. Was that the bell that just rang, or was it her imagination?

"Aamaa." Prasanti was panting.

"What happened? I asked you not to be here."

"Guess who I just saw?"

"Who? The Sharmas' new son? The monkey-faced idiot?"

"No."

"Then?"

"Don't get angry."

"Why would I?"

"You've shouted at me a few times already."

"Because you deserve it. Stop wasting my time and tell me who you saw."

"It's Ruthwa—he's here."

"You're an idiot."

"No, he is here, I promise—should I let him in?"

Her not being able to face Bhagwati wasn't such a big problem anymore.

Two

So, why did I go home? Why would I go to a place where I was unwelcome?

I don't know.

No, that's a lie. I went because of one reason.

I went to see Prasanti.

Whom do I first see? Prasanti, the *hijra*, after all these years. Thirteen years. Thirteen damn years.

Ah, Prasanti. We go way, way back.

Ah, Prasanti, the eunuch, the half-sex, the *hijra*. Eunuchs and I have something of a history.

Before my downfall as a writer came, I received good money, especially from Western papers, to write frivolous claptrap on shit-knows-what masquerading as cultural commentary. All I had to do, really, was sell these unsuspecting publications Facebook notes of my travels around India. This is from one of those edgy men's magazines whose readers love reading about the exotic. Every bit of what's mentioned in the piece happened to me.

Yes, I, too, wouldn't believe me if I were you.

Robbed by Eunuchs

Nothing quite prepares you for the show that ensues when a gaggle of eunuchs descends on you.

On my recent visit to Delhi, I got into an auto-rickshaw, a CNG-run three-wheeler that quivers—and I do mean quivers thunderously as it moves—rendering conversation an impossible shouting match.

The peculiar construction of the auto-rickshaw—it has no doors or windows, and you get in from an open side, while the "closed" side has two horizontal bars—makes its passengers easy targets for beggars and lepers because hastily rolling up windows as panhandlers approach is not an option. Beggars can touch you, run away with your belongings, and incessantly pester you about the money you're giving them not being enough, and stories of their snatching some Good Samaritan's wallet as he or she tries withdrawing change are plentiful.

As such, Indian eunuchs love the auto-rickshaw as much as they love a red light. The combination of the two, complemented with a clueless passenger, makes for a big payday.

Now, why would I be afraid of eunuchs? Would I really have to give them money if I didn't want to? I mean, c'mon, aren't there panhandling laws in India, you may ask?

Well, if you aren't familiar with the subculture of eunuchs in South Asia, here's a synopsis: They are the most powerful people here. It's believed that snubbing one means getting cursed, so this enterprising group plays off this widely held superstition and pushes itself to a superior bargaining position almost everywhere in India.

The eunuchs have no shame—one has, on one occasion, flashed my friends and me her mysterious private parts on a bus—and they use that to their ultimate advantage while demanding money from you.

A birth in your family? A group of eunuchs will be there to bless it—it's auspicious. A wedding? Sure, they're there—they supposedly bring luck. What if you don't want to give them money? You risk bad luck and potential embarrassment in many ways, a perpetually pinched penis (notice the failed attempt at clever alliteration to distract you, the reader, from the horror of what actually goes down) being one of them.

Hardly had I traveled a mile and was stuck in the worst traffic I had ever seen when a eunuch came running to my car, got in next to me, and asked for money. A nervous wreck always makes for easy bait, and I overwhelmingly fit into that category.

The traffic showed no signs of clearing up, and I knew that my new friend would not let go of me until I gave her money.

Being the smart-ass that I am, I handed her a hundred-rupee bill with sweaty, excessive trepidation, the kind she probably sees only on her luckiest days.

Little was I to know that this was one expensive eunuch: one hundred rupees wouldn't do.

I'd have to pay her a grand, which she'd split with her girlfriend, who had mysteriously appeared from nowhere and proudly unbuttoned her *kurta*, a loose Indian shirt, revealing what looked like semi-formed breasts with plenty of hair, or something close, if I was seeing correctly.

Finally, as the traffic showed signs of movement, and they had successfully swindled me of Rs. 300, the eunuchs went on their way, blessing me and probably discussing what an easy day it was.

Yeah, that's the closest I've come to tits—well, kind of—since my arrival in India.

Groups of eunuchs are found more commonly in the plains than the hills. Because most hill cultures do not favor their presence at weddings and celebrations—I can't think of a single Nepali wedding at which eunuchs danced—*hijras*' moneymaking rackets are worse suited to Gangtok than, say, Siliguri, which they migrate to in large numbers.

In the hills of Gangtok or Kalimpong, you may find one or two eunuchs, ridiculed more than elsewhere because they don't have to their benefit a power in numbers.

Prasanti was one such eunuch.

The tale she narrates about how she came to work at our place is different from everyone else's story.

Aamaa says she found her on a train and took pity on her. Prasanti says she was dancing at a wedding and Aamaa liked the way she livened the atmosphere so much that she brought her home.

The eunuch's story is highly unlikely because, first, she is a pathological liar; second, it's something Aamaa, or anyone else for that matter, doesn't substantiate; and, third, few people in Gangtok have much use for *hijras* at weddings.

Whatever the truth, Prasanti had become family in a way the other servants, such as Didi, the old woman before her, never had.

Aamaa built a small house for Didi once her son was trained and trusted enough to take care of our factory in Kalimpong. My cunning grandmother often points this out as an example of her altruism, but truly she got rid of the old servant because the rheumy woman's usefulness had expired. Keeping her around was a liability.

Prasanti, it was evident, wouldn't go away even if her entire body was paralyzed.

She had become too much a part of Aamaa's life for her to be ejected to Kalimpong once her functionality declined. This gave the eunuch many advantages.

Before Prasanti's arrival, no servant, driver, or gardener who worked for us could sit on our furniture. When watching TV, they brought their own wicker stools, on which they sat out of everyone's way, like figurines adorning the corners. Prasanti broke the rule within three weeks of her arrival—she said *hijras* couldn't sit on the hard stools because of their sensitive behinds. She took to sitting in a chair that she didn't share with anybody.

It soon became Prasanti's chair.

Prasanti got away with a lot. Her mouth, for example, could put a Khalpara pimp to shame.

The Nepali word for *butt*—*condo*—is often a bad word, straddling between grudging acceptance in some households and downright intolerance in others.

In the hierarchy of filthy words, it doesn't rank as high as the Nepali terms for *vagina, whore,* and *penis,* but it's still a word the Neupaneys wouldn't use at home.

It's also a word that, like *fart,* provokes endless laughter.

Prasanti had no qualms about liberally sprinkling the word as noun—both common and proper—and adjective in her speech.

In the beginning, Aamaa scolded her, gave her dangerous looks, and even boxed her ear, but when nothing could diminish Prasanti's zeal for the word, my grandmother gave up.

Condo became acceptable vocabulary at home, which certainly appalled the relatives.

"Why do you keep shouting my name, *oie condo*?" she'd scream when we called out to her. "Do you need me to come scratch your *condo,* you *condo*-like people?"

If Prasanti was in an especially bad mood, she'd bestow a form of *condo* on the neighbors, too.

Physically, when she had no makeup on, Prasanti looked like your everyday male or perhaps a transvestite.

Her rapidly thinning hair she anxiously tried growing long. She may have had breasts, too, but we couldn't be sure.

Often, we accused her of being nothing more than a very feminine male, a myth she threatened to debunk by exposing her nether regions to us. She never followed through with her warning, but we were all curious.

We sometimes struggled to gauge if those bumps on her chest were breasts or simply fat.

Because her choice of outfit was a lumpy *kurta*-pajama, it was easy for me to assume the garments housed breasts. Agastaya declared that they didn't, but it was just like my older brother to claim that anything sexual didn't exist.

I once rummaged through Prasanti's tin box, which was placed on another tin box in her room, to see what I'd find there and was struck by the number of lacy bras in it.

When I told the others about my discovery, they wouldn't believe me.

When I was about ten, a child who knew more about sex than his older brother, I saw Prasanti's bra strap peep from under her *kurta*. I directed Agastaya and Bhagwati's attention to it. Agastaya, in keeping with his personality, looked away. Bhagwati, on the other hand, stared, transfixed.

"What are you looking at?" Prasanti asked, annoyed. "Or is your *condo* itching?"

"Nothing," Bhagwati remarked, still a little shocked at the sight.

"Oh, this?" Prasanti snapped the strap. "Well, we women have goods to take care of, don't we?" She giggled.

"What goods?" I asked good-humoredly.

"Oh, you men are such *bokas*," she said. "Such *bokas* and dogs." She was blushing. Agastaya vacated the room. "Another dog has left."

"I am a dog," I said.

"Do you want to see my God-given gifts?" Prasanti asked Bhagwati, chattering nervously. "I can only show them to women. You don't want to get the men too excited."

"No, not even if someone threatens to kill me," Bhagwati said, covering her face. In English, she added: "This woman is insane."

This always infuriated Prasanti. She hated being left out, and people perpetually used English to abandon her.

"What's the *phusuk-phusuk* in English?" she demanded. "Are you talking about me?"

Of course we were talking about her. We had never, up to that point in our lives, encountered this blatant a conversation about one's sex organs, however nebulous. That it came from a servant—so what if she had taken it upon herself to hoist her status to something much higher?—was even more bizarre.

Bhagwati continued in English: "Imagine if we were like her. Whom would we fall in love with? A man, a woman, or a yak?"

"Yes, yes, make fun of me," Prasanti grumbled. "I treat you like my own brothers and sisters, and you think I am a *hijra* and nothing else."

"Prasanti, just because I declined your offer to have a look at your breasts doesn't mean you should cry and moan," Bhagwati said. "Just do your work."

This reminder that she was a servant enraged Prasanti more than anything else. Off she went marching to Aamaa, with us in tow. We were curious what the eunuch would say and nervous about Aamaa's reaction.

Aamaa was in her office, barely visible behind a mountain of paperwork and a fog of *beedi* smoke.

"These people are teasing me," Prasanti whined. "They are calling me names. Their shit is stuck in their *condo* if they don't make fun of me at least once a day."

"Stop listening to them," Aamaa said distractedly. "Just do your work."

"Today, they threw sanitary napkins at me and asked me if I had any use for them," the eunuch lied. "No one asked me that question even when I danced at weddings. I treat them like my brother and sister."

Aamaa saw an easy solution to the problem.

Tihaar, the Hindu festival of lights, was only a month and a half away.

The Nepali Hindus celebrate its last day as a dedication to their brothers. Whereas many non-Nepali-speaking Hindus have their *Raksha Bandhan* to commemorate the sacred relationship between brothers and sisters, we observe our *Bhai Tika*. Manasa thinks there's sexism at play—she often babbles something about the entire concept of sisters worshipping brothers so the brothers can protect them being an insult to her gender, but no one cares about Manasa's feminist rants.

Long story short, on the day of *Bhai Tika*, everybody with a sibling of the opposite sex gets blessed. When an opposite-sex sibling is lacking, cousins are involved.

"They are your brothers and sisters," Aamaa said to Prasanti. "You will celebrate *Bhai Tika* with them."

Bhagwati and I exchanged disbelieving looks. "You mean applying *tika* on us?" I asked.

This couldn't be true.

The glittery *tika* that my sisters applied on my forehead and I on theirs was a fun affair. We managed to take the tedium out of a religious ritual and made it colorful and happy and even hilarious.

With seven colors at our disposal and the forehead as our canvas, we had a riot. The base of the *tika*, made up of rice paste, didn't make me itch like the red *tika* concocted with grains of uncooked rice and yogurt that Aamaa spread on our foreheads during *Dashain*.

The year before, I daubed the image of a dog on Bhagwati's forehead, when a simple circle with its surface speckled with colors would have sufficed. Manasa painted on my forehead a bird, or something like it, when a vertical base made up of the rice paste to be filled with colors was all that was required.

"Yes, putting *tika* on you all," Aamaa said before leaving for the factory in Kalimpong.

Our favorite custom would now include Prasanti. She was an interloper.

But there was an issue: would the eunuch offer *tika* to Bhagwati and Manasa, as Agastaya and I did, or would Agastaya and I put *tika* on her, as we did on our sisters?

Aamaa didn't seem too concerned.

We didn't confront Prasanti about the sanitary-napkin lie. We thought it was unimportant then because we had to share the news of the *Bhai Tika* development with Agastaya and Manasa.

Prasanti, on her part, victoriously swayed back to the kitchen.

She could have snapped her bra strap, but I might have been imagining things.

When *Bhai Tika* arrived, after we lit crackers on a dog's tail and made fun of *Deusi* participants, who sang carols and were keeping alive a custom that we as public-school students couldn't ever aspire to, we sat down for our *tika*.

We were still curious about whether Prasanti would fulfill a male role or a female one.

Decked in her yellow wedding finery—the sari and blouse she wore in her previous life when she danced at weddings with her brethren—Prasanti, our sister, took her sisterly role seriously. By the time she was done, Agastaya and I had vegetable oil—we had never until then involved oil in our ritual, but Prasanti said that she knew better because she was a priest's daughter—dripping from our heads and ears. Each of our foreheads also showed off a perfect vertical line, so meticulously filled with colors that not a dot strayed beyond the base, convincing Manasa and Bhagwati that destroying the eunuch's artistry to make space for a silly dog would be sacrilege. There were no animals on my forehead that year, no colors childishly smeared.

Agastaya and I reciprocated by applying *tika* on Prasanti and the sisters.

Prasanti accepted our monetary offering of fifty rupees and exclaimed that she hoped what was in her envelope was equal to the amount in my sisters'.

We thought that was where her role ended, but Prasanti insisted we weren't done. She now applied *tika* on my sisters the way Agastaya and I did. In a weird, distorted logic that made no sense—because brothers make monetary offerings to their sisters—Prasanti, our brother, demanded money from Bhagwati and Manasa.

"That's one advantage of being a *hijra*, an in-between," she said with a giggle and ensconced her four envelopes in between her bra strap and shoulder with a loud snap.

To see this *hijra*—who'd add some much-needed detail to my third book, my first nonfiction book, my first book since the downfall—on my return home is to be taken back in time. Somehow, it seems as though everything will be all right.

•

She stares at me as though I am an apparition.

Then she touches me, first with her index finger and finally with her entire hand.

This description may read poignant, similar to a reunion between star-crossed lovers.

It isn't.

In fact, Prasanti almost pushes me.

"Aye, it's . . . you," she says, momentarily flummoxed about maintaining pronoun propriety, the variation of the Nepali *you* to employ.

I am too old for her to use *tan*, reserved for intimates, lowlifes, and those younger than you, and which she, when dealing with an adolescent me, with alarming regularity substituted with *timi*, the great equalizer between *tan* and *tapaai*, the latter being the *you* that accords respect.

And to her I am still somehow too familiar, still the cheeky brat who demanded that she show me her chest and rifled through her underwear drawer, for her to yet elevate me to a deferential *tapaai* despite how grown-up I must have seemed.

She finally settles for a neutral *timi* before running away to inform Aamaa about this unexpected arrival.

I wait for the world to fall apart and for the dogs to be set on me.

Nothing happens.

First, I see Agastaya, whom I had last seen in New York a year ago.

Fat, ugly. Bald, bespectacled. Hands shaky, making me wonder if he had any right to conduct surgery.

Words exchanged: "Hey," "hey." Eye language: *Is that really you?* Not a word about my going into the house. I remain at the threshold.

Manasa and Bhagwati close behind. Bhagwati pretty in a slutty way. Think an angel dressed up as a whore for Halloween. A splotch of sweat under her arm when she nervously scratches her head. Manasa her lady-in-waiting. Nah, grandma-in-waiting. Wrinkly. Dark. Miserable.

I had seen Bhagwati but not her husband on the same trip during which I met up with Agastaya, when I flew from New York to Denver.

It had been two years since my last rendezvous with Manasa, and two years had added ten to her face. The husband must be getting tail somewhere else because he sure as hell couldn't be tapping someone this hideous.

Words exchanged: "Hey," "hey," "hey," "hey." Eye language: *Are you kidding me?*

"Is no one going to invite me in?" My gaze moves from one sibling to another.

"It's not our house to invite you, Ruthwa." This is Manasa, just like her namesake, the damn snake goddess, full of venom.

"How Western," I point out.

"Talk values—it's you talking values." Manasa again.

"Father-in-law still giving you problems, Manasa? What's it now? Giving his peenie a little shake before bed?"

"Cunt, you're an absolute cunt." To Bhagwati and Agastaya she says, "Oh, don't look so shocked, you two. How American of you to take offense at the word. Nothing describes him better."

"Stop fighting. Come in, Ruthwa. But be prepared for Aamaa." Bhagwati the peacemaker. Bhagwati the goddess. The *bhaagney-keti*, the girl who ran away. The reject playing mediator.

I walk into the house where my first novel was set.

"Didn't know you were coming." Ah, Agastaya. Sexless. Friendless. Lifeless. Role model whose academic standards I was expected to live up to and whose accomplishments it was hoped I'd replicate. An internationally acclaimed book didn't do it. Everything would pale in comparison to the oncologist's achievements.

"I wouldn't miss it for the world." I laugh. Nervous laughter from the others follows. "Aamaa's eighty-fourth birthday—c'mon, I wouldn't miss it."

"You do know there will be a lot of drama," Bhagwati, who should know a thing or two about drama,
warns. *PhD, Engineering Drama* should be the letters
trailing her name, her low-caste name.

"He's here for that," Manasa conjectures, and with a
repetition of the sentence she declares it, guarantees it.
"He'll write about it. Bastard."

"Name a publishing house that will touch me."

"Some reality-TV production that branches into
publishing—who knows?" says Manasa—acerbic, full
of vitriol, her father-in-law's crutch, her father-in-law's
darling. "It will be right up your alley."

"Nah, I want to write a book about putting an Oxford
degree to good use, like a sister of mine is doing. Where's
the devil?"

"She doesn't want to see the devil." Agastaya laughs
at his own wit.

America has bestowed upon him a wiggly paunch and
a proclivity for platitudes.

The *hijra* darts down the stairs, clearly excited about
informing the others of my presence. Once she sees us in
the same room, she stops short, disappointed.

"Aamaa doesn't want to see you," she says.

"Wouldn't I know?" I smile at everyone.

It doesn't matter who wants to see me and who
does not.

I am here.

I am with family.

•

Prasanti waltzes into the dining room with a can of
strawberries, most definitely brought by one of my siblings from abroad, and places it on the table.

"Here," she says. "We have all finished dinner. Because your grandmother doesn't want to see your face, you should celebrate with something sweet."

Before Manasa can chastise her and ask her for spoons with which to fish the berries out of the syrup and for bowls out of which to eat them, Prasanti disappears.

"The way she does everything," Manasa says. "Half-baked."

"Makes sense," I offer. "Half is who she is."

Manasa and Bhagwati laugh cursorily.

"The house is the same, huh?" I look around. "The ceiling is still wavy and uneven. Even the dining table looks very much the same as it did when I left Gangtok."

"What did you expect?" Manasa replies. "Marbled stairway and beautiful granite countertops?"

"Talking about beautiful granite countertops, I was at the factory recently. It looks even better than it did during our days."

"Wait—why would you go there?" Manasa asks. "What new troubles are you creating for the family?"

"Yeah, what, exactly, were you doing in Kalimpong?" Agastaya pinches a strawberry out of the can and eats it with relish. "You couldn't have gone there to see the factory."

Strawberries are beautiful. Yet, almost always, they taste disappointingly flat. I have concocted a warped analogy that compares them to extremely attractive women who are terrible in the sack.

In *Himalayan Sunset,* I spent close to a page describing the analogy.

"Nothing." Would I find a copy of *Himalayan Sunset* in the house? "Just relaxing."

It is late. Everyone wants to seek asylum in sleep.

Safe subjects are exhausting. Other topics are hazardous.

A cantankerous Manasa, a catatonic Agastaya, and a conciliatory Bhagwati stare ahead of them.

I feel outnumbered—the pressure to entertain rises as the number of words exchanged diminishes.

"Do any of you want to update me on what has happened so far?" I ask.

"I don't."

"I don't."

"No."

"Where's the bookshelf?" I make for the sitting room. "Maybe I should look at the books."

"Where it was when you left Gangtok." Manasa heads upstairs. "I am off to watch mindless TV."

In the relative privacy of the sitting room, I open the sliding door of the shelf to see if it houses my books.

There it is: *Himalayan Sunset*. The yellow cover. The sun peeping from behind the mountains. The sun setting on the British Empire. How easy writing was then— how easily it came to me.

Such a clever book, critics said. In reality, it was a story that thrived on stereotypes. The Brahmins in *Himalayan Sunset* were stingier and more conservative than those of my real life, the eunuchs more flamboyant, the Western gays more promiscuous, the Indian gays even more deeply closeted, the Americans far more ethnocentric than those I came across, and the refugees all worked as dishwashers. Cobwebs in India dangled more freely, mosquitoes here sucked blood more vehemently, and roaches multiplied more aggressively.

Of course, you must stick to pigeonholes in your writing; otherwise, there's all that talk about inauthenticity.

The East seethed at the unflattering portrayals of various members of my community, called the book a betrayal, but once the Western stamp of approval—with a nudge and a wink from literary critics—was plastered all over the book, the East came around soon enough. For the West, India is cool, and Sikkim's former Himalayan-kingdom-ness even cooler.

I conduct an experiment of my youth by allowing the book to open up to the best-read page. At the TNA library, that's how we found smut. At the Neupaney Oasis, too, *Himalayan Sunset* opens to a sex scene. It is the part about Aamaa's rape.

Who has been reading this well-thumbed book? Who is getting his or her jollies from my well-reviewed rape scene? Every one of the pages where the rape was alluded to is dog-eared.

Aamaa can't really read English. Could it be Prasanti? Prasanti barely recognizes the letters of the alphabet.

Finding your book wherever it's been set can be weird. Finding the pages of the rape scene of the owner of the house you are in can be downright unnerving.

I place the book on the shelf, and then I push it back, farther and farther back until I hear it fall to the floor behind the shelf.

I pray that is the only copy in the house. I also pray I don't find the other book. If *Himalayan Sunset* made me famous, there was another that brought me notoriety of the worst kind.

•

Manasa sneaks up to me from behind and makes herself comfortable on the sofa.

"Look at someone looking at books—like his two books haven't polluted the world enough," she quips.

"I thought you wanted to watch your Star Plus shows. Is that what an MBA from the Said Business School gave you a taste for?"

"I decided against it. Are you writing again?"

The other two follow her, as though they can't bear being alone with each other for a second. "Yes."

"Really?"—Bhagwati.

"A novel?"—Agastaya.

"Nah, nonfiction."

"How the mighty have fallen."—Manasa.

"What's wrong with nonfiction?"

"With you there's so much nonfiction in fiction that one just can't say."—Manasa.

"Thanks for the support."

"What's the book about?"—Agastaya.

"I am undecided." It would be wise not to blabber about the topic being eunuchs. "At the moment, I am just trying to write. I've never had writer's block this severe. I stare at the computer for hours and still come up with nothing. I'm doing everything the writing greats have suggested—making notes, trying to write every goddamn thing I can think of, writing a certain number of words a day, dabbling in poetry, screenplay, rewriting my old interviews. Nothing works."

"Sure."—Manasa.

"Have you tried changing routines?"—Agastaya. He would know because medicine and writing are so similar.

"Want to hear something I wrote? It's a short poem."

"Ha. Who was the writer who kept ranting about poetry being the most insincere form of literature?"—Manasa.

"How fun, Manasa. You're at your best today."

"Sure. Read it."—Bhagwati.

"No, why should we encourage him, when he will use his writing to get back at us?"—Manasa.

In the book, I described Aamaa's rape, not Manasa's.

It was Aamaa's identity that was compromised, not Manasa's.

It was Aamaa's hirsute vagina that the readers of *Himalayan Sunset* got a glimpse of, not Manasa's.

And it was a blight on Aamaa's character when my unreliable narrator, so sensitive and respectful of women, declared that a middle-aged Aamaa "must have enjoyed it. All these years, there had been no sex. The breasts may have sagged, but the desire not so much."

But again, it's Manasa I am talking about. She can be a horror, a bitch.

"It wasn't your rape I described," I say, looking away from Manasa. "It was the old lady's. What ails you?"

"Everyone knew it was her. Everyone knew whose family it was."

"Didn't you say in London that you now belong to a different family?"

"Don't play games. You know what I mean."

"I described the rape of a woman who bought her first factory with money she extracted using the most questionable means. She deserves to be in jail." That bit is true. After my parents died when the jeep they were in collided with a bus, and their vehicle fell into the River Teesta, a bawling Aamaa went to the then-chief minister's office and lied to him: her son and daughter-in-law, she sobbed, had been on this trip to Kalimpong to buy some property. The large sums of money they had with them had gone down along with the jeep and its passengers. The money the charitable chief minister offered the relatives of the deceased wasn't compensation enough for Aamaa. She emerged from the meeting with enough money to eventually purchase the Kalimpong factory.

"Even if she's the biggest villain on earth, you have no fucking right to write about her rape, you conscienceless prick."—Manasa.

"Oh, like Aamaa has a conscience."

"You don't get it. No fucking man in this country gets how serious rape is. I can't reason with you."

"I am going upstairs," I say.

"Where?"—Bhagwati.

"To hell."

"It could be worse than hell. She's made trouble about everything since we arrived."—Agastaya.

"Like what? I thought I was the only one who rankled her."

"You've forgotten about a Damaai granddaughter."—Bhagwati.

"A bachelor grandson."—Agastaya.

"And me."—Manasa.

"What's her problem with you?"

"Everything. I didn't bring my husband to her awful *Chaurasi*."

"Why not?"

My ugly sister glares in silence.

"All right, I'm going to bell the cat." I am such a showman.

"Not tonight. It's too late. Wait until tomorrow."— Bhagwati.

"Where do I sleep?"

"Probably the couch. VIP treatment for you."—
Manasa.

•

I wake up on the morning of Kukkur *Puja* to ululating
street dogs.

Gangtok has a canine abundance that people incor-
rectly think doesn't quite hamper the place's beauty.
Dogs—mangy, drooling, flea-ridden—populate the entire
damn town.

During the day, the capital belongs to humans. At
night, curs reign supreme.

For most of the year, dogs are either neglected or ill-
treated. On Kukkur *Puja*, devotees run after them, garland them, and ply them with feasts.

Tomorrow the dogs can fornicate in peace, but today
those orgasms will have to be delayed because some pious
human needs to absolve his or her sins.

It isn't even light yet. No one is awake.

I can't sleep because the couch of my yesteryears isn't
cooperating. Wads of feather and sponge from the sofa
cushions are strewn all over the floor in evidence.

On the table is what looks like a place card with my
name written on it in Manasa's unmistakable curli-
cue. The inside of the card contains a message: *Darling
Ruthwa, now that you are writing again, I thought you might
require a book for inspiration. Please find V. S. Naipaul's* Half
a Life, *which you love so much, on the table. Of course, your
love for it was well documented in* In the Foothills of the
Himalayas. *Enjoy the journey, brother. Love, M.*

The nerve of the bitch . . . she needs to be throttled
to death.

•

Bold. Deep. Sad. Beautiful. Pitch-perfect. Chilling. Perfectly done. Poignant. Real. Visceral.

A right-wing London newspaper declared the depic-
tion of Aamaa's incident in *Himalayan Sunset* as "the most
visceral description of rape written in the last fifty years."

I took that as a big compliment. I take it I wouldn't have
received it if I admitted to everybody that the account
was repeated verbatim—the litany of ellipses connoting
pauses of pain—from my grandmother's narration.

Besides, I was always doubtful—in fact, I still am—of
the veracity of Aamaa's rape story.

She's, therefore, the better storyteller than I.

That was *Himalayan Sunset*. There was also another
Himalayan-titled novel: *In the Foothills of the Himalayas*,
where, let's say, things . . . er . . . didn't work out quite
as well.

•

I walk into Manasa's room upstairs so I can throw *Half
a Life* on her hideous head but find Bhagwati sleeping
there.

"Where's the bitch?" I demand.

"Couldn't you sleep, either?"

"Nah. I just woke up. That's one uncomfortable sofa."

"It's still dark. What time is it? Are you looking for
Prasanti?"

"No, for Manasa. What a frustrated, fucked-up piece
of shit she is."

"What did she do?"

"Salt. Old wounds. Left a Naipaul book on my table."

"The one from which you plagiarized?"

"Aaargh. Yes."

"That's funny." Bhagwati laughs. Even when she's just awoken or had a sleepless night, she's glowing.

"She has no conscience."

"She thinks the same about you."

"Well, we are descendants of the great Chitralekha Neupaney. How would we have consciences?"

"Why, exactly, are you here again?" Bhagwati rubs her eyes and yawns.

"Only if you promise not to tell anyone."

"I do."

"An old friend at an Indian publishing house—I am not disclosing which one—has asked me to write a proposal for a nonfiction book."

"Even after the plagiarism scandal?"

"Yeah, he's from Darjeeling. A Nepali helping a Nepali out or something."

"What will you write on?"

"The eunuchs of the hills."

Her sleepy eyes exude skepticism.

"Think of it—there have been so many books on eunuchs living in the plains. None on the hill ones. No one even knows they exist."

"Will it have buyers?"

"It should. I'm writing it. I don't know."

"Why Kalimpong?"

"Wanted to do some research there—start with Prasanti's family."

"And what did you find?" Bhagwati sits up now.

"Nothing really," I lie, and then improvise. "Nothing of consequence really."

Prasanti's mother was dead. Her father was dead. Her stepmother, of whose existence I was unaware, was dead. When I finally tracked down a miserable half sister, she refused to talk to me. Even my accented Nepali backfired. So, I offered her money. One hundred rupees. Four hundred rupees. One thousand rupees.

"You're stalling," Bhagwati declares.

"Well, I did find her sister. She gave me nothing."

The truth was different. The half sister did reveal that she remembered a few things about Prasanti's childhood. Prasanti—well, Prasanti was Prasant, a boy, then—had received all the love and affection from the parents. The father had been a priest and the mother insane. That was Prasanti's mother, not the half sister's. Prasanti had apparently run away from home when she was eleven. A few neighbors had by then gathered around us and pronounced the story true. Yes, Prasanti was last seen at her uncle's funeral in Melli.

She wasn't exactly voluble, this pricey sister, so I asked her if I could see the other sisters. All three of them had been married to men from Nepal. One of them had even run away with a *Jaisi*, a lower-category Brahmin, and was now cut off from the rest of the family. I should have continued flashing the sister a new 1,000-rupee bill while layer after layer of secrecy was peeled off until the body of Prasanti's early life was mine to devour.

"I could have pestered the neighbors to talk, friends and relatives to gossip, but I left," I say.

"Because you were bored?" Bhagwati asks.

"One could say that."

I tell my sister about the strange tension rippling in Kalimpong. The townspeople looked upon the new vigor brought to the Gorkhaland movement as a positive turn of events, but the more educated among the group huddled together in concern. A "suggestion" was made by the *Gorkha Jana-shakti Morcha*, the political party that over-promises and under-delivers, that everyone should wear traditional clothes during *Tihaar*.

In these parts, a suggestion is often a mandate, and enforcers of suggestions are often self-appointed. Add to these enforcers the moral police of the hills in the form of a bunch of party-appointed young men—nay, boys—and Kalimpong was becoming an unrecognizable place. Dictatorial.

The guardians of our culture—these political hooligans—gave inciting speeches, and people cheered. Loudly. The guardians of our culture banned alcohol while people made bootleg purchases. Frequently. The guardians of our culture eschewed Nepali in favor of Gorkhali while people became hopeful. Sadly. The guardians of our culture made promises and swore Gorkhaland would happen while people chose to believe them. Again.

My run-ins with the guardians of our culture because I wore shorts and T-shirts became more frequent. One particularly bad experience later, I packed my bags for Sikkim.

"So, you're back to writing about one of us?" Bhagwati asks. "Can't you find other topics—like this tension in Kalimpong, for instance?"

"That's a good idea."

"Think of it—it is a relevant issue. And it's better than writing about Prasanti."

"Do you care?"

"To be honest, I don't."

"Then why ask?"

"It seems to bother the others. Aamaa's rape . . ."

"Which very well could have been a lie."

"Even then."

"So, how's your marriage?"

"I know what you're trying to do, but I can't undo it, Ruthwa. I can't undo what I did. You can, and I don't think writing yet another book about one of us is the way to go about it."

"I am resurrecting my career, Bhagwati. It was horrible to be hailed as the next big thing in South Asian fiction when the first book came out and declared finished with the second one. This nonfiction book will help."

"Why did you do it?"

"Do what?"

"Lift those lines from Naipaul's book?"

"I didn't do it intentionally. Who plagiarizes intentionally, especially from an author who's read everywhere? It happened. I read and reread that cranky old man's book to see where the magic lay. The words seeped in, registered—his words became my words. It was a big, fucking mistake, yes, but it wasn't my mistake alone. The editor missed it. The copy editor missed it. The proofreader missed it. But I alone had to take the hit."

"So, another book, huh?"

"A friend did me a favor, Bhagwati. I can't go around demanding new topics. I am thirty-one. I can't live the rest of my life clouded by that one mistake. I haven't worked this hard before. I am trying everything. I am writing poetry, or trying to, at least. It's awful. I am making mundane lists of my memories. I've never tried this hard to get back to writing. I can't screw this opportunity up."

"You could do other things."

"And wonder for the rest of my life what would have happened if I hadn't quit writing altogether?"

"Do you think the plagiarism scandal was God's way of teaching you a lesson for including the rape in the book?"

"I didn't think the rape story was true—that's why I included it in the book. I still think it's a lie."

"You turned it into a joke."

"You accuse me of being insensitive to rapes. Believe me, I am not. I cannot see someone as formidable as Aamaa being raped."

"I am not convinced."

"Tell me this: do you believe it actually happened to her?"

"No."

"See? I don't either. Yes, women get raped. Yes, strong women get raped. It's tragic. It's infuriating. It's fucked-up. But I know Aamaa wouldn't get raped. She's too . . ."

"What? Ugly?"

"No. Fuck that. Strong. She's too . . . It's Aamaa. She exudes power. Who'd dare do it to her?"

"I know. But why would she keep insisting it happened to her?"

"Again, it's Aamaa. Probably to let us know that setbacks happen? To prove how hardy she is? It's Chitralekha Neupaney—anything is possible. Gives more punch to her rags-to-riches story."

"Let's talk about other things."

"How're you doing financially?"

"Why does everyone think I am so poor?" Bhagwati says, exasperated. "If you want to catch Aamaa, now might be a better time to do it than later. At least no one is awake."

With that, she covers her pretty face with the ugly quilt. It's my cue to leave her alone.

•

Downstairs, in the sitting room, I accost Agastaya, who's half asleep, about his opinion on my career. He echoes Bhagwati's sentiments regarding my writing about the Gorkhaland movement.

He then staggers to the bathroom. That reminds me—I *have* to pee.

He doesn't close the door. I follow him.

"What the hell?" he inquires, his penis half out of his drawers.

"My bladder is about to burst." I flick my dick out; it anoints the sink with a sprinkle of urine.

"I have no idea what's happening," Agastaya says, shoving his junk back into his briefs. "Couldn't you use the upstairs bathroom?"

"This is like the good old days." The jet doesn't stop. "Like Aamaa will open her door so I can pee in her bathroom?"

"This is awkward."

"How the hell?"

"Because we are grown men."

He leaves the bathroom.

I let the tap run and spit into the sink.

Agastaya waits for me to finish, enters the bathroom, looks away from the sink, and locks the door.

Once he comes out, I ask him if he will listen to something I've written. He says no.

"So, then, I should write about the Gorkhaland move-ment?" I ask him again.

"Fucking write about whatever the fuck you want." He closes the door to his room with a bang.

Who is he now? Manasa?

•

I try coaxing the door to Aamaa's room open. I knock at it insistently. I push it with all my might.

No one knocks in this family. No one has boundaries of privacy. No one has a sense of space.

The door is locked from the inside. She who scorned privacy, who always maintained that there was no need for it, is now clinging to it.

"Aamaa, can you hear me?"

"Aamaa." Once, twice, three times.

The red door opens, creakily, uncertainly, reticently.

Inside, through the small opening, looks out Prasanti, a man in a woman, a woman in a man. "It's still dark, you ghost," she whispers. "She's in bed."

"I'm hungry. Can you give me something other than strawberries to eat?"

"At this time in the morning?" She is still whispering, as if Aamaa is actually asleep.

"Yes, stones in the stomach," I whisper, too.

"Go down. I'll be there in a minute."

I wait by the door. God, the Neupaney Oasis needs a paint job.

Prasanti emerges, covering whatever is on her chest with a scarf. Quickly, before I can figure out what she is doing, she inserts a key into the keyhole and locks the door. The key, along with its family of jangling siblings, goes into the vicinity of the eunuch's bosom—that sanctum sanctorum where all is safe.

Inside, the snubber of privacy is locked in her private sanatorium.

My plan to sneak in is thwarted. I'd have to find some other way to see the old hag.

Someone snores.

"I can't make anything elaborate," Prasanti says. "Can you do with noodles?"

"Wai-Wai?"

"No, Maggi."

"No Wai-Wai?"

"No."

I pull a chair from the dining room into the kitchen.

"What? Will you watch me cook?"

"Just want to talk."

"No one wants to talk to you. I am surprised those people did. Aamaa wasn't very happy."

"You haven't aged a bit."

"I know. I am a beauty queen." Prasanti pours some water into a saucepan, breaks the Maggi in half, and throws the two pieces into the vessel with the same gracelessness that I vividly remember. "What happened to your *dara*?"

"Went to a dentist, got braces—they fixed my teeth."

"Your *gas* must like your repaired teeth."

Gas, where I come from, in addition to being the kitchen equipment you use for cooking and the cylinder on which said equipment works, of which there is forever a scarcity around here, is also your girlfriend. Don't ask me why. The educated use it mockingly, disparagingly. The masses say it with solemnity, as if no other synonym would do justice to the love of their lives.

"Don't you say *condo* these days?"

"No, I've grown up." Prasanti smiles. "I don't use bad words anymore."

"I don't believe you. *Condo* was your favorite word."

"Now it is *laro*."

I laugh in shock at her brazenness, at the lowliest word for *penis* she just used.

"Wow," I say, because I don't know how else to convey my delight. "Wow. Wow."

"What wow-wow?" Prasanti chides. "Wow-wow-wow—like an *Angrez* who doesn't know any other word. Will you make me your topic now?"

Ah, *topic*. A word I come across every day but whose meaning now was so far removed from the connotation it held in my adolescence. Your *topic* was the object of your sexual affection.

"Topic of your *chattisey*, huh?" Prasanti asks.

I am slack-jawed.

Chattis is *thirty-six*, the number.

Chattisey, with the suffix, somehow means thirty-six strokes of the penis for the purpose of self-pleasuring. The number of strokes it is purported for your member to spit semen out. *Chattisey* is the most creative—if substandard—Nepali word I know, but it is just one of the many clever words we have concocted. We Nepali-speaking people use our language ingeniously. We are lovers of neologism.

"I have some *sel-roti*," Prasanti remembers. "I made them all a few days ago. Would you like some?"

"Nah, not this early in the morning—we'll eat them later. For now, Maggi is enough."

"You loved *sel-roti* as a child."

"I liked all food as a child."

"Has that changed?"

"Nah, still like all food."

"Then why did you say no to my *sel-roti*?"

"Because I'll be full with all that Maggi."

"You just said you were very hungry."

"All right, give me a *sel-roti*."

"No *sel-roti* for you now. My *sel-roti* isn't for picky people like you. I am dispatching half of what I made to those idiots at the Kalimpong factory. They say it's the best *sel-roti* they have ever eaten."

She is behaving like a woman difficult to get into bed.

"Do you still dance?" I ask. A showman recognizes another showman. We know better than to let go of an opportunity to perform.

"I dance only for special people like Aamaa." She hands me the soupy Maggi in a bowl. "It's hot, fool. Be careful."

"So, you won't dance for me?"

"You're Aamaa's enemy. You're my enemy."

"Entertain me while I eat."

"All right, I'll sing." She can't keep the desire to perform suppressed even for a minute.

Prasanti clears her throat a few times, holds her balled-up fist to her mouth, and sings "*Deusi*," a carol sung by groups of men during *Tihaar*. "*Jhilimili, jhilimili,*" she sings softly and bellows: "*Deusurey.*" The words preceding the *Deusurey* are barely audible, but the *Deusurey*, the chorus, rumbles out several decibels louder and keeps getting louder and louder until at the door stands Manasa and the *Deusurey* becomes softer and softer.

"Stop it." Manasa is furious. "Stop it. I am trying to sleep."

"He asked me to," Prasanti says with mock fear in her eyes.

"Does that mean you have to do everything he asks you?"

"Yes, I am a servant."

"You're a servant only when you feel like it. When you have real work, you're a *Maharani*."

"Or a *maharandi*," Prasanti says. The clever play of words, by which she relegates a queen to a whore, makes me laugh uncontrollably.

"You, too, stop, Ruthwa," Manasa says in English. "Don't encourage her. She's not one of your whores."

"*Maharani, maharandi*, who knows?" Prasanti says. "Deep within even a *Maharani* could be a *maharandi*. *Randi, Rani. Rani, Randi.*"

This is too much. I have to set aside the bowl of Maggi somewhere so I can laugh without spilling any soup on myself.

"Look at him—laughing *galala*." Prasanti points at me, using an onomatopoeic deliciousness whose English translation—maybe *uproariously*—would do zero justice to it. "Here, give your bowl to me. Laugh freely. The wrinkles don't show on you like they do on this one."

Which is when Manasa loses it.

It is one of those slaps—perfect in its thunder, in the four-finger imprint it leaves behind, and in the shock it causes the slapped. Had baby slaps preceded it and pinches trailed it, the slap would have lost some of its perfection. No words trivialize the slap. No justification adulterates it. It is a swift slap, a half-a-second slap, and the venue where it is delivered will smart for hours. Hell, every part of the body of the slapped will throb for hours.

The dispenser of the perfect slap heads back to bed, whereas the perfectly slapped hurries to her room.

"Aamaa, can you hear me?" I shout from downstairs, then laugh to myself at the absurdity of the question, the absurdity of the situation.

It isn't even six a.m.

This is going to be one long day.

THREE

Prasanti Paradise

Prasanti had stopped spitting into people's food a long time ago. She did not feel any satisfaction in her victims not knowing what she had done to their food, so these days, she threw stones into their rice. Choosing these pebbles was an art, for she had to pick out barely visible, tiny white stones and hide them in mounds of rice only after the food had been apportioned onto the plates. She couldn't throw the stones into the rice cooker because they would swim everywhere when the rice boiled, and those people she didn't want assaulted by her weapon of choice would inadvertently end up crunching on one.

A foil to this otherwise foolproof tool of revenge was not knowing which seat and plate the recipient of her evil designs would select. Prasanti, thus, set aside the pebbles for second helpings. When someone she wanted dead demanded more rice, she'd serve this person a mound with the tiny bowl she sometimes used as a ladle and into which she would have already introduced a few pebbles.

Prasanti usually stuck to a plan. She would not follow through with her plot the very night someone ill-treated her but wait a day or two, play nice with this person, pretend she had forgotten everything about the mistreatment meted out on her, and then strike. Today, though, she wasn't going to delay her payback. Her cheek still stung, and the humiliation of a slap at this age was too painful to swallow.

After the showdown at dawn, Prasanti had disappeared into the darkness, retreated beyond the garage, and cried. The encounter with Manasa gave rise to one unpleasant memory after another. She, therefore, did what she always did when she felt defeated: she had her dialogue with God.

"How dare she treat me that way?" she asked God.

"You shouldn't have made fun of her," Prasanti answered as God.

"But she is horrible. Treats me like I am a servant."

"You are a servant, and you have to put up with her only for a few days. She will be gone."

"I hate her."

"And she hates you."

"Why am I made this way?" she asked God.

"Because you're special," God replied.

"Is this how special people feel?" she demanded of God.

"Yes, sometimes even special people feel misery," God answered.

"Why couldn't I be one—man or woman?"

"Because you're special."

"Sometimes I feel you say that only to make me feel happy."

"Think of it this way—how many people in the world can claim to be like you? How many people in Gangtok are like you?"

"Perhaps two."

"Yes, of the *lakhs* of people in the city, it's just you and the dancer who has run away to Siliguri."

"And she's the butt of all jokes."

"That she is," God replied.

"Why are we such jokes? Why do they always laugh at us? Why does no one take us seriously?"

"You could be serious. They'd take you seriously. But you are always laughing, always dancing, always jumping. You want to be taken seriously, behave differently."

"I try doing that. Sometimes, I never smile. But it makes me miserable. I want to be my own self again. Am I really special?"

"You are special. I wanted you to experience life as very few humans can. You are living a good life."

It was a mechanism that had always worked. It would work forever.

Today, the day of the worship of dogs, Prasanti would give that little bitch called Manasa the best meal of her life.

Manasa was a light eater and seldom asked for second helpings, so Prasanti would have to slightly tweak her regular plan of action. The tiny stones the eunuch had picked up were so delightfully shaped, sized, and colored that they didn't look very different from grains of rice. They wouldn't even jangle on the plate. All she had to do now was figure out where Manasa would sit.

Manasa was the first to arrive when Prasanti let everyone know with a squeal that lunch was ready. As her mistress's daughter turned to the sink to wash her hands, Prasanti surreptitiously sprinkled some stones into the rice on the plate closest to Manasa's back. Feeling more self-congratulatory now because she was certain Manasa would perch herself at her usual spot, right in front of which was the stone-laden plate, the eunuch stirred the stones into the rice a bit. They blended perfectly with the grains.

Manasa sat in her usual chair, made a face at the barely disassembled cauliflower florets in the curry, studied the plate in front of her, and asked Prasanti if she had portioned out rice for elephants and not humans. She moved the plate to the place to her left and ladled a tiny amount of fresh rice from the cooker into an empty bowl. Aamaa, who had voluntarily exiled herself to her bedroom for breakfast with no resistance from her family members, came in at the same time as Agastaya and sat next to Manasa.

"How was it?" Aamaa asked, adding cauliflower and *daal* atop the hill of rice on the plate intended for Manasa. "The monastery? Did you find God there? What do you find in monasteries that you don't find in temples? This *daal* looks too thin."

"I go to monasteries to look at paintings, Aamaa," Agastaya said as he scooped out some yogurt and added it to a mix similar to Chitralekha's. "Buddha, Kaali—I believe in no one."

"That's how I brought you up—to question your own religion and be cynical about everything, marriage included."

Bhagwati trailed in after Agastaya as though still unsure of her place in the dining room. Prasanti was unbearably uncomfortable. She had never subjected Chitralekha to a stone treatment. Her mistress didn't deserve it. Worse, she had once admitted to Chitralekha—in one of those moments of mistress-servant bonding—that she had mixed some pebbles into the food of the minister next door when he came to discuss with Chitralekha his plans of vertically expanding his building. Aamaa had lightly reprimanded her but seemed more amused than offended at the breach of hospitality. Chitralekha would probably know what was going on.

Ruthwa swaggered in and sat opposite Aamaa. It would be nice if the tension between grandson and grandmother made Aamaa forget that she had food in front of her.

"The entire family is here," Ruthwa said.

No one else said a word.

"Silence?" Ruthwa continued. "That means I am forgiven. Ah."

For a while, things worked as Prasanti hoped they would. Aamaa would make little balls out of the rice, cauliflower, and *daal* and then break them. She repeated the process a few times. She was too distracted by Ruthwa's presence to eat.

"For no fault of mine, everybody stopped talking to me," Ruthwa said. "Now, everyone seems fine with me. Aamaa, I have missed out on a few years of your life. Fill me in—what has happened since the prodigal grandson elevated this family from obscurity to fame?"

Prasanti heard Manasa laugh. The fool would have been grimacing had Prasanti's plans not been foiled.

Bhagwati cast a look at Manasa and asked Prasanti for a glass of water.

"Do you still eat rice for all three meals, Aamaa?" Bhagwati asked. "What a *bhaatey* you've always been."

"All Nepalis love their rice," Aamaa said, suddenly chirpy. "All Brahmins love their rice. Doesn't your family love it, too? Bhutanese and Damaais don't? I thought they did."

"Bhagwati will become an American soon," Manasa said. "She will then eat bread—did you know that's what they eat in America, Aamaa? How would you? You haven't been outside India, yet you think you know everything."

"Yes, I know," Aamaa replied. "I know what it is like to be the grandmother of a thirty-three-year-old who's yet unmarried."

Prasanti stood at the threshold of the kitchen, praying that Chitralekha would toss her plate at Manasa in fury. That would take care of two things: the stones and Manasa.

Manasa took a sip of water and placed it on the table not very gently.

"Soon, we will have . . ." Aamaa said. And then it came—the first crunch.

"A pebble?" she said to herself. "That hasn't happened to me in a long time." She spat out the food on the table and moved her plate to conceal the goo. "What would we old, dying people know?" she continued. "Our opinions don't matter."

Another crunch. This one was slightly louder than the last. Chitralekha spat it out and hid the debris with the steel glass.

"One grandson and unmarried."

"Shut up, Aamaa," Manasa said. "You have two grandsons, and both are here right now."

"No worries if she doesn't consider me one," Ruthwa said. "I always knew I was adopted."

"Just one," Chitralekha said, before taking a mouthful. A second later came a loud crunching. "Did some blind person cook the rice today? How can one get three pebbles in three bites?"

"Oh, is that your way of denying that you have two grandsons?" Manasa said, more hostile than she had been up to that point.

"Who cooks food here?" Chitralekha spluttered. "Prasanti, three pebbles? Come here, you idiot."

Prasanti forced her feet to move forward. "I think I need to see the eye doctor," she sheepishly said.

"I know what it is." Chitralekha got up, overturning the plate and causing it to clang to the floor, its contents splattering as far as the walls. "I know what it is. Yes, the minister—you did this with the next-door minister, too. You are angry with me because I asked you to mind your own business, you witch."

"No, it was a mistake. It really was."

"Shut up. I know. She was defending this Damaai. The Damaai has probably weaved some kind of black magic on this *hijra*. She kept supporting her. You give me half-caste great-grandchildren and dissolve this family's name in mud and then recruit my loyal servant to win over my affection. I am surprised I even let you inside my home."

"No, it wasn't her," Prasanti said. "It wasn't her idea."

"Shut up. You're a servant," Chitralekha hissed. "You've probably forgotten it because of the good life you have here. One more mistake, and you will be out begging in the streets. This does not work at all. Every-body takes advantage of me, even a good-for-nothing *hijra*. Tell me, you *kukkurnee*, you did it because I told you I didn't need your opinions yesterday, didn't you? What will you do next? Poison me? I should call the police. You'll probably poison me."

Police wasn't a good word for Prasanti. It brought back memories, the same that surfaced when she had her con-versations with God.

"Sorry!" she sobbed. "It was for Manasa. Manasa slapped me this morning. It was for her. Ask her. Please ask her. She ate out of that stupid bowl today. She slapped me—slapped me like I was a child. I am a woman in her thirties who gets beaten. How bad is that? I did it to teach her a lesson."

By the time Chitralekha stormed upstairs and the others finished eating and rinsing their mouths in silence, the film of tears obscuring Prasanti's vision cleared, and her eyes met Manasa's, where she spotted sheer disgust. Desperate for sympathy, she turned to Bhagwati, who sat frozen in a chair, her eyes on the plate Chitralekha had thrown on the floor.

Even a dialogue with God wouldn't solve this problem. She was an idiot to throw away all the goodwill she had built. Her mistress—the one person she had always made happy—couldn't stand her now. Manasa knew of Prasanti's hatred for her. Given how the dynamics in the family had changed, Manasa would easily be able to convince her grandmother to get rid of Prasanti. What was she but a servant? Easily disposable, with no onerous duties to perform, a *hijra* with a skill level so low that those clueless *Adivasis* from Doars could easily do her job with a day's training. All these years of injecting laughter into the house had been quashed with the humiliation she's just inflicted on Aamaa.

She understood Aamaa, and Aamaa understood her. She knew that the key to Aamaa's heart was raunchy humor. Anything that entailed sex, sexual characteristics, excretion, and flatulence made her mistress's day. She could titillate her mistress. She knew Aamaa as well as she knew herself.

Prasanti's life had been different from the dancer *hijra*'s—all because of Aamaa. She was so far removed from her past in Bombay, when she lived in a *koti*, danced at people's homes, and was expected to eventually prostitute herself. The *hijras* she'd lived with were lying when they promised her that, in them, she'd eventually find companionship, in their lifestyles, acceptance and society. Now she had a roof above her head, a nice, strong roof, good food to eat—the same food her mistress ate—and good clothes to wear.

Yet, she took her life here for granted.

The *hijras* of her past, in an effort to feel better about their sorry lives, invented naïve stories. They claimed that they were blessed by Lord Rama and were his chosen ones. In one of the many ridiculous versions of the tale they had a penchant for repeating—as though the retelling made it more truthful—the eunuchs brayed that their ability to jinx people's fates was bequeathed to them by Rama himself. It was some silly story dating back to when Rama was sent into exile. His subjects followed him to the forest, and Rama, the benevolent prince, asked them all to return, to allow him to serve penance alone. Fourteen years later, on the way back to his kingdom of Ayodhya, he discovered that people were waiting for him outside the forest.

"Why are you still here?" Rama asked.

"Well, Lord," one of the people said. "You asked all men and women to go back. We are neither men nor women, so we stayed."

Moved by their devotion, the god gave them the power of the curse—anyone who crossed them would be destroyed.

That's what the *hijras* believed. Prasanti, as hard as she tried, couldn't bring herself to accept the story.

She had given up that life for this, and this was a far better life.

Her room was right below the stairs, which made the ceiling slant—it was low toward the entrance and very high at the other end. She had spoken to Aamaa about moving the door to the end with the higher ceiling, but Aamaa put it off, saying she'd promote her to an actual room—one of the grandchildren's rooms—if she behaved. Prasanti couldn't pace the area without hitting her head at some point. And yet, as she looked around her space, she couldn't help wondering if she should complain about the construction quirk. She had a nice bed. She didn't sleep on the floor. On the bed was a soft mattress, different from the rags she'd put together in the *hijra* house. The sheets were clean and had no holes. She had no memory of sheets from the *hijra* house—they had most likely been absent, like dignity and self-respect. She had so many clothes—new and hand-me-downs—that she was sometimes tempted to discard some of them.

Prasanti couldn't cry anymore. It was as though she had exhausted her last teardrop.

The *Godrej* wardrobe, which she had obtained without permission from one of the rooms upstairs, rattled as she opened it. She inspected the contents of her safe-deposit box: an envelope with a thick stack of 500-rupee bills, some earned, some stolen; three pairs of gold earrings, one gifted, two stolen; a dozen gold bangles, half presented, half stolen; and a stolen necklace. Prasanti ran her hands over the crispness of each bill, as though she were examining a fine piece of cloth, and counted. She had accumulated more than Rs. 40,000.

She wasn't a poor woman. She was worth more than all the servants she knew. Even if she were thrown out

of the house, she had enough in cash and gold to be able
to live. If she chose to move to a village, she'd even be
considered well off. Then the cold reality of this alterna-
tive life set in: she couldn't live outside the house. She
wouldn't get a moment's peace beyond the compound.
She would be taunted, beaten, and destroyed, all because
she had more of an organ than some and not enough of
one as others. She had to live here. She'd have to live
here. She couldn't risk an altercation like the one that
had just occurred.

Prasanti made up her mind. She would do her job.
She would please everyone—even Manasa, impossible as it would be not to fight with her. She would
stir up no trouble. In fact, she would start now. She
would hang marigold garlands around the windows. It
didn't matter that Bhagwati had said she'd do it. It didn't
matter that Aamaa had confided in Prasanti that she
wanted Bhagwati to do it with Agastaya, so Bhagwati
could goad Agastaya into seeing some woman. Prasanti
would do everything around the house. She wanted
to show everyone she could work hard, that she was
irreplaceable.

In the sitting room was the basket that contained
the garlands she and Bhagwati had sewn together in the
morning. Prasanti grabbed a garland and proceeded to
deck the main door with it. Ruthwa asked if she needed
help. Her condition had moved this brainless, heartless,
selfish devil to take pity on her. She didn't need his assis-
tance but said nothing.

"Is everything all right?" Ruthwa said. "Are you
okay?"

This display of concern—insincere as it may have
been—brought back the flood of tears.

"I have work to do," Prasanti said. "I have a lot of work to do."

She couldn't go back to living alone as a *hijra*. She couldn't go back to living with other *hijras*.

She couldn't return to her old life—any of her old lives.

Four

It's just the right moment for me to intervene. Prasanti is at her susceptible best.

She keeps telling me that her story isn't anything extraordinary, that it is an everyman story—well, an every*hijra* story.

With the labor divided between Prasanti and me—and she in the mood to bleat about her past, which only quickens the pace at which she hangs the *malas* around the windows—it doesn't take very long for all the windows and doors of the house (with the exception of those in Aamaa's room) to be garlanded with marigolds.

It takes a far longer time to write the piece on Prasanti. But what a marvelous sample chapter this will be to accompany my proposal on a book about the *hijras* of the hills.

A Hijra Story

She had been born Prasant Acharya—the son of a Brahmin priest and his second wife.

Within six short years of his first marriage, Pundit Acharya was the burdened father of four daughters. Already nearing sixty and prone to sicknesses whose diagnosis varied from doctor to doctor, the priest was afraid he would die without a son to perform his death rites.

The thought of a stranger incinerating his fat, pudgy body bothered the priest. The stranger would be some relative—flesh and blood, yes, but flesh and blood many times removed. The pundit was certain his cremator wouldn't abstain from salt for thirteen days after his death. The image of this man sucking on a sliver of chicken ten minutes after setting the priest's body on fire made our learned friend despondent.

Pundit Acharya had tried again and again to impregnate his wife, but she dutifully isolated herself in the cowshed month after month to menstruate in peace. No child—male or female—arrived.

When he had married his first wife, Nirmala, slightly older than a child bride and slightly younger than a woman, those thighs had been so full of promise. And he couldn't fault her—for she delivered, quantity-wise. But what good was quantity when not one of his four offspring could immolate him?

Nothing made his sick heart cry more than when he saw his younger brother's twin toddlers run around naked, their tiny penises glistening in the sun. Pundit Acharya seldom saw his nephews clothed from the waist down. It was as though the little boys' overactive bladders, which engendered a frequent change of clothes that started early in the morning, and Pundit Acharya's brother's acute poverty, which guaranteed that the harassed mother would run out of clothes into which to change the sons by the third urination of the day, was a mocking reminder from God about what the priest lacked.

Adopting one of the two nephews wouldn't be the same as siring a son.

So, Pundit Chavi Raman Acharya called a meeting at which he discussed his problem with fellow priests, all of whom thought similarly, and all of whom pitied this poor man whose sicknesses received confused diagnoses and whose wife hadn't yet borne him a son.

The Pundit had an idea.

"Would it be inappropriate for me to say that I'd like to get married to your daughter, Parajuli-*jee*?" he asked one of the gathered men.

Parajuli was a young priest who had married very early. Pundit Acharya was an old priest who had married very late. Parajuli had a nineteen-year-old daughter who talked to herself. A week before, she had cut her mother's hair with a knife when the exhausted mother was asleep.

The nineteen-year-old daughter still played with seven-year-olds.

"But there's a problem," Pundit Acharya said.

It wasn't that the bride-to-be was retarded.

"It's a caste problem."

All the priests had already started nodding in understanding.

"I am Acharya," Acharya said.

The priests continued nodding in understanding.

It wasn't the difference in their castes; it was the similarity. The bride-to-be and her husband-to-be belonged to the same *gotra*—they both were from the *Kaundinya gotra*, descendants of the *Kaundinya* Rishi. The union would be a form of consanguineous marriage—at its complicated best—even if Pundit Acharya and Pundit Parajuli would have to go back seventy-seven generations to find common DNA.

"But it's not a problem we can't solve," Acharya said. "We create the rules here. I am the oldest pundit in Kalimpong. This relationship I declare nonconsanguineous."

The others were in rapt attention. Acharya-*jee* was an erudite man.

The six pundits agreed. All of them had, at one point or another, received tutelage under Acharya. Pundit Acharya had married hundreds of men to hundreds of women and conducted the death rites of hundreds of dead bodies. Because everyone agreed that the priest needed to be married a second time so he could have a son who'd cremate his dead body, the very slight murmur about the nature of a wedding between an Acharya and a Parajuli was quickly hushed by experts on punditry.

The marriage was simple.

The retarded wife wore red. The groom wore *daura-suruwal*. The groom's first wife wore green. The wife's father wore a *dhoti* waist down and his sacred thread waist up. The groom's brother conducted the ceremony. The groom's four daughters wore frilly frocks. The brother's sons, the two nephews, played in the sun, fully clothed.

At last, God had stopped laughing at Pundit-*jee*.

Sumitra, the new wife, had to be reprimanded a few times by her father during the ceremony. When instructed to sprinkle rice into the sacred fire around which she and her groom sat, she threw some at her soon-to-be step-daughters' faces and laughed. When asked to take the sacred rounds, she refused to have the loose end of her sari tied to her husband's cloth belt. Once Round One was completed with difficulty and a few pinches from her father, Sumitra wouldn't take Round Two.

Pundit Parajuli looked apologetically at Pundit Acharya and said a slap or two was necessary to discipline his retarded child when she was like this.

Pundit Acharya asked his first wife to take note.

Ten months later, Sumitra gave birth to a child, dangling between whose brittle legs was a penis.

Pundit Acharya could have kissed the tiny protrusion in joy.

He showed the little bundle to his four daughters and nearly slapped the second one when she tried touching her little brother.

Sumitra wailed and wailed. Her favorite toy, the biggest doll she had ever seen, was snatched away from her and handed over to the first wife for safekeeping.

Sumitra was allowed a few minutes at a time to play with the constantly crying doll when it would suckle on her.

Other times, no one was allowed to touch Prasant but the priest and his first wife.

Prasant was a delightful baby who wore delightful clothes—shorts with frills, shirts with frills, and pants with frills, all sewn with frock pieces salvaged from his sisters' wardrobe.

The father had grand ambitions for the child. He wanted his three-year-old to grow up to be not a teacher, a policeman, or a driver like many of his fellow priests' sons were choosing to become, but a pundit.

Like father, like son, everyone would say.

Pundit Acharya couldn't really tell one daughter from another. One had stopped going to school because she was stupid. Another had formed a close bond with her stepmother. He was growing old, and he often forgot the daughters' names.

With his son, he was better. He was a proud father when the son, Prasant, was fed his first spoon of gooey rice. Prasant spat it out.

When his son's long, lustrous hair was cut for the first time at age three, and his head shaved, Prasant looked exactly like him. Everyone who attended the *Chewar* commented on the similarity.

Prasant cried when he saw his shaved head in the mirror. All said he didn't recognize himself.

The Pundit wanted to conduct Prasant's threading ritual soon after the *Chewar* so that, should he die, he could die knowing that his son would set him on fire. The *Bratabandha* ceremony, during which Prasant would wear the sacred thread, would fully qualify the son to perform his parents' last rites.

The Pundit didn't notice that his oldest daughter had started making monthly trips to the cowshed. He was distracted because he was figuring out an auspicious date for his son's coming-of-age function.

Sumitra loved fire. A few times, she set on fire things whose combustible characteristics the Pundit had serious doubts about, guavas being among them. One day, she burned her head. Had one of the daughters not seen her running around with her hair on fire, the Pundit's retarded wife would have died. With a head devoid of hair, like her favorite crying doll's, she was sent home, minus the crying doll.

"I just can't deal with one more child when I have five of my own," the Pundit said to his fellow priest, who understood.

While Sumitra was resettling into her natal home, her son was dancing to a radio song.

Prasant was sent to Rockvale, an English-medium school, unlike his sisters.

He refused to wear shorts to school. His stepmother and he reached a compromise with pants, which he soiled with enduring regularity.

Prasant wouldn't write a thing when asked to.

Prasant wouldn't hop when asked to.

He wouldn't run when asked to.

He wouldn't jump when asked to.

He wouldn't skip when asked to.

He wouldn't stop dancing when asked to.

Prasant couldn't be promoted to Lower Kindergarten because he hadn't learned how to write a single letter of the alphabet.

The priest wondered if the mother's slow brain had somehow been passed on to the son.

Prasant refused to go back to Rockvale the following year. He went to the village school with his sisters.

At the threading ceremony, in which he was required to shave his head, Prasant wouldn't allow shears to come near him. He spat at, pinched, scratched, and bit any hand that tried.

It was the first *Bratabandha* ceremony the priest had overseen whose participant was not tonsured.

The white cloth that would be girdled up around his son's loins as a *dhoti*, his son quickly improvised into a baby sari. Everyone said the poor boy was so used to females in the house that his child's mind hadn't gathered that a sari was meant only for women.

At eight, Prasant came home from school with all his nails painted.

The Sanskrit *shlokas* the priest tried shoving down his son's throat Prasant converted into a song and danced to.

When he was nine, a group of older boys at school thrashed Prasant, threatening to beat him up even more if he called himself Prasant.

Very agreeably, Pundit Acharya's son, from then onward, called himself Prasanti.

He wouldn't answer to Prasant, happily saying that his face would be punched if he answered to Prasant, so everybody called him Prasanti.

At ten, he dressed himself in his sister's green dress, much too short for him, and walked around the neighborhood.

Some said he was insane, like his mother. The Brahmins said it was because he was an offspring of two *sagotris*.

At eleven, when his uncle—the father of the naked babies who had taunted Pundit Acharya—died, Prasant disappeared from the funeral in the small town of Melli.

A year later, Pundit Acharya died in his sleep. His twin nephews cremated him. They were naked only from the waist up.

Prasant-Prasanti got on a bus to Siliguri. Siliguri was only three hours away, but it was big—far bigger than Kalimpong—and it was in the plains.

"Where have you come from, my sweet boy?" the conductor asked.

"Kalimpong."

"And your parents?"

"They put me on the bus. My brother will pick me up in Siliguri."

"Where in Siliguri?"

"The station."

"You talk like a girl."

"I know," Prasant said. "I am a girl."

"I thought you were a boy. Your clothes."

"People make those mistakes."

"What can we do?" the conductor said to the other passengers. "It's the age. Girls look like boys and boys like girls."

"Your hair is like a girl's."

"What is your name, *chori*?"

"Prasanti."

"What caste?"

"Baahun. Prasanti Acharya."

"Are you related to the pundit of Pudong?"

"No, I am from Lava."

"That pundit ate so much *kheer* when he came for a *puja* to our place," the conductor said to the other passengers. "He just wouldn't stop eating."

The others laughed at Prasanti's father. She felt an odd satisfaction.

Prasanti had been to Siliguri a few times before but never on her own. When the bus pulled into the Tenzing Norgay station, she waved at an imaginary figure.

No one suspected her lack of a brother.

She wandered the streets, took in the sounds, and absorbed the sights.

Some people looked Nepali. Many did not.

The honking was perpetual. The cars went by faster than they did in Kalimpong.

The crowds were bigger—much bigger than on Haat Day in Kalimpong. Perhaps today was Siliguri's Haat Day.

It was hot, really hot. No April in Kalimpong was this hot.

She'd now put her Prasanti-ness to the test.

At a small store that sold sweets lodged in glass bottles, she said, in Nepali, "Aamaa asked me to ask you to give me Lacto-King worth ten rupees."

The shopkeeper didn't care who she was, didn't balk when she handed him a hundred-rupee bill.

"And that nail polish."

"Anything else?" he growled in Bengali.

"Do you have any eyeliner?"

"No, this isn't a cosmetics shop."

"Why do such young girls wear eyeliner?" a disapproving woman said, in Hindi. "You're naturally beautiful."

Prasanti blushed a happy blush.

She wanted to hug the woman and narrate her life story to her, but the woman picked up her heavy bags and tried crossing the street. The traffic wouldn't allow her to.

"Where are you going?" Prasanti boldly asked.

"I have to cook at a wedding," she said.

"At Pradhan Nagar?" It was the only Siliguri address Prasanti knew of.

"No, just there." She pointed.

Across the street stood a big house decorated with colorful lights. The lights hadn't yet been lit.

Weddings served food. Weddings played music. Weddings were so full of people that no one would know whose daughter Prasanti was.

The party was unlike any Prasanti had seen before.

She had been to many ceremonies in Kalimpong over which her father presided, but this was grander than all of them. They served Coke and Fanta and Sprite.

Sikkim Supreme orange juice was as extravagant as it got at the weddings she had attended.

Prasanti guzzled one fizzy drink after another as she swayed from side to side to the songs blaring from the loudspeaker.

A group of boisterous women who looked like men arrived in a procession that could rival the groom's party in loudness.

They had long hair, wore saris, donned makeup, and danced with abandon. Yet most of them had the faces of men.

One of them played a drum that was tied around her neck with a red cloth while her friends danced to Hindi songs.

The groom gave them some money. They asked for more.

He gave them some more money. They asked for more.

Some wedding attendees cheered. Others jeered.

"Who are they?" Prasanti asked a couple who looked Nepali.

"*Hijras*," the husband replied. "Whose daughter are you?"

"My mother cooks here. I came to attend the wedding."

The explanation sufficed.

"Are they men or women?" Prasanti asked.

"They are both," the irate husband replied.

Prasanti knew what she'd do.

At first the *hijras* tried sending her back to the wedding house. She wouldn't let go of the sari of the prettiest one.

"I want to be like you," she said in Nepali.

"What about your parents?" someone asked.

"They are dead."

"We can't take you. How old are you?"

"Thirteen," Prasanti lied.

"Are you a boy or a girl?"

"A girl," Prasanti lied.

"Liar," the pretty *hijra* said, staring at the outline of her *soo-soo*.

"I am a boy, but I want to be a girl."

"Like us," a *hijra* sadly said.

"I can dance," Prasanti said. She danced the way she had seen them do. She frequently clapped with the flat of her hands. All the *hijras* smiled. Soon they all laughed.

"We still can't take you," the pretty one said. "You're too young—you will attract too much attention. What about the police?"

"I could be your daughter," Prasanti said to her.

"She could be my *chela*," the pretty one said to everyone else.

"Too dangerous," the oldest-looking in the group said. "You have to go back."

"I have nowhere to go."

She trailed them to their shack, where she saw more like them.

"How was it?" an elderly woman asked.

The dancing *hijras* ignored her questions about the wedding and told her about the curious little boy they had found.

"We can't risk having him here," the elderly man-woman said. "The police are always accusing us of abducting young boys and forcing them into being *hijras*. This one is too young, and look at her hair."

"But I can grow it," Prasanti said in desperation.

"She can be my *chela*," the pretty one said.

"You've barely been here a month," the leader said. "It's much too early for you to be taking on a disciple."

"Don't forget, this little boy is like us," the pretty one said. "He's going through what we went through. Look at how fair and pretty he is."

"Are you Nepali?" the leader asked.

Prasanti didn't know what the safe answer would be, so she said, "Yes."

"From Nepal?"

"No."

"Then?"

Again, she didn't know what the safe answer would be. "From Siliguri," she lied.

The look of concern that came to everyone's face suggested it was the wrong answer.

"From Siliguri," the leader repeated. "Did you hear that? His family will come looking for him here. We will spend the rest of our lives in jail. You have to let go of him."

"At least let him stay the night," the pretty one said.

"What if they come looking for him tonight?" the leader asked. She recruited the pretty one to take the boy back.

"I don't want to go anywhere," Prasanti cried.

"You have to."

"I want you to be my mother," Prasanti said to the pretty one once they were out in the open.

"Okay," the pretty one said. "You can be my *chela*. I will be your guru."

"But what about them?"

"Don't worry about them."

She gave Prasanti a wig to wear. It was the prettiest Prasanti had ever felt.

Prasanti and she boarded a train.

"Where are we going?" Prasanti asked. It was the first time she had been on a train.

"Somewhere far—where they will never find us."

"I have some money," Prasanti said. She handed her new mother, her new guru, a fifty-rupee bill.

"We will make enough money," the guru said. She sat down on the floor by the toilets. Prasanti followed suit.

The train started. "Are you hungry?" the guru said.

"No, I ate a lot at the wedding."

"Clever girl."

"Where are we going?"

"Who knows? Delhi? Bombay? You will be safe with me wherever you go."

"What will we eat there? Will my fifty rupees be enough?"

"We are *hijras*—we will make money."

Those walking by them to go to the toilets looked at them warily, cautiously.

"They think I have kidnapped you," the guru said.

"What if they steal me from you?"

"They won't," the guru said with confidence. "They won't do that."

A man with a threatening mustache and a threatening name-tag asked them to show him their tickets.

"Aye, *saahab*, you should be ashamed to ask a *hijra* and her sister for tickets," the guru said somewhat amicably. "We are here to bless the passengers. We'll start soliciting tomorrow morning. Right now, I am tired and need to sleep."

"Who is she?" the man asked.

"My sister."

"Your *hijra* sister or your real sister?"

"She's my real sister who's also a *hijra*."

"You look so much darker than she does."

"She took after my mother. I took after my father."

"I still need to fine you. How about some money for tea for me?"

The guru sprang to her feet and shouted: "Everybody, hear me, this man is asking me for bribe money. Cursed be your family. Cursed be your children." She lifted her sari up to her knees and clapped her hands the way she and the other *hijras* had done at the wedding.

But then, there had been a lot of laughter. Right now, there was aggression.

People from nearby compartments thronged to inspect the scene.

"He takes bribe money from the poor," the guru said. "Cursed be these *babus* who serve our nation."

She let her sari go farther up. "Okay, don't make too much trouble," the man with the mustache said. "Don't make too much noise."

Embarrassed, he left, and the passengers tittered and went about their ways.

The guru procured some eggs from one of the salesmen.

"Here, eat this," she told Prasanti.

"I can't. I am vegetarian."

"Not even eggs?" the guru asked in wonder.

"No. I am a Brahmin."

The guru laughed bitterly. "You aren't Brahmin anymore. You aren't Hindu anymore. You're a *hijra*. We *hijras* are Muslims."

Prasanti kept the egg balled in her fist and threw it away when her guru wasn't looking.

When they reached Bombay three days later, they had made 1,100 rupees between them. The master—the guru—embarrassed men who weren't ready to part with money by touching them, pinching them, and threatening to lift up her sari.

The disciple—the *chela*—collected money in a black purse. She learned to return fifty-*paisa* coins by the fifth compartment.

With families that had children, the guru blessed the babies by touching their heads with both her hands. The *chela* smothered their cheeks.

With the elderly, the guru sat for a while and asked them if their age troubled them. The *chela* touched the old people's heads with both her palms.

With the traveling salesmen whose wares she fancied, the guru asked for free *bindis,* lipstick tubes, and key chains. The *chela* demanded the same things the salesmen gave her guru.

Guru and *chela* bypassed female compartments. "They aren't worth our time—they are difficult," the guru said.

They spent the most time in a compartment of teenage boys. Prasanti figured they were barely three to four years older than she was.

"We will give you more money if you show us where you pee from," one of them said.

"From here," the guru said, pointing at her butt.

The boys laughed.

"Show us, show us," the boys chorused. "Hurry up now before our teacher comes back from the bathroom."

"Don't you know you will be cursed if you see a *hijra*'s pee-pee?" the guru asked.

"We don't care," one of them said. "Show us. Show us. Show us." The others joined in.

"Okay—you twenty rupees, you twenty rupees, you twenty rupees, you twenty rupees, and you fifty rupees," the guru said in English.

"Why should I pay fifty rupees?" the loudest among them asked.

"Because you're sexy," the guru said. The boys cheered. "Money? Now."

The boys gave the cash to Prasanti, who pecked each one on the cheek as she collected it. Loud cheering followed each peck.

The guru lifted her sari. Prasanti saw a *soo-soo*-less man for the first time. Just roots where a tree had once been.

"Can he touch it?" The loud boy pointed at his friend and laughed.

Everyone laughed.

"What did you do with it?" the loud boy asked.

"Had an operation." The guru let her sari slide down. "More answers for more money."

The boys deliberated among themselves and said they had seen and heard enough for the day.

"Wait until our sir comes back," the loud boy said. "You should harass him and ask him for a hundred rupees."

"Teachers have no money," the guru said, and she went her way. "Don't do naughty things with your *laro* after what you have seen today."

"Yuck," the loud boy said.

"Yuck," the others said.

Prasanti was the happiest she had ever been.

Two years later, Prasanti ran away from her house in Bombay.

She and her guru had become members of a new house near the Dadar railway station.

Her guru now had a new guru, who introduced her to the world of prostitution.

"I owe it to her," the guru said to Prasanti. "I don't like doing it, but I owe it to her because she paid off my debts to the old *hijra* house. She also allowed me to keep you as a *chela* although I am new here. I should be grateful."

Prasanti's guru was to pay Rs. 150 a day to her new guru, irrespective of how good or bad the day had been.

"Earlier, I was a *badhaai hijra*—I was vital to people's celebrations," the guru grumbled to Prasanti. "Now I am a whore. What have I done with my life?"

Prasanti was sent off with the other *hijras* to solicit money from shops around the railway station.

The men often remarked on how beautiful she was.

Prasanti knew she was fair—mountain fair. Fair was beautiful here. She thought her guru was far more attractive than she, but her guru was dark, so not many people in Bombay found the older woman as gorgeous.

"The house will get your *nirvanan* done soon, and then no ugly stick sticking out of your body," her guru said. "Then you can have customers like I do."

Prasanti had heard a lot about the operation.

All *hijras* respected those who had undergone it.

A few months after Prasanti's arrival, the *nayak*, the leader of the house, had declared that she should be circumcised.

"We are Muslims," the guru said. "We can't keep turtle-like foreskins."

It had been painful.

Prasanti's guru gave her many pills to swallow.

The big ones were so her breasts would sprout.

The small ones were so her voice wouldn't crack.

The medium ones were so her facial hair wouldn't grow fast.

She took to wearing bras.

Her voice cracked, grew bigger, hoarser, manlier.

The hair on her face grew fast. She once tried shaving it and received a beating from her housemates. She could only tweeze her facial hair, they said. Only men shaved.

She learned how to drape a sari.

She learned how to eat meat—only Halaal.

She learned how to tweeze her unibrow.

There'd be some elaborate *puja* before she and her fellow *hijra* Kalyani would be sent off to some town in Karnataka to get their penises removed.

The *hijra* god, Pothiraj Maharaj, would be worshipped. Surprisingly, he was a Hindu god.

There'd be dancing, singing, and merrymaking in the house. *Hijras* from the neighboring houses would be invited.

Prasanti was fond of her penis.

She enjoyed her penis.

Her penis was a part of who she was.

She liked her rapidly growing breasts, and she liked her penis.

But a penis was unwelcome on a *hijra*'s body.

So, she did what was expected of her. She and Kalyani took the train to Bangalore, on the outskirts of which was the hospital where they'd have their operations.

The surgery wasn't painful. She was fully conscious, enthralled by the doctor who conducted it and anxious about what life would be like memberless.

Two hours after the operation, she awoke every patient in the secret clinic. She screamed that where her penis had been burned, itched, hurt. Kalyani held her friend's hand and tried covering her mouth to muffle the screams. Kalyani forced black tea down Prasanti's throat. A cup. Two cups. Three cups. Nothing worked. Finally, after hours of shrieking, she slipped into an uneasy sleep.

When she awoke, Kalyani was packing up her belongings.

"I can't stay," her friend said. "I can't have the surgery."

Prasanti couldn't lie to her. She wasn't going to tell her friend the surgery was life-changing. It wasn't. When Kalyani looked at her for reinforcement, there wasn't any forthcoming.

It hurt when Prasanti peed into the catheter. It hurt when she moved.

Kalyani-less, she learned to walk. She had peed sitting down even when she had a penis, and she continued sitting on her haunches. But it was different now.

No one would forgive her for Kalyani's breakout. Her *hijra* friends would say that Prasanti could have talked her into the surgery.

Prasanti didn't belong with the *hijras* even if she was one. In the house, they came from everywhere—from Madras and Hyderabad, from Lucknow and Nagpur— some trying to get as far away as they could from where they were born. Among all these people, she wished to find one person who spoke Nepali. Her guru spoke a little Nepali, but the guru was mostly away, getting drunk and getting raped by men who didn't pay.

The sense of community that had so impressed Prasanti was now suffocating.

She longed to be an individual. She craved the mainstream, even if the mainstream was determined to shut her out.

So, Prasanti ran away. She left behind her saris in the clinic and took with her the one she wore. With the little money she had managed to save, she got on a train, unconcerned about where it would take her.

The train was going to Guwahati. Of the hundreds of trains she could have taken, she found herself on the one heading to her part of the country.

At Howrah, she got bored and went from compartment to compartment to solicit money.

A group of schoolgirls laughed at her but wouldn't give her money.

A group of old men paid no attention to her.

A scared, good-looking man gave her ten rupees, and she blessed him even though she laughed at his naïveté.

A *beedi*-puffing woman scolded her co-passenger for giving Prasanti money.

"Yes, give them money and spoil them," she admonished. "That's why they don't work."

She spoke as if Hindi wasn't her first language. She spoke as if she struggled with the language. She spoke as if Nepali was her first language.

So, they got talking—eunuch-beggar and *beedi*-smoking woman.

Prasanti told her everything. The woman listened.

Prasanti told her who her father was. The woman puffed on her *beedi* and said she knew him.

Prasanti cried. The woman consoled.

Prasanti—penis-less, homeless, *hijra*-membership-less—said she needed protection. Chitralekha, my grand-mother, took her home.

•

Manasa barges into the room of my yesteryears, where I venture today because Prasanti has benevolently cleaned it.

"Not a good time," I say.

"Like I care," Manasa replies.

"My editor finds everything I've written irreverent, tongue-in-cheek."

"That's a bad thing?"

"Apparently so. He doesn't want my nonfiction book to be a joke."

"Poor Ruthwa. Always the victim."

"Oh, thanks for the Naipaul book, by the way," I tell Manasa without looking up. "It didn't hurt at all."

She does not acknowledge my gratitude. "What was that about?" she asks.

"What was what about?"

"I am talking about the devil-may-care attitude at the lunch table."

"I don't know what you mean."

"Creating trouble?" she asks, as though she's unsure.

"Whatever. You have way too much free time on your hands now that there's no father-in-law to pick up after."

"Why is your room so clean?"

"I cleaned it."

"She did it, didn't she? The eunuch cleaned the room. That little scoundrel will get another slap from me. Is that why you helped her hang the *malas*?"

"Yeah," I lie.

"Liar—you wanted something else. What is it? Tell me."

"What would I want from her?"

"I don't know. How would I know? You're a promiscuous beast—you probably want to sleep with Prasanti—who knows?"

"She's more attractive than you."

Manasa looks at me to qualify the joke. When she sees I am serious, she examines herself in the closet mirror and sighs. "That Prasanti creature has even wiped your mirror spotless," she says.

"She does a job well when she wants to."

"What are you working on?" Manasa tries reading the contents of the computer screen.

"Bhagwati thinks I should write about Gorkhaland, about what the movement is doing to its people with the strikes and mandatory this and mandatory that."

"I like the idea."

"You do?"

"All right, enough Ruthwa talk. I can't handle it."

Bhagwati walks in and asks if I was drunk at lunch.

"Where would I find alcohol in this house?" I ask.

"I don't know—you must have brought some from Kalimpong or somewhere."—Bhagwati.

"The sale of liquor is prohibited in Kalimpong—some Gorkhaland rules," I reply.

"What about those Nepali cultures that require alcohol to be a part of their celebrations?"—Bhagwati.

"Blah, blah, blah, I am bored with this Gorkhaland talk. By the way, what were you doing in Kalimpong?"—Manasa.

I let her know that a blast from the past, a pretty thing with bad teeth from Scotland, was volunteering at

Dr. Graham's Homes, and the trip to Kalimpong was to surprise her.

And to fuck her, but that is understood.

"You're creepy."—Manasa.

"Well, glad that answers your question," I say. "I have some serious writing to do. My cunt of an editor, who thinks I don't know how to write nonfiction, has spoken to a friend of his at the Kolkata *Telegraph* to get me some column space in the hope of rebuilding my career as a serious writer. Looks like a Gorkhaland column is coming your way."

Bhagwati stays quiet. Manasa scowls.

"If each one of you would get the hell out of this room, I'd appreciate it," I say.

They both walk out quietly.

An Open Letter to Gorkhaland Leaders

At the outset, I'll tell you this: I am from Sikkim, but I believe in the cause of Gorkhaland.

I see no reason a Nepali-majority region should be under the regime of a Bengali-majority state.

I feel for you. Yes, I may have been brought up in Gangtok, with its many abundances, but growing up, I spent every winter break in Kalimpong, which is my grandmother's natal home and where she owns her biggest factory. We aren't very different, after all. It's just that we in Sikkim lucked out; you didn't.

I have seen your hopes rise. I have seen them ebb. I get warm and fuzzy when I see the proposed Gorkhaland map—it's so colorful and full of hope.

But enough is enough.

You know we need to go through your roads to get to the airport in Bagdogra. Yet, you declare the roads closed.

You force boarding schools to shut down for days, affecting so many of our children studying there.

Inconveniencing us will get the central government's attention—understandable. Bringing the hills to a standstill is the best way to make yourself a squeaky wheel—I get it.

But now you're taking things too far, and we won't stand for it. In fact, even your people won't stand for it, you see.

I was in Kalimpong recently. I am not going to complain about the once-glamorous town, a must-stop on the Silk Route, being reduced to a shell of its former self. Or of the water scarcity.

A group of yellow-clothed young boys stopped my cab near the famous Munnu paan shop. They were teenagers—some barely— and polite. They wanted to check the taxi's trunk.

"What for?" I asked, in English, to intimidate them.

"For alcohol. The Gorkha Jana-shakti Morcha forbids the consumption of alcohol these days."

"We are Nepalis—drinking alcohol is part of so many of our tribes' cultures," I countered.

My Gorkha policemen were soon joined by a bunch of young women dressed in their gunyu-cholos. So many beautiful women in their traditional outfits—it was a great sight.

But the feast for my eyes soon turned sour. One of the women asked me why I wasn't dressed up.

"Well, I am," I somewhat cheekily replied.

But jeans and T-shirts weren't what they were looking for. They wanted daura-suruwals and Dhaka hats on all males. It was apparently mandated.

Aha, what?

Yes, compulsory.

The Gorkha Jana-shakti Morcha had declared that everyone in the district of Darjeeling, soon to be Gorkhaland (soon, soon, soon . . . since the eighties), a separate state from West Bengal, should wear traditional costumes on that day.

I could have told them I was from Sikkim, but my curiosity was aroused.

"What happens if I don't want to wear it?"

Before they could answer, a prepubescent pseudo-policeman jubilantly cried out, "He has a bottle of Teacher's whiskey."

My alcohol was confiscated, and I was casually asked to buy daura-suruwal.

"If you can afford to reserve a taxi, you can afford to buy the clothes," said one of the women, seizing my whiskey.

Before I could say good-bye, I asked them to empty the bottle. After some hesitation, the leader of the pack threw the whiskey onto the pavement.

The alcohol flowed out, directionless. Like the movement. No one made an effort to contain it. Like no one made an effort to contain this movement.

Tomorrow you will ask us to wear underwear with your party colors on it.

People won't stand for it, Mr. Moktan. This is just not the way. This is Gorkhaland, not Hitlerland.

FIVE

Fireworks

Bhagwati was at her pious best on Lakshmi *Puja*. Although the goddess of wealth blessed her faithful devotee with abundant financial hardship in return, the oldest Neupaney's fondness for the festival didn't dwindle a bit.

There would be fireworks in Gangtok—rocket-shaped crackers, miniature atom bombs, and onion-like explosives—and there would be fireworks at home. Bhagwati only hoped that the inevitable accusatory conversation between the wronged grandmother and the erring grandson wouldn't happen today. It was a relief not to be the biggest villain in the house for once, yes, but the spectacle could be postponed until Lakshmi *Puja* was over. The plate-throwing pandemonium yesterday was rough. Prasanti and Aamaa, two members of the same team, had split up unceremoniously. Ruthwa and Aamaa's interaction today would result in more turmoil.

People worshipped cows today, but because the Neupaneys had no cows of their own, they would participate only in the evening ritual. They would invite the goddess of wealth into their lives as a family—the five-member family they were trying hard to become again. They'd light earthenware lamps and perch them on windowsills. Prasanti and Ruthwa, the unlikeliest of allies, had already decorated the doors and windows with marigold garlands. The worship space, which was a room in itself, needed a thorough cleaning. Prasanti's slapdash mopping of the floor and sloppy wiping of the marble statues of various gods and goddesses wouldn't do today, so Bhagwati set to work. All the while, she compared her altar in America to the one here. Her husband must have already tidied up their apartment in Boulder in the hopes that Lakshmi would finally include him in her altruism this year. When surrounded by gods and religious paraphernalia, any memory of Ram, even after all these years, was entwined with the cold, hard truth of his caste, so Bhagwati determined that Aamaa might not like her playing this active a role in the *puja*. She was, after all, not a Neupaney anymore. She would instruct Prasanti to do the cleaning while she stood watch. It was a fate Bhagwati was resigned to.

Prasanti was not in her room, but her personal altar, which contained spotlessly wiped diminutive statues of Ganesha, Shiva, and Lakshmi, was fragrant with incense. Curious whether the servant's negligent cleaning efforts extended to her personal space, Bhagwati did a quick survey and was struck by the neatness of the room. The eunuch wasn't unskilled. The sheet on Prasanti's bed was fresher than the sheets on theirs. The floor had been swept and mopped. In the *Godrej* wardrobe, the clothes were neatly folded. Some were even ironed. In the trinket box was a stack of 500-rupee bills. Deeper in it were jewelry pieces—earrings, bangles, and a necklace.

If Prasanti and she were to compare their net worth, the eunuch definitely had more money. To be made aware of this wide gap in income between her and a servant on a day like today was cruel. Yet, Bhagwati's faith in the goddess of wealth did not waver. She would pray even more fervently this year than she did previous years.

Ruthwa was puttering around the kitchen in pajamas and a torn T-shirt. They were his sleeping clothes, his house clothes, and his going-out clothes. Her brother did not believe in being impeccably turned out.

"Good morning," Bhagwati said.

"Oh, hey, you're up early."

"So are you."

"Is it so we can have our alone time like we did yesterday morning?"

"It's my favorite day of the festival."

"Yeah," Ruthwa said, slathering Amul butter on a piece of bread. "Just thought I'd take a walk around town or go to some of the viewpoints." He made a face before spitting the bread out into an overflowing trash can.

"This early?"

"Why not? I want to experience Gangtok's beauty in the morning."

"When will you be back?"

"Back for what?"

"It's Lakshmi *Puja*. Please tell me you knew about it."

"Oh, yeah, it is Lakshmi *Puja*," Ruthwa said in a tone that suggested he could have been mocking her. "I'll probably be back in the evening for the actual *puja*."

"Wasn't the purpose of your visit to make amends with Aamaa? Go talk to her in private."

"Nah, I saw her at lunch yesterday. You don't expect me to wait around all day so I can have a glimpse of the queen, do you?"

"Just saying. It's Lakshmi *Puja* today. I hope there are no fights."

"Like the one between mistress and servant yesterday?" Ruthwa laughed.

"Yes, it wasn't pretty."

"How nice it feels not to be at the center of these family feuds."

"I feel exactly the same way. I am glad I'm not the cause of all these fights."

"Now that Aamaa is running out of people to have fights with, she's quickly crossing over to picking them with nonfamily members," Ruthwa said.

"Prasanti is hardly nonfamily." Bhagwati boiled water for coffee. "She's probably more family to Aamaa than I am."

"Or I am," Ruthwa said.

"You're a bully. Bullies are afraid of bullies. She's scared of you."

"So, I thought Aamaa didn't want you in the kitchen. Are you allowed in?"

"I don't know what the rules are. I have to admit I thought of cleaning the *puja* room but then stopped myself because I have no knowledge of the rules."

"The one who married the outcaste touched the gods—what nerve," Ruthwa said.

"It's a shame. I just love Lakshmi *Puja*."

"And the goddess has been so good to you."

"She will be soon."

"You need to let one of them help you. You probably won't accept my financial support because I am, you know, Ruthwa. Not that I have very much."

She wouldn't talk about money today. "And I am, you know, Bhagwati—worse than you are. You simply portrayed Aamaa in an unflattering light, and very few people outside the family even know it was her life you wrote about. People who know us barely understood the book. They said all the big words drove them to the dictionary from page one itself."

"The way you spoke to me yesterday—with all that talk asking me to stay away from Prasanti's story—I'd have thought the book had a far bigger impact than that."

"What I am trying to say is that in the pyramid of the unforgivable, I am higher than you are, and Aamaa talks to me, so she will talk to you, too. Just make an effort."

Ruthwa made for the bathroom.

"See you later?" Bhagwati was hopeful.

"Yeah, if you're lucky."

All these years, when they were forced from one country to another and to another, from one home to the next, one camp to a different one, Bhagwati often wondered how happy her brothers and sister were.

When a person had been as poor as she had for as long as she had, it was easy to assume that all her siblings, who would never lack money, were far more content than she'd ever be. In addition, not one of them would have caste issues to contend with. Her formal education, which Bhagwati often used to demarcate herself from the rest at the camps, had ended at high school, its posh public nature notwithstanding. Her siblings had gone on to receive advanced degrees. While she, the oldest, preferred obscurity, the youngest had become a critically acclaimed writer. Bhagwati had always been sure that her siblings were all so much happier than she was.

Now, as she explored her home, the house from which she had run away, she realized she had been wrong.

Manasa's life showed in her face. Her sister, the satisfied one, the happy one, had become the exact antithesis of her adolescent self. Manasa had a marriage that was going wrong and a career that was stalled. What had she worked so hard throughout life for? What good was a 93.75% in her board exams? Did Manasa get an Oxford degree, the proof of which stood so proudly framed on the windowsill by the landing, to become a home-care aide to her father-in-law? With an arranged marriage to a Brahmin from a well-known family, Manasa had won the lottery. But lottery winners paid for their luck after the initial jubilation died down, and Manasa was doing just that.

Agastaya was a doctor—shouldn't he have had the most fulfilled life of them all? Yet, he was so guarded, so cautious. Bhagwati admitted that adulthood made you cynical, but to be as mundane as Agastaya was to not live at all.

And Ruthwa? For all his appearances, here was a boy trapped in a man's body. Was he happy? Bhagwati didn't think so. He was trying hard, too hard, to live up to the image he had created for himself. Yes, with the scandal he had been through a lot, but it didn't appear as though he regretted it. If anything, her brother was remorseless—how happy could an unrepentant person be?

She may have been a dishwasher—a fired one—but she now had little doubt that she was more content than her siblings. It had taken her this trip to realize that she had been an idiot to question her joyless life all along, to hold her siblings' nonexistent happiness as a benchmark.

Feeling guilty that besides a hasty e-mail that she sent him soon after arriving in Delhi, she had had no interaction with her husband, Bhagwati called him from the landline. It wasn't Lakshmi *Puja* in Boulder yet, but Ram would feel nice about being thought of when this rare moment of positivity gripped her.

"Is it time for the *puja* yet?" he asked her right after picking up.

"No, no, it's just morning here. Another eleven or twelve hours left. I've just made a beautiful discovery. You, Mr. Self-Help, will be so pleased."

"Okay, I'll call you back right away"—because phone calls from America to India were so much cheaper than those from India to the United States.

"Happy Lakshmi *Puja* to you," he said when she picked up after the first ring.

"And to you, and to Virochan and Aatish—how are they?"

"The same." He laughed. "Want nothing to do with Lakshmi *Puja*."

"Why aren't you at work?" She was afraid he might have gotten fired again.

"I will be in another twenty minutes."

"How's it coming along?"

"Good—not as bad as the last one. By the way, how are you doing, money-wise?"

"This is Gangtok." It was slightly odd that Ram should ask the question. "I haven't set foot outside the house since I arrived, so I've spent no money."

"Good," he said.

Something was definitely amiss. "Wait, what's going on?"

"Nothing, to be honest."

"You're a horrible liar," Bhagwati said. "Tell me what's up."

"First tell me how much money you have in your Chase Bank account."

"I think I have about a thousand dollars."

"Oh, thank God."

"But there's a problem—about eight hundred and fifty there is Agastaya's. Remember he purchased my ticket? He hasn't cashed the check I sent him."

The line went silent for a few heavy seconds. "May I ask you for a favor?"

Just what was going on? "Go ahead."

"Can you ask Agastaya not to cash the check?"

Ram had always been adamant about not using her family's money. For him to make this request was disconcerting. She said nothing.

"I feel horrible, but something has come up," Ram said.

"Is it one of the kids?"

"No, no, they're fine."

"Then, what is it?"

"I was learning how to drive."

"Are you hurt?"

"No, I'm fine, by the grace of God."

"Did you finally get a learner's permit?" Molly, their Christian friend at the International Organization for Migration, had told them time and again that they shouldn't take driving lessons without a proper permit, which they could easily acquire by passing a written test. Both Bhagwati and Ram had been putting off taking the test all this while.

"I am sorry to say that Ravi Daai, of the second floor, and I took his car for a ride."

"And you do not have a permit." She knew the answer. "What happened?" she asked.

"It wasn't anything major. I didn't slow down enough when making a turn, so I ended up driving the car into a ditch. I am so sorry, Bhagwati."

"Does Ravi Daai not have insurance?"

"He told me the premium would go up if he noti-fied the insurance company. He has been kind enough to allow me to compensate him after you return."

"He could've simply called the insurance company."

"The repair center estimated the damages to be around eight hundred dollars."

"Eight hundred dollars that we don't have."

"I am so sorry, Bhagwati."

"I am, too. Excellent news on Lakshmi *Puja*."

"I am not driving another car until I pass the driver's test."

"Good decision, Ram—too bad it's already too late. I have to go."

"Wait, what was the amazing discovery you made?"

It didn't matter. It didn't matter how happy she had felt. Somehow, she wasn't feeling chipper anymore.

•

Agastaya had a sinking feeling in the pit of his stomach.

Bhagwati had three times asked him about see-ing some girl—a pediatrician six years younger than he who had recently graduated from JIPMER, his alma mater. The third time, he had been impatient with his older sister, asking her to stop masquerading as Aamaa's mouthpiece, an insinuation at which she appeared hurt. She didn't deny the accusation, though, so he was sure that she and Aamaa were in cahoots to see him married off.

That, though, was only a small problem.

The bigger issue—again—was Nicky. For days, his boyfriend hadn't replied to any of his texts or calls. The first message Agastaya sent Nicky after arriving in

Gangtok was to let him know that he had finally reached home. The second one asked Nicky how he was doing. The third wondered if everything was all right. The fourth was to ask his boyfriend if he was sick. The fifth message was a plea to call him. This, Agastaya followed with a handful of phone calls, all of which went straight to Nicky's voice mail.

Agastaya had last felt this nauseated only when Nicky stormed out of One If by Land, Two If by Sea on their anniversary. The reason: Agastaya had asked his boyfriend of a year to go easy on the Dom Pérignon.

"I can't have you dictate every damn thing in my life," Nicky had said.

"But you're slurring." They hadn't even begun their main course.

"As I should. It's our anniversary dinner."

"Please be quiet." He could sense that other patrons, out on romantic dinners, were distracted by Nicky's belligerence.

And, out of the blue, Nicky had dropped the bomb. "I think we should take a break from each other. You're a control freak and boring."

Agastaya lost all appetite for his lobster bisque. Before he could say anything to placate Nicky, his boyfriend had made a dramatic exit. The two-day-late text that Nicky deployed to explain his misconduct stated that he had been feeling suffocated for a long time and that perhaps they should consider dating other people. Agastaya was aghast. Nothing in his partner's comportment had suggested that things weren't all hunky-dory in their relationship.

Yes, when Nicky was a handful, Agastaya did consider leaving him, but Nicky was not just the first man

Agastaya had been with—he was also the first person. The highest extent of Agastaya's physical intimacy pre-Nicky had been two drunken makeout sessions with barely conscious women in college. Agastaya hadn't ever courted women (or men) and hadn't ever been on dates. Nicky, one of his nurses at Beth Israel, had initiated him into the world of nonplatonic relationships and helped him navigate his way through it.

The more Nicky talked about how difficult a time his friends were having finding "the one," the more Agastaya became convinced that eschewing his relationship in favor of the unknown wasn't a wise idea. Agastaya was not interesting; he was not beautiful. Financially, he did all right, but he would hate to be out on a date where his biggest selling point was the size of his wallet. Agastaya was aware that he was a difficult person to date, not because he threw temper tantrums or was high maintenance but because his partner would have to go without letting many people know that they were in a relationship. It'd have to be kept secret from Agastaya's world—no introductions to his friends, no movie nights with relatives. It was a solitary, isolating relationship. That was a big sacrifice, and for three years, Nicky had put up with it.

To win Nicky back after the restaurant incident, Agastaya had asked him to move in. It had meant some big adjustments—firing Sabitri, his Nepalese maid, for one. To live together was what Nicky wanted, and this Agastaya had found out when he checked their e-mail. The e-mail, by the way, wasn't just Agastaya's. It wasn't just Nicky's. Coined by a conflation of their names, Nickgastaya @gmail.com was the e-mail address Agastaya had created a few months before. Nicky had said the new ID made him want to vomit, but he was mighty pleased to have his name kick it off. Sneakiness, not sappiness, had driven Agastaya to create the joint address: he could now keep track of his boyfriend's goings-on. Nicky soon migrated from Hotmail to Gmail once he discovered how much more user-friendly the latter was.

With the password still unchanged, Nickgastaya @gmail.com became Nicky's primary e-mail. And with that, it also evolved into an all-encompassing source of anxiety and stress for Agastaya. He read and reread e-mails between Nicky and his friends, tried discerning flirtations, and wondered if he was being cheated on. When the contents of his boyfriend's e-mail gave him sleepless nights, Agastaya would try to wean himself from checking the account. But he would always relapse a few days later, when, like a man possessed, he'd rifle through every e-mail he had missed out on and obsess over it.

When things were going very well or terribly, Agastaya would check the e-mail twice a day. As the relationship returned to normalcy—a place between too much love and too much hate—he'd stay away from Nickgastaya @gmail.com, password: gastayanick. Things were bad now. His boyfriend wasn't responding to any of his texts or phone calls. Agastaya needed to check the account desperately, but at eight in the morning, on Lakshmi *Puja*, he was sure no Internet café would be open. He wished he had brought his laptop. At the last moment, in character for a person who was living a secret life, Agastaya had left his MacBook Air behind in New York. In Gangtok, notions of privacy were left at the door the moment he stepped into his grandmother's house. He wouldn't check his e-mail on the decade-old desktop computer even if it had Internet connectivity, which he doubted. He wasn't about to risk being outed by one of his siblings to all the other members of the family. Nothing in his family was a secret. He decided he would activate the Internet on his phone for the rest of his trip.

Outside, in the garden, as though with thoughts as heavy as his to bog her down, nursing a cup of coffee and staring at the balcony upstairs, was Bhagwati.

"Beautiful day," she said when he approached.

"Yes, it's getting colder, though." He shivered.

"Would you like some coffee?"

"I'll pass."

"Are you angry with me?"

Of course, he was. "For what?"

"For talking to you about the doctor woman."

"I've made it clear to you that I don't want to get married," he said, glad he could talk about the issue in private before everyone was in his face. "You need to be in the right mood for it. I don't feel like marriage now. Perhaps I'll be up for it in a few years."

"That's fine. But what harm is there in going for lunch with a girl or two?" Bhagwati said. "Who knows if you might click?"

"And how is that any of your business?"

"It's not. But I want to see you happy. Marriage made me happy."

"Huh?" Agastaya said.

"What?"

"Nothing, Bhagwati," Agastaya said. "It will sound too mean. Forget it."

"No, no, tell me."

"Sure, if you want to hear it. You're hardly the person I'd look at as a model of happiness."

"Because I'm poor?"

"Among other things. Look at you—so self-righteous. How about you concentrate on getting your life in order before straightening mine out?"

Bhagwati was sullen. He might have said too much. "I am sorry," he said. "I sound as insensitive as Ruthwa. I'm just tired of all this marriage talk."

"You don't have to look at it like it's prison, Agastaya. You're thirty-three. Marriage will do you good."

"I know. It's just not the time now."

"Look at you—you're so unhappy," Bhagwati said. "You need some fun in life."

He clenched his fist. "Again, how do you know I am unhappy?"

"I can tell. Everyone can."

"What if what you see of me is not who I am?"

"It's a very unhappy face that you decide to present to the world, then."

"What's it to you, Bhagwati? Seriously, I'd understand it if it was a lady of leisure analyzing my unhappiness. But don't you have your plate full? You need to start with admitting your kids to a private school. Do you know how bad state schools in the U.S. are?"

"From what I know, they're better than private schools in Bhutan," she said defensively.

"Is that what your target is? If it's better than what it'd have been in Bhutan, it's good enough for your children? Dream big."

"We were talking about suitable women for you."

"And now we are talking about your poverty. Marriage is a topic that makes me scream. Poverty is a topic that makes you see red. We're even."

"If that's the way you want to look at it," Bhagwati said, taking a big gulp of her coffee. "If that's the way—fine."

He had to get out. It didn't matter if the Internet cafés didn't open until later. He needed to get the hell out of there.

Up a dingy flight of waterlogged stairs on MG Marg was a cyber café that was just opening for the day. The skullcaps on all the three workers' heads explained why. *Become even more in-your-face with your faith during some other religion's festival,* Agastaya thought, surprised at the vitriol in him.

Urdu conversation droned in the background. The Internet became even more lethargic in the foreground.

Username: nickgastaya

Password: gastayanick

Agastaya felt guilty about checking the e-mail, but then again, he was only going through what was jointly theirs.

There it was. The e-mail. The answer to everything. The answer to Nicky's behavior. And, yet, the answer gave way to so many questions. It made way for so many emotions. First, Agastaya was elated. Then his mouth went dry. The hair on his hands stood up. He hoped the men around him wouldn't see his torrent of tears. He was curious about so many things, and he wouldn't find the answer to them in the cacophony of Urdu that grew louder by the minute.

Deep in thought, grave in demeanor, Agastaya walked to the window and stared out on to the square, where, sitting on one of the benches and smoking a cigarette was his younger brother—legs spread wide apart, the hair on his head an unruly mess, and his eyes on the posterior of every woman who walked by. Gangtok was such a small place.

Agastaya called Ruthwa's name. His younger brother continued smoking.

"Hey, look up, Ruthwa!" he shouted.

"Ha." Ruthwa strained to see in the sun. "What are you doing here?"

"Came to check my e-mail. Want to go for a coffee?"

"Nah. I like the sun."

"Why don't I grab some coffee and join you in the sun?" Agastaya asked.

"Yeah, do that."

The skullcapped men had no change on them, so Agastaya asked them to keep the hundred-rupee bill.

"Lakshmi *Puja*?" one of them asked.

"No, no change on you, and no change on me." Agastaya hurried out. He hated Muslims today. He was a bigot today. He hated everyone today.

Baker's Café was closed for the holiday. Agastaya purchased a bottle of Coke from one of the stores lining MG Marg and strode over to his brother, who was scratching his groin.

"You, too, couldn't bear it, could you?" Ruthwa said.

Agastaya was quiet.

"The house and its forced festivities—couldn't bear it?"

"I had to step out to check my e-mail. I had a little tiff with Bhagwati."

"Yeah, I had a talk with her, too. I wouldn't call it a tiff. It was more a talk—not pleasant but not wholly a tiff."

"She's been going on and on about getting me married," said Agastaya, suddenly willing to talk about marriage with Ruthwa, with whom he had never been very close. When a bigger issue presented itself, it was Agastaya's nature to seek refuge in smaller ones. It was easy to pour his anxiety about Nicky into his annoyance with Bhagwati's marriage talk. It would take his mind off his boyfriend.

"She's been going on and on about Aamaa to me."

"It seems she's in a mood to talk sense into everybody when she should be worried about feeding, clothing, and sheltering her family."

"I don't think her situation is that dire. I wonder if she talks about marriage-rescuing with Manasa."

"I strongly suspect she has been recruited by Aamaa to do this marriage talk. I told her off today, and now I feel bad about it."

"Good thing no one asks me to get married."

"Why are you here again?"

"To see my loving family."

Agastaya asked Ruthwa if he had another cigarette. "I need to smoke."

Ruthwa elevated his left eyebrow. "Since when?"

"Since now—I'm stressed."

"Yeah, family does that to you."

"So, are you here to avoid Aamaa?"

"Are you going to get married?" Ruthwa asked.

"Are you ever going to stop being an asshole?"

"Are you going to stop channeling Bhagwati? Or Manasa?"

They both laughed in between puffs. A combination of laughter and nicotine accounted for Agastaya's feeling a whole lot lighter. But then, almost as soon as they had left, Nicky-related thoughts came back. The heaviness returned.

•

Manasa had awoken early, too, but chose to stay in bed when she heard Bhagwati talking to Ruthwa in the kitchen. Then she heard voices from the garden, which was right outside the guest room, and this time it was

Bhagwati talking wedded bliss to Agastaya. With her sister at her pontificating best, Manasa decided that she wasn't going to leave the room for a long time now.

But an hour or so later, someone drummed at her door. When the knocks grew more urgent, Manasa finally left her bed.

Prasanti, excitement writ large on her face, stood outside.

"What, Prasanti? Are you going to throw stones at me because your plan yesterday backfired?"

"There's someone at the gate," Prasanti said. "He's a foreigner—looks like an over-boiled potato."

"So, what am I to do?"

"I can't speak to him. I know no English."

"He must be lost."

"No, he keeps asking for Agastaya," Prasanti said. "*Agusta, Augusta, Oogoostoo*, he says. It took me some time to figure out." She tried a few more permutations of Agastaya's name.

"Where's Agastaya?"

"Gone to town, I think."

"Can't Bhagwati talk to him?"

"She is cleaning upstairs."

"Yes, because that's not your job."

Prasanti pretended not to understand. Manasa grabbed her robe and rushed out to the garden with Prasanti following her. Outside the gate stood a tall, lanky white man.

"May I help you?" Manasa asked.

"Hi, I'm from New York."

"Yes?" Manasa said somewhat rudely. Being a New Yorker didn't give one the liberty to show up at people's doors in foreign countries unannounced.

"I am an acquaintance of Agastaya's," he said. "He told me he'd be home, and I was paying Gangtok a visit, so I thought I'd stop by. Finding Neupaney Oasis isn't difficult—everyone knows where it is."

"Oh, okay. I'm sorry if I was rude."

"You weren't."

"Agastaya has gone to town, but he should be back soon. Why don't you come in?"

When he walked in, the American hit his head on the ceiling of the wicket door.

"Sorry," Manasa said. "It's not used to people over six feet. I am Manasa, Agastaya's sister."

"Very nice to meet you. Do I detect a slight British accent?"

"I live in London."

"So, you're also visiting?"

"Yes. My sister from Colorado is here, too. As is the youngest sibling. In fact, all of Agastaya's siblings are here. You do know that we have a festival going on, don't you?"

"Yes, the Diwali."

"The Nepali-speaking people call it *Tihaar*," Manasa corrected him. "You've come right on time for the festivities. And tomorrow is our grandmother's birthday."

"I hope my presence isn't an imposition."

"It isn't, but I've just awoken. I need to freshen up. Why don't you sit out in the sun for a while? I shall have someone bring you tea."

"Prasanti!" Manasa shouted. The servant had been observing them unobtrusively, choosing to spread on a mat fermented leaves of mustard, cauliflower, and radish, which she'd soon use as a base for *gundruk*, Manasa's favorite soup. "Bring this man some tea and biscuits."

Inside, Bhagwati was scrubbing the stairs.

"Since when did that become your job?" Manasa asked.

"It's fine. I woke up early. I had nothing to do."

"A friend of Agastaya's from New York is at the door. Can you entertain him for a while? I need to use the toilet."

Bhagwati agreed. "What's his name?"

"I realized he didn't tell me, and I didn't ask him. How rude of me. Let me go find out."

She returned a minute later.

"Nicholas," Manasa said. "Nicholas is his name—he's not bad-looking."

Not one of the water geysers in either of the two bathrooms was on. That was the problem with Gangtok—Manasa had to plan a shower at least an hour in advance in order to have ample hot water. She quickly brushed her teeth, rinsed, examined with indifference the blood in her saliva, wiped her mouth, and counted the number of days left before she'd be back in Kathmandu and then in London.

The bathroom was filthy. She did not understand why people in India had a partiality for wet loos. All it took was for the shower area to be barricaded, but with the shower being bang in the middle of the bathroom, this was nearly impossible. Manasa was always conscious that the commode not get wet when she bathed here, so she covered the toilet with a dirty towel before she let the shower run. Hairs of various lengths and shapes spun about in puddles on the floor. This wasn't very different from being greeted by Himal's beard hairs, lumped with his shaving cream, that she often found in the sink of their London bathroom. Beard and books and the foul discharge from his ear—she had given her husband so much grief about them. She had forced him to install a small shelf above the flush, but a day or two later, all his books—their titles ranging from *Donald Trump: Master Apprentice* to *How to Win Friends and Influence People*—were back on the floor, open at various pages, big words underlined aggressively. The sink would be cleaned meticulously the day she shouted at Himal but was back to its hair-covered glory the next day. Himal would keep complaining that his perforated eardrum wasn't a big deal and that he had no time for surgery. It was maddening.

London would be awful once she returned. She would soon be surrounded by the forced feel-good spirit of Christmas that her father-in-law wanted to be a part of. She had to wheel him to ridiculous shopping centers where the lights were, where the celebrations were. The thought of that life—her life, her real life—being only three days away filled her with dread. She would do herself a giant favor, she decided as she dried herself, by attempting to enjoy her last few days here.

She ran a dryer over her hair and avoided the sight of her body in the mirror. She wasn't fat, but she couldn't bear to look at her naked frame. She was afraid of things she might find—stretch marks, flab, wrinkles—but it was her face that scared her the most, and her face she couldn't help inspecting. All one had to do was look at her Facebook profile picture from two years before to see how much she had aged. Sometimes, when she saw her reflection in a windowpane or a car mirror, it took her a few seconds to recognize the woman looking back at her.

She heard Nicholas and Bhagwati chitchatting outside. Manasa hadn't done very much since her arrival in Gangtok and wanted to visit a few old sites. She wasn't a big fan of the city's modern avatar and disliked that almost every third building in the MG Marg area housed a hotel of some kind. The Gangtok of her childhood had been slower, less flashy. Tourists were fewer and poorer. These days, big spenders from the West fought with middle-class Bengalis for a piece of the city and state to taint. No one saw the harmful effects of tourism and excessive commercialization. Manasa was nervous for her hometown. She'd perhaps ask the others to join her on her sightseeing trip to the outskirts. If they weren't willing to accompany her, she'd go solo. Life was sometimes better alone.

"I was telling Byaagg-wuti how understandable her English is," Nicholas said when he saw Manasa come out. "I can't believe she's been in America only two years. Her accent is perfect."

"And what is a perfect accent?" Manasa asked.

"Well, for us ignorant Americans, anybody who doesn't speak like us has an accent."

"That's the entire world outside America." Manasa registered the look Bhagwati shot her.

"I know," Nicholas said. "I apologize for my countrymen's shortcomings. We should see the world outside of America. You're from London—wow!"

"That I am," Manasa said, her voice still icy.

"The weather must drive you insane."

"It's no worse than New York—at least the summers in London don't get as hot."

"I'd not have minded the cold in London if the sun so much as ever shone," Nicholas confessed. "The bleakness gets to me."

"I'd choose London over New York any day."

"At least October in New York is beautiful," Nicholas said. "But October in Gangtok is even better."

"I haven't been to either New York or London," Bhagwati declared. "Boulder is a good place to live. I might just live there all my life."

"I like India the best," Nicholas said. "I don't get why upper-middle-class Indians would want to move to America. You have it so easy here—servants, chauffeurs, and living like kings."

"What do you do?" Manasa asked.

"I am a traveler," Nicholas answered dreamily. "You could say a pseudo-anthropologist."

"You take what you have for granted," Manasa scolded Nicholas. "Everyone in India thinks you Americans have the ideal life. Grass greener—you see."

Before Nicholas could launch into another silly rationalization about how the upper-middle-class Indian had it best, Manasa ordered Prasanti to get the cordless. This conversation was inane. "We should call Agastaya," she said.

"That's fine," Nicholas said. "I'm quite enjoying my time with the two of you."

She took no pleasure in this banal discussion of weather and the stupidity of India's upper middle class. Bhagwati, on the other hand, seemed enthralled by the new arrival. The sooner Manasa dumped him on Agastaya, the quicker she'd start enjoying whatever few days of freedom she had left.

"We're on our way," her brother said on the phone.

"Who's 'we?'"

"I am with Ruthwa."

"There's a surprise waiting for you." Manasa smiled at Nicholas.

"I think I know what you're talking about. Is my friend there?"

"Yes, Nicholas from New York is here. Hurry up."

"I am almost there."

Manasa relayed the message to Agastaya's friend.

When her brother finally arrived, he and Nicholas shook hands and exchanged awkward hugs. "I see you've met the two sisters," Agastaya said. "My brother went to buy some cigarettes and should be here later."

"Yes, we have been having a great discussion," replied Nicholas.

"About New York, London, and the upper-middle-class Indian," Manasa said, hoping the despair with which she looked upon the topics hadn't crept into her voice. "I'll let you gentlemen catch up in peace."

Bhagwati, too, excused herself.

"What a boring fellow," Manasa said to Bhagwati once they were inside the house. "Making the most basic of points and thinking he's some intellectual. 'What's the weather like in London? What's the weather like in Boulder?'"

"I quite liked him," Bhagwati answered.

"You were all over him."

"He isn't that good-looking."

"But he's white," Manasa teased. "His whiteness had you going crazy."

"I was just being polite," Bhagwati said, not very pleasantly. "You were rude."

"For good reason—I hated him."

"How can you form an opinion of someone within two minutes of talking to him?"

"I can. At least I don't have this ridiculous post-colonial hangover where I believe that every whitey I come across is worthy of being fawned over. The way you were so pleased when he called your accent perfect was absurd. You were like a teenager in heat."

"I wasn't fawning over him. I treat people with hospitality. You should learn that."

"What now?" Manasa said. "Are you going to lecture me, too? Lecturing Ruthwa early in the morning not enough for you? Lecturing Agastaya early in the morning not enough for you?"

"Who told you?"

"I heard. I sleep right next to the kitchen and right by the garden, dammit. I keep getting woken up in the mornings. Today it was your nonsense. Yesterday it was Prasanti's. I am moving to another room, I swear. Maybe I'll share the bed with Aamaa. I haven't slept well in days."

"Those weren't lectures."

"Sure, they weren't," Manasa said, uncertain why she was so peevish. "Is Aamaa paying you to talk Agastaya into getting married?"

Bhagwati sighed. She said nothing. She hiked upstairs. She didn't look at Manasa.

It wasn't supposed to have come out that way. She could have left money out of it. Manasa wanted to kick herself.

Her plan to ask Bhagwati to play tourist with her would have to wait. Her resolve to take full advantage of her last few days in Gangtok wasn't exactly going well.

•

Chitralekha would stay in bed all day. Her grandchildren would beg her to conduct the *puja*, and she'd join them only after an entire day's sulking.

Tomorrow was her big day. The priest would be in later to examine the kiln. Dignitaries had been invited for an extravagant lunch. Friends and richer family members would join them. The poorer relatives would come by later for dinner, which would be cobbled together from leftovers of the previous meal.

Tonight, the *Bhailo* singers, mostly young girls, would hop from house to house singing Diwali carols all night and disrupt Chitralekha's peace. Bhagwati volunteered to take offerings out to the girls and had readied a plate on which she placed some uncooked rice, a tiny copper pot that held a marigold, and an earthenware lamp. As the girls arrived, Bhagwati would count the strength of each group and accordingly place money on the plate, the ornateness of which was very often sidelined by the amount of money it bore. The task of paying the girls, thanking them, and sending them off usually fell on Prasanti, who, Chitralekha was aware, cut the amount to be paid to each group by half and pocketed the remaining money.

What Prasanti had done yesterday was inexcusable, but after Chitralekha's fury had subsided, she decided that her servant had just made an unfortunate mistake. Yes, she'd pardon the brainless eunuch, but Chitralekha hadn't had a moment to declare to Prasanti that all was forgiven. Her servant hadn't brought her tea and hadn't even asked her down to breakfast. Chitralekha was ready to overlook yesterday's indiscretion, but she didn't like this lack of follow-up.

The eunuch wasn't the only person who should have been begging her for exculpation. Ruthwa had knocked at her door early last morning with all the earnestness of the remorseful but quickly disqualified himself for redemption when he shouted, "Aamaa, can you hear me?" following it with a chortle. To her grandson, everything was a joke. What he did to her was a joke. What he did to the family was a joke. His cruel laughter had rung in her ears until she again fell asleep. She could have slapped him, but an old woman's slap on a thirty-one-year-old man would not have the kind of effect she desired. If anything, it would invite ridicule from all the grandchildren. Yet another story in the endless book of tyrannies Aamaa had supposedly inflicted on the children.

Her heart had palpitated after the outburst with Prasanti. She felt old—as though she didn't have in her the will to fight anymore. The realization alarmed her. Isn't that how old people—people who had given up—felt? A part of her didn't want to let go, but there was another part—this one, these days, more victorious—that constantly commanded her to rest, to spend her days in reflection at the great life she had led, to twiddle her beads and contemplate where her cenotaphs would be. She was sleeping and dreaming so much more these days. She felt useless.

If she had no ambition left in her, she'd have happily moved to Kalimpong. Gangtok was wonderful, and it was home, but there was always too much going on. The central location of her house didn't help matters. People who had no business dropping by stopped by all the time. Some were there to talk trade and commerce. Others didn't want to use public restrooms on their trips to town, and Chitralekha's bathroom was a convenient choice. Many wanted favors. Some came to offer her their respects, as if she was some guru. Others wanted her blessings because an old woman supposedly had the power in her to sway the minds of gods.

She had piled too much on her plate the last few years. Her level of civic engagement was at an all-time high. Why would a school invite her, a person with a second-grade education, to give away prizes? And why would she, a person with a second-grade education, accept the invitation? Yes, allying herself with the right political candidate was important at one point in her life, but, for a long time now, Gangtok had had no opposition party, no politician worth being friends with other than Subba. And Subba was already her friend, so there was no reason, really, for her to go to parties, to be seen at rallies, to give rousing speeches. She didn't look forward to attending these events—she went as a creature of habit. Cutting down on these commitments would be difficult—no, impossible—if she continued living in Gangtok. She often discussed with Prasanti the temptation to post a sign that read *Please come in only if you're expected* at her gate to lower the number of visitors. There was just no respite.

Moving to Kalimpong wouldn't have been much different from staying in Gangtok if she settled in her bazaar house there, but she had no intention of doing that. Her textile factory in Sindebong was four acres of paradise, two and a half miles away from town. It was well connected by road to the market but amply far from it so she would never have to encounter a traffic jam for miles.

The two bedrooms on the third floor of the factory were more manageable than this big house. She could take Prasanti with her, but Prasanti had become too much of a city girl to like living in the country. Didi, the previous helper, was now based in Kalimpong, but she was old and frail. Old and frail people irritated Chitrale-kha. She'd have to raise Prasanti's pay if a Kalimpong move occurred. If the lack of something to do bothered her (or Prasanti) too much, she (or Prasanti) could simply head down to the workroom to supervise the sewing, dyeing, and tanning. She wouldn't think of expansion, of making more money, of destroying her competitors. Kalimpong was also warmer. It would be good for her health.

But what was good for her body wasn't necessarily good for her mind. The first few days would be peaceful, and then she'd feel stifled. The factory, as idyllic as its location may have been, would not have views of the Kanchen-dzonga. Even if it did, she couldn't possibly stare at the mountain the entire day. She still had so many things to sort out here. She wasn't about to retire with no one in sight to continue her legacy. One grandson was opposed to marriage, and she'd avoided thinking of the other all these years. What harm would it do one of them to give her an heir? At least she could be on her way to death knowing that the Neupaney family wouldn't die after her grandchildren's generation. The only great-grandchildren she had didn't count. Shouldn't her frustrations, therefore, be forgiven? Wasn't her behavior justified?

Manasa's reedy voice put an end to Chitralekha's reverie.

"Aamaa, are you going to eat breakfast or not?" Manasa asked from outside Chitralekha's room. "You must be hurting because your beloved has betrayed you, you poor thing."

Chitralekha stayed silent. Manasa let herself in.

"It's Lakshmi *Puja*," her granddaughter said. "We have a white male Lakshmi in the garden."

"Who?" Chitralekha asked.

"Agastaya's friend. Irritating man."

"He must take good care of his grandparents."

"Yes, he probably does," Manasa said. "By dumping them in old-age homes. We should have done that with you."

"I'd have been better off there than here."

"Yes, probably. You'd have found a man for yourself there. Isn't that what life is all about if you're female? Find a man and live happily ever after? I hit the jackpot."

"Yet you think you should throw it all away."

"I like my man, even if he is spineless. It's the father-in-law, who looks like he'll even outlive you, that I am not fond of."

Bhagwati walked in with a bowl of oatmeal. "You have to eat something, Aamaa," she said. "You didn't even eat dinner last night."

Chitralekha was famished, so she took an unsure spoonful of oatmeal. It was hot.

"I thought you'd never eat anything touched by Bhagwati," Manasa said.

Chitralekha didn't answer. She swallowed another mouthful.

"Is Bhagwati not the evil one anymore?" Manasa said, while her older sister made faces at her. "Aamaa and I were discussing marriages. I am sure you have plenty to add, Bhagwati—you're an expert at making a marriage work. You love talking about marriages."

"I still think Prasanti is better than all of you." Chitralekha took the last spoonful of her oatmeal. Then she remembered the crunching of stones from yesterday's rice and spat out what she was chewing.

"Even when she fed you stones?" Manasa asked with all the innocence she could muster.

"Those stones were meant for you, and you deserved them."

"More than Agastaya, who's shelving marriage? More than Bhagwati, who got married to a Damaai? More than Ruthwa, who wrote about the most harrowing experience of your life for the world to read?"

"All of you deserved it," Chitralekha said. Yes, they deserved it.

"But you don't deserve all this, right, Aamaa?" Manasa said. "You, the victim, don't deserve this life at all."

Bhagwati asked Manasa not to taunt Aamaa, to which Aamaa said, "I can defend myself, Bhagwati. I don't need your help."

"No, Aamaa," Manasa continued. "I want an answer. How is it that all four of your grandchildren are now your enemies?"

"I am an unlucky woman," Chitralekha said with resignation. "Look at the way you all treat me. What did I do to deserve it?"

"Everything, Aamaa. Why can't you look at the bright side of things? We've come all the way from various corners of the world to help celebrate your birthday. Why don't you appreciate that?"

"I am going to sleep," Chitralekha said. "Please pull the door shut on your way out."

"No, Aamaa." Manasa was relentless. "Why don't you appreciate what we do for you?"

"Manasa, that's enough," Bhagwati said. "She doesn't look well."

"I am perfectly well, Bhagwati," Chitralekha said. "No need to defend me."

"Yes, pick on her, Aamaa," said Manasa. "Pick on the weakest. Why don't you say anything to Ruthwa? Because you're afraid he's going to write about you and make you a caricature again, aren't you?"

"Manasa, let's go downstairs," Bhagwati said. "There's a lot to prepare for tomorrow."

Chitralekha had turned to her other side when they left, so she couldn't see who banged the door closed. It had to be Manasa. Her younger granddaughter had so much anger in her. Manasa was right in her interrogation, though. When had her grandchildren become her enemies? How did she only see faults in them? Why couldn't she let them be and let them go?

She'd ask the one person who wouldn't shy away from giving her an unbiased opinion. "Prasanti!" she shouted. "Prasanti."

Prasanti meekly opened the door. "Did you call me?" she asked, her face toward the floor.

"Yes, I called you. Isn't your name Prasanti?"

"Yes, but I thought you were angry with me."

"For what you did yesterday? That I am."

"I am sorry," Prasanti said. "I am sorry. The stones were for Manasa. They weren't for you."

"I know. No reason to apologize."

"I was afraid you'd send me away." Prasanti cried harder. "I was afraid this wouldn't be my home anymore."

"Where would you go, you slow girl?" Chitralekha asked. "To your father's house in Kalimpong or to your *hijra* house in Bombay? This is your house."

"But you were so angry yesterday," Prasanti said, sobbing. "You've never been that angry with me."

"I am angry with you all the time. You don't do good work around here. Yesterday, I just decided to show it."

"I am sorry." Prasanti sniffled. "I am really sorry. I'll be good to everyone—even Manasa."

"Don't you dare be good to Manasa. Continue treating her badly. She deserves it."

"Okay. And I am trying to find a way to get Bhagwati and Agastaya to be alone."

"Try harder."

"I promise," Prasanti cried.

"Okay, now stop this. I didn't call you here so you could ruin my bed sheet with your tears and snot. You will have to wash the sheet yourself—you know that."

"I'll do my work properly from now on. I will work hard."

"Pfft. Tell me—and be honest—do you think I am unnecessarily hard on the children?"

"But you were not just a grandmother to them," Prasanti said, her tear ducts finally worn out. "You were a father and mother, so your expectations from them are higher."

"So you think I am right to pester them to get married, have children etc., etc.?"

"Yes, you are, but . . ." The servant stopped herself.

"But what?"

"I am stupid, I know, but why would you worry yourself about that? Nobody could tell you how to live your life, so nobody should tell them how to live theirs."

It made sense. What the eunuch said was clear. Why did they have to fulfill her wants? Why did they have to live life her way? But why not?

"But why not? I gave them so much. Can't they give me something in return? A marriage? Children? A little push to make their marriage work?"

"There's one of them who has given you all three."

"She's different."

"Why continue holding a grudge? Your being angry with her isn't going to change anything. Even if she divorces her husband, her Damaai babies aren't going anywhere."

That was true. If only forgiveness came that easily.

SIX

Nicky

Thankfully, his sisters—with their newly formed, if feigned, Western notions of privacy—left them alone. But it wouldn't last long—someone would barge in sooner or later.

Agastaya was glad he had read Nicky's e-mail earlier that morning. He would otherwise not have known how to react to his lover's arrival. The e-mail, sent to Anthony, was revelatory—it showed that Nicky had a side that cared.

Hey love,
Giving Foolito a surprise. Heading to his hometown. Will be there by the 21st or 22nd. Some silly permits required for his state, like its a country within a country or something. What do us ignorant Americans know? Will be there a full week before schedule. Wonder what India will be like. Probably hot, polluted, and hairy men. As long as there not as hairy as A . . . just kidding, he's perfect the way he is. My love to Tony II.
    Nick

First, it was euphoria that set in. He was described as "perfect" to Nicky's old lover. That was the nicest compliment Agastaya had ever received from Nicky. Elation had then given way to panic when the magnitude of what Nicky was about to do hit home. His boyfriend would show up in Gangtok. What after that? Giving surprises was Nicky's forte, but this was taking it a little too far. Had Nicky booked a hotel, or did he foolishly think that he would stay in Aamaa's house?

Well, Nicky was here now, and Agastaya would have to deal with him.

"God, you are here!" Agastaya said.

"Something makes me feel that's not an exclamation of happiness," Nicky replied.

"You look good."

"Once again, not an expression of happiness."

"Thanks for the surprise."

"Are you sure you're grateful for it? Your face says otherwise."

Yes, it was a very generous gesture on Nicky's part. Yes, it was good to see Nicky.

"I just can't believe it—you in my home world," Agastaya finally said because he didn't know how to keep the conversation moving.

"I know, right?" Nicky exalted. "Don't worry—to everyone, I am an anthropologist."

"I guess I should feel grateful."

"What the fuck? Oops, am I allowed to use the f-word here?"

Hadn't Agastaya imagined Nicky in this setting just two days before? His boyfriend had met half his family and would soon meet the other half. How careful Agastaya had been about divorcing his New York life from his family life. Now the two had collided. "I am sorry. It's great to see you. I'm just slightly taken aback. You know how it is with me and surprises."

"This was supposed to be the greatest surprise of your life," Nicky said. "And now you've ruined it."

"How have I ruined it?"

"You're so . . . what's the word? . . . whatever . . . You're so difficult to please."

Agastaya looked around to see if anyone was within earshot. Ruthwa would be back at any time. Nicky's making a list of his shortcomings now in his loud voice wasn't safe. Agastaya wouldn't put it past any of his siblings to listen in on this conversation. Worse, the eavesdropper would report the exchange to everyone. This garden wasn't a secure place at all. Someone was probably behind the curtains right now, judging his body language.

"Where are you staying?"

"At the Mayfair—so beautiful, so Thai. They treat me very well there, but my room is booked only until tonight."

"And after that?"

"I don't know. It's your town. Figure shit out. This wasn't the response I expected. I hate this. I should never think of doing anything good for you. You always have a problem."

Nicky had still not realized the gravity of showing up unannounced. He now wanted credit, teary-eyed gratitude. If they were somewhere else, Agastaya would have asked his partner if he was right in the head, but he couldn't afford to be melodramatic here.

"I'm sorry," he said. "It's my family—you know what they do to me."

"I quite liked Byaag-wutti. Manasa was a little bitch."

"Yes, she can be difficult at times."

"Isn't Roota here, too?" Nicky asked.

"He is."

"Manasa told me—that little gossip. Is he as hunky as he was in those pictures?"

"Still doesn't shower."

"He doesn't need to with a face like that."

"Smokes like a chimney."

"Hence the smell, I'd think."

"Oh, no, that's from me. I smoked a cigarette today."

"Good for you." Nicky lifted his hand for a high-five. "Indulging in a vice or two might be right for you."

Agastaya wouldn't high-five back. "I was stressed."

"Who isn't? I was, too, especially when crossing the border into Sikkim. Why does one require a permit to come to your state when you're already in the country? Why do we need visas to visit this country in the first place? I don't get it. It's not like any American would want to live here forever."

At least Nicky's tirade wasn't against him.

"If we have to apply for visas to go to America, why should you be exempt from visas to enter India?"

"First world," Nicky said. "First world, third world."

"India is second world now."

"Yes, second world with all those slums. The kids in the slums were so cute—even cuter than those in *Slumdog Millionaire*."

"Where did you see slums in Gangtok?"

"All of Delhi is a slum. The kids waved at me as I passed them. I wanted to hug every one of them and shower them with kisses."

Nicky's desire for children wasn't going to change even if he changed continents. Wholeheartedly believing that trivializing his boyfriend's hankering wasn't enough, Agastaya tried sexualizing it. Perhaps that would make a difference. "That sounds creepy. Please don't say anything like that."

"Anything involving kids is creepy to you," Nicky said.

"Well, you did sound like a pedophile when you said that." Agastaya was being cruel.

"I am this close to yelling. You welcome me to your hometown by calling me a pedophile. I think I should leave."

"Now, don't take everything so seriously."

"What the fuck am I supposed to do, then? You just called me a pedophile. You look more like a pedophile than I do."

"I was joking," Agastaya said.

"You don't joke—ever. You have no sense of humor. The nurses at Beth Israel think you're weird. You aren't funny. Your jokes aren't funny."

"You're raising your voice, Nicky. Can we talk about this later?"

"When? In Agra? Outside the Taj Mahal? Let's solve our problems outside the most romantic place in the world."

"I didn't mean that, Nick. It's just that this house isn't the place to do it."

"I hate you," Nick said.

"I know," Agastaya said. "At the moment I hate you, too."

Bhagwati's face materialized on the balcony. She asked Agastaya if he might want some tea.

"No, thanks," Agastaya replied.

"And, Nicholas, you?" Bhagwati said.

"Chai-tea would be great."

"And we will also have some *sel-roti* coming your way. It's a special Nepali bread."

"How exciting," Nicky said. "I feel the need to feel special."

Once Bhagwati went inside, Agastaya warned: "She was probably standing there. She must have heard us."

"Paranoia, paranoia—all your doing."

"She has been pestering me to get married since I saw her. She wants me to meet some doctor girl."

"Doctor or not, the girl has no penis—that disqualifies her."

"I can't say that to Bhagwati."

"Why not?" Nicky said. "Just why not? It's not like you have to come back and live here. You see these people once every two or three years. Why do you care?"

"We've been through this, Nicky. Plenty of times."

"Yes, we have, and I'm tired of it."

"Are we doing this here again?"

Prasanti put an end to the silence that followed by marching outside like a drill sergeant. "Would you like your tea inside or outside?" she asked Agastaya.

"Outside."

She reemerged, armed with a tray of tea and *sel-roti*.

"Thank you," Nicky said as she placed the tray on a stool.

Prasanti giggled.

"Do you speak English?" Nicky asked.

Prasanti giggled in reply.

"She doesn't," Agastaya dismissed, and in Nepali said to the eunuch: "Prasanti, why are you behaving like a spoiled child in front of my friend?"

Prasanti provided her answer in a giggle.

"If she can openly be a trannie, why can't you?" Nicky said.

Prasanti, covering her face with the tray, giggled again and marched back into the house.

"Left-right, left-right," she bellowed. "This will be the new tune I'll march to."

•

Desirous of taking full advantage of her last three days of freedom, Manasa made a call to book a spa treatment at the luxurious new Mayfair Hotel.

She had planned the massage partly because of Ruthwa's unflattering opinion on the way she had aged. She had noticed a new sagging above her jawline, and her hair had stopped brushing in the direction she steered it. The problem with her hair could be attributed to the water in Gangtok, but she couldn't be too sure. The lifelessness she felt inside showed outside, she knew, but she also had an excuse—Bua couldn't be left alone while she gallivanted from beauty parlor to beauty parlor. She rarely wore nail polish these days—that's how far vanity had been demoted in her life.

Bhagwati had just showered and was sunning herself in the garden. That beauty needed no spa.

"I've booked some treatments at the Mayfair," Manasa said.

"Good—you have fun."

"I've booked the both of us in."

"I can't afford such luxuries," Bhagwati replied.

"It's a gift from me."

"I was being sarcastic," Bhagwati said, on her face a duplicate of the disgusted look she'd had earlier when Manasa asked her if Aamaa was paying her to talk sense into Agastaya. "Do you think I can't afford a spa trip? You seriously think I am worse off than a beggar, don't you?"

Manasa couldn't think of a way to defend herself, so she kept quiet, which infuriated Bhagwati further.

"I feel insulted by you, Manasa," Bhagwati said, her tone uncontemptuous. "All the time, with your smug attitude. Money isn't everything, you know. If it was, you'd have been far more blessed than any of us."

Manasa meant to tell her older sister that all her money-related comments had been inadvertent, but she was tired of treading on eggshells with Bhagwati. "I don't mean to be rude, Bhagwati, but why do you become so sensitive when money comes up?"

"Because you're all constantly implying that I am poor. Yes, I am—so what?"

"I never purposefully tried to do it. It's just that every time there's money talk, you become stiff. I don't know what to do."

"So, it's my fault now?"

"Look, I am sorry. Can we go to the spa? We need to look nice for the party tomorrow. I feel hideous. I look so dark these days."

"I don't need to go to a spa," Bhagwati snapped. "I am whiter than a quilt cover."

"The quilt covers in this house have yellowed, so, yes, you are whiter than they," Manasa replied.

"Terrible joke." Bhagwati started filing her nails. Even her nails were shiny. How could someone's nails— nails!—be so pretty?

"Okay, I know you don't need to go to a spa—you're gorgeous. You don't even need to wear makeup, but can you please accompany your ugly sister?"

"I didn't mean that," Bhagwati said, softening. "I didn't mean I don't need to go to a spa because I'm beautiful. I just don't like spas. I feel they're a waste."

"See? I misconstrued what you said," Manasa said.

"So?"

"You've been misreading all my money-related comments. Maybe you're sensitive about money the way I am about my looks."

Bhagwati smiled. Perhaps she understood.

"Yes, everyone here is so worried about my poverty," she said. "But now please shut up about it. Don't come up with examples that make no sense. You're making things worse."

"So, you aren't coming?"

"No, and I wouldn't mind being left alone for some time."

Her noble intention rebuffed and her nobler attempt at drawing a connection between misinterpreted remarks trampled upon, Manasa called the spa to cancel her reservation.

Being misunderstood for no fault of her own wasn't amusing, but Manasa wouldn't let her sister's surliness affect her. She had promised herself that she'd have fun these last few days, so when she saw her brother and Nicholas involved in deep conversation, she called out to them.

"Aamaa wants to meet Nicholas!" she shouted.

"What will she talk to him about?" Agastaya replied.

"About life," Manasa said.

"In what language?"

"I'll translate for them," Manasa offered. "Or you can."

"I'd love to meet your grandmother," Nicholas said.

"Nicky, please, don't," Agastaya said to Nicholas.

"Why not? She sounds like a lovely lady."

Manasa galloped to Aamaa's bedroom, where her grandmother was changing channels.

"The *gorey* wants to come up and get your blessings," she informed the old lady.

"What blessings will I give a beef-eater?" Aamaa replied without looking away from the TV.

"I am a beef-eater, and you bless me. Oooh, they are here. Get up. You want him to have a nice impression of you."

"The most important thing in my life a day before my eighty-fourth birthday," said Aamaa, "is to impress a *gorey*?"

"And please don't smoke in front of him."

Aamaa fished out from her pouch a *beedi* and lit it up just as Agastaya and Nicholas entered the room.

"Aamaa, this is Nicholas," Agastaya said in Nepali.

Aamaa smiled shyly at Nicholas.

"Nicky . . . Nicholas, this is Aamaa, my grandmother," he said in English.

"Hello," Nicholas said.

"Won't he do *Namaste* to me?" Aamaa looked at Manasa.

"She's asking you why you don't wish *Namaste* to her," Manasa translated to Nicholas.

"Oh, *Namaste*," Nicholas said and in a theatrical gesture brought both his hands together.

"He's even fairer than those people from Belgium," Aamaa said to Manasa.

"She says you're very good-looking." Manasa stretched the truth.

Agastaya fidgeted a bit.

"Oh, thank you." Nicky smiled.

"Aamaa, aren't you going to ask him to sit?" Manasa asked.

"Sit? Where? Do these *goreys* sit on the bed? Tell him to remove his shoes if he wants to put his feet on my sheet."

Manasa laughed at her grandmother's newfound concern for hygiene. Agastaya smiled.

"Aamaa has seen on TV that some Westerners don't take off their shoes when they go to bed," Manasa said to Nicky. "That's how well informed our grandma is. She says you remove your shoes if you have any intention of placing your feet on her sheet."

Manasa laughed harder. Agastaya's smile narrowed as his forehead creased.

"I'm fine," Nicky said. "I'll stand. What's that cute thing she's smoking?"

"It's a disgusting cigarette—favored by lowlifes," Manasa said.

"What's he asking?" Aamaa asked.

"He wants to know why you won't give up your terrible habit of smoking," Manasa said.

Chitralekha smiled. "Come, come," she said in English, and she signaled for Nicholas to walk to her.

Nicholas hesitated but inched toward the bed. Aamaa handed the *beedi* she was smoking to him.

"She wants you to smoke it," Manasa said, looking unsurely at Agastaya but delighted by Aamaa's generosity.

"I'd love to." Nicholas took a puff of the *beedi*. He coughed and choked but made another go.

"These *goreys* can't smoke a harmless *beedi*," Aamaa said. "How could they have ruled us for all those years?"

Everyone but Agastaya laughed. Agastaya didn't seem very amused. Manasa found that even funnier.

•

Aamaa's room was a mess when Bhagwati walked in—a smoke-filled, people-filled, cough-filled, laughter-filled mess.

"They are bonding," Manasa said to Bhagwati. "Look at how strangers bond over *beedi*. *Beedi* is a universal language."

This was like trespassing into a Hollywood comedy in which the characters were all smoking pot. But no one here was high. Everyone was just being silly.

"Shouldn't we eat lunch?" Bhagwati asked. Then, in Nepali, she asked the same question to Aamaa.

"Ask him what he likes to eat," Aamaa said, which Manasa submissively translated.

"Curry," Nicholas replied.

"I understood that," Aamaa said. "But what curry?"

Manasa did the two-word interpreting: "Which curry?"

"Chicken curry."

"This is a vegetarian Upadhyay Baahun's house—no chicken here," Aamaa said. "He will be thrown out if he wants chicken."

Nicholas may have sensed her meaning. "Okay, vegetables, then."

As Aamaa got up and led her merry entourage downstairs, a confounded Bhagwati focused on the sole sullen person left behind.

"What, exactly, is going on?" she said.

"She wanted him to try the *beedi*, and since then they've become best friends," Agastaya answered.

"I assume he is staying for lunch," Bhagwati said.

"He doesn't deserve to, but it's Aamaa's house, and she's already asked him what he wants to eat."

"How do they even speak to each other?"

"Manasa has volunteered to do the translating. She orchestrated all this."

"That's what boredom does," Bhagwati said.

"I know. This guy is a leech. He'll never let go of my side—or any of your sides now."

Downstairs, Ruthwa was already seated with the trio.

"Have you been introduced?" Agastaya asked Ruthwa.

"Oh, you are Roota," Nicholas said.

"How do you do?" Ruthwa said in a stiff manner.

"Very nice meeting you," Nicholas replied.

"So, I am not the only gatecrasher around here?" Ruthwa asked no one in particular.

"Is this the entire family, then?" Nicholas surveyed the entire table, where Prasanti was yet to serve food.

Aamaa wanted Manasa to translate what the *gorey* said.

"Everyone but the spouses," Aamaa said.

"I am not going to translate that," Manasa said to Aamaa.

Bhagwati felt a wave of anger overpower her. This easy acceptance by Aamaa of a stranger—a non-Hindu, a non-Nepali, a non-Indian, a white man—was jarring when Bhagwati had for the last year and a half been toiling to get Aamaa to approve of her children. Aamaa had remained resolute, unmoved, but here she was, best friends with a man whose last name she didn't know. What had happened to her beef-eater/non-beef-eater nonsense? Her grandmother's mouth had even gladly puffed on the same *beedi* that the beef-eater had smoked.

"I will." Bhagwati offered to translate. "She says all the family members are here but the spouses."

"Oh, yes, all but the significant others," Nicholas said. "Why are your partners not here?"

"Mine is an untouchable, so he couldn't come," Bhagwati said.

"And you?" Nicholas directed the question at Manasa.

"I didn't bring mine because . . . too long a story," Manasa said. "I didn't bring mine because I didn't want him around."

"And you, Roota?"

"It is *Ruthwa*," Ruthwa corrected the American.

"What about you, Roota?"

"I don't believe in monogamy."

"Good for you. And what about you?" Nicholas turned his attention to Agastaya. "You're loaded and a catch. Don't you have anybody you could bring to the event?"

"No one, really," Agastaya said.

Bhagwati seized the chance. "He berates me for asking him to get married," she said. "He needs to find a nice girl . . ."

"*Key kuraa gardaichan?*" Aaamaa asked Manasa.

"I don't want to be the translator anymore," Manasa replied. "Someone, please take over."

"I will," Ruthwa said.

"Not you," came Manasa's reply.

"Why not?"

"All right, you're more than welcome to," Manasa deigned. "Aamaa, Ruthwa will do the translation."

Aamaa pursed her lips.

"Prasanti, where's the food?" she shouted. "We have a guest."

"I am a guest, too," Ruthwa said in Nepali.

Prasanti brought everyone's plate—each had some rice on it. She laughed when she placed Nicholas's plate in front of him.

"I'll slap you if there is any stone in my rice," Manasa said to Prasanti.

"Do you eat the rice by itself in Sikkim?" Nicholas asked.

"Yes, we do," Manasa said. "We can't afford vegetables in India."

"Ignorant American—get it, get it." Nicholas proudly looked around.

Prasanti emerged again bearing two bowls with two ladles and placed them on the table. She portioned onto Nicholas's plate a ladleful of *daal* from one and the squishiest squash Bhagwati had ever seen from another. The solid vegetable chunks had all been battered into a paste.

"What's that guacamole-like thing?" Nicky asked.

"Serving done only for the guest," Prasanti said, and she giggled.

She repeated the process for Chitralekha and added, "And for the *ghar*-Aamaa. The others should serve themselves."

"It smells like heaven," Nicholas said.

Ruthwa scoffed. Agastaya glanced at Ruthwa.

"Be careful," Ruthwa said. "They frequently find pebbles in the rice here."

"Can you tell him we usually eat more than one vegetable?" Aamaa asked Manasa. "What if he thinks this is what our everyday diet is like?"

"No, I'll not tell him that," Manasa replied. "Are you worried about your social status with a stranger?"

"Can I eat with my fingers, too?" Nicholas asked. "It's always been a dream of mine."

"We aren't a dictatorship, Nicholas," Manasa said. "You do what you want."

"It's not as easy as it looks," Bhagwati said. "When I had American guests over in Boulder, they all gave up."

Ruthwa lifted his left hand and brought all his fingers together in demonstration. "It's easy—this is it, right?"

"Wait until you try it with the rice," Bhagwati warned.

"Tell him he can't eat with his left hand," Aamaa said to Bhagwati, which Bhagwati conveyed.

"But why?" Nicholas asked.

"We use the left hand exclusively for fun things in the bathroom," Ruthwa explained.

"I needed something *that* well described to whet my appetite for this repulsive food," Manasa said.

Nicholas took a few grains of rice, yellowed on contamination with the other contents of his plate, between the fingers of his right hand and made a small ball of it with the squash and *daal*. He then tilted his head, and, with his mouth facing the ceiling, lifted his hand up in the air, aiming for the rice to drop into his mouth in a shower. Half the grains entered their desired destination while the other half fell onto his shirt.

"Prasanti, come look at this!" Aamaa shouted, delighted with the spectacle.

Nicholas was a great performer. He slurped his food, made "mmm" sounds to pronounce its deliciousness, accepted a second helping before dropping on himself almost all of what was served, and continued eating, distracting and delighting Prasanti and Aamaa, who had stopped chewing because she was so engrossed in the *gorey*'s rice-eating skills.

"So, is it acceptable for him to sit at your table, Aamaa?" Bhagwati quietly said. "He's not an untouchable?"

"He is different," Aamaa said.

"How, different?"

"He's not the husband of one of you," Aamaa said. "He'll never be married to any of you."

Manasa, momentarily forgetting that she had given up the role of interpreter, translated Aamaa's commentary for Nicholas. "She says it's okay for you, a beef-eater, to be seated at the same table as us because you will never be married to one of us."

"Yes, she has a point," Nicholas said. "She has a point."

Bhagwati didn't say anything to that. Aamaa continued being fascinated by Nicholas's adventures with food. She called out to Prasanti again when some rice—the biggest fistful so far—fell to the floor.

The piety Bhagwati felt every Lakshmi *Puja* was slowly and surely deserting her today.

•

Prasanti had secured decorations from the driver's cousin and made a pageant of chaining the string of lights to the roof.

"Where are all the *condo* men when you need them?" She was out of breath. "Why do I have to do everything here?"

Manasa and Agastaya were immersed in deep conversation up on the balcony . . . in English. Ruthwa and

Bhagwati were playing cards while occasionally talking . . . in English.

"Come, come," Chitralekha said to her grandson's
friend, who was touring the garden by himself. "Help,
help."

She hadn't given it much thought when they were
growing up, but she found it odd that all her grandchildren talked to one another mostly in English. She found
it even more peculiar that the children even spoke to one
another. They were a fractious bunch as youngsters. As
adults, they seemed to have set aside their differences,
if for a few days, and that made her wonder why she
couldn't become like them. It'd make her life—and the
lives of those around her—so much easier if she simply
faked forgiveness for the time they were here. They'd all
be gone after that. She'd maybe see them for a few days
once every two years. A protean Chitralekha for her protean grandchildren—that would be an ideal world. But
she wasn't used to living in an ideal world.

"Prasanti, those lights aren't attractive at all," Manasa
said. "I like the marigold garlands by themselves better—
the décor is more natural that way."

"Look which *condo* is talking about beauty," Prasanti
said. "A *Chaurasi* comes only once in a lifetime. Subba
will be here. Ministers will be here. We have to make
this house look like a palace."

"Except it's looking like a *hijra* house right now,"
Manasa said.

Agastaya's friend—Chitralekha still couldn't pronounce his name—gave Manasa an expectant look.

"He must be feeling left out," Chitralekha said to
Manasa. "Why don't you translate what you just said
to Prasanti for him?"

Thankfully, Manasa complied without argument.

An exchange occurred between the white man and her rude granddaughter. This one was speckled with laughter on both sides.

"He likes the lights," Manasa explained to Chitralekha. "He thinks they are important for a festival but even more fitting for a birthday that falls on a festival."

Ruthwa whispered to Bhagwati, and they both laughed.

"Ask him if they have something like this in America," Chitralekha said. "I don't know how to say his name."

Manasa and the friend tossed words at each other.

"He says American festivals are boring, and he wants you to call him Nicky. All people who like him call him Nicky."

"Nicky, Nicky," Chitralekha practiced while Nicky beamed. "That's not difficult at all. It could even be a Nepali name."

Manasa did what she had to.

"Nicky wonders if you'll give a speech tomorrow," Manasa said to Chitralekha.

"A speech? Now, why?"

Words were swapped between Manasa and Nicky.

"It's like stones rattling in a plastic bottle." Chitralekha described what she thought of the give-and-take in English to Manasa, who was still mid-dialogue with Nicky. Only Ruthwa heard her and smiled.

"I know," he said.

Chitralekha looked in the direction of Bhagwati and Ruthwa, who were playing some puerile card game. "Playing *joot-patti* like five-year-olds," she said.

Once the babble of English voices died, Manasa said, "He thinks you should deliver a speech tomorrow. It is a very big occasion. It's a very important birthday. All those invited need to be inspired by you."

"Is this an election rally?" Chitralekha asked. She thought for a moment. The idea made sense. A roomful of people—well-wishers, VIPs, dignitaries, jealous neighbors—would hang on every word that came out of her mouth. And it would be a novel thing to do. No one delivered speeches during personal celebrations.

"People in America give speeches," Agastaya, even quieter today than his usual self, said.

"Maybe I could do it," Chitralekha said.

"Please don't," Manasa begged. "No one does that here."

"That hasn't stopped me from doing things no one has done before," Chitralekha replied. "Had I not done things that hadn't been done before, I am sure I'd have been able to give you the best of everything."

"Embarrass the whole family if you want," Manasa said. "Do it. I'll hide when you give the speech."

"Nicky—Nicky has good ideas," Chitralekha remarked. "What else should we do?"

"He thinks you should also dance," Manasa said after an exchange with Nicky.

"I am not a cheap dancer." Chitralekha waited for a response.

"He thinks you should dance."

"That I won't do. Prasanti will do the dancing for me."

"I only dance for Aamaa these days," Prasanti said, untangling a knot of wires. "You unlucky people will not have me dance on your birthdays. And I give up on these *condo* lights. Two men in the family, and I have to do this alone."

"I am a guest, so I shouldn't be expected to help," Ruthwa said.

"You helped me yesterday, *condo*—and I thought you were a changed man," Prasanti huffed. "Now I know it must be because you wanted to ask me about my past."

"Wait, he asked you about your past?" Manasa said. "What did he want to know?"

"Oh, this and that. My father and mother's story. Made me cry. This man isn't a good man."

"Wait a second—you told him everything?" Manasa asked.

"Yes, everything—even about my operation. He was the most interested in that. Do you also want to get a surgery, *chakka*?"

"He'll write a book about you now," Manasa said. "Everyone will know your story."

"And then I'll become famous," Prasanti retorted. "And people will make a movie about me."

"Did he promise you that?" Manasa asked.

"No. I know. I know these things. I know. And you will be even more jealous of me than you are right now. Don't think I've forgotten the slap."

"Isn't it time for the *puja*?" Bhagwati asked.

"It is," Prasanti said. "Will this *gorey* also come?"

"Let him watch it from the outside," Chitralekha said.

"Do I also have to watch it from the outside, then?" Bhagwati asked.

"You and your siblings have already defiled the entire house—what would it matter if you were to degrade one more room?" Chitralekha responded. She was very pleased with her answer.

The *puja* ushering the goddess of wealth had always been a short affair in their house. It defied tradition in almost every way—the brevity, the absence of incantations, and the general lack of knowledge of what precisely was to be done on a *puja*, any *puja*. Participants would stand in front of the altar, pray in silence, and Chitralekha applied a red dot of a *tika* on each one of them. They'd then light the lamps, gamble, and welcome the *Bhailo* singers. This one was no different, but again, this one *was* different—the entire family was celebrating the festival under one roof after eighteen years.

And it was her birthday that enabled that. This was a singular affair.

When Chitralekha offered *tika* to Bhagwati, Bhagwati might have been crying. When she applied it on Manasa's forehead, Manasa stuck out her tongue and made a monkey-like face. When she put *tika* on Agastaya, he touched her feet with his head. She looked away when she gave Ruthwa his *tika*. After she applied the red dot on Nicky, he hugged her. She turned red.

Outside, the first group of *Bhailo* girls chorused:

Blessed be he who gives us a handful of gifts with a
     roof of gold
Blessed be he who gives us a bagful of gifts with a
     golden shed
Blessed be he who gives us a quintal of donation
     with a golden mansion . . .

May this house be blessed with a lot of cattle
May this family flourish and prosper
May the elderly have long lifelines like those of
     banyan trees
May the stone the elderly touch turn to gold
May the mud they touch turn to paddy
May the water they touch turn to oil . . .

Nicky took pictures. Manasa and Bhagwati changed into blue saris, which did nothing to accentuate the appearance of the former yet immensely flattered the latter. Agastaya and Ruthwa played cards. Prasanti lit a sparkler near a nervous Nicky. Chitralekha asked Prasanti to double the offering for the young girls who had just finished their singing.

"Give them three hundred rupees," she said. "They're the first to come—they'll bring us luck. This has been a good year."

SEVEN

At the ungodly hour of six in the morning, Aamaa's Toyota Innova snakes its way through the many curves north of Chandmari to get to Hanuman Tok.

We whizz by a stuttering jeep, hanging from the back of which are three standing men.

Nicky dives into his backpack for his camera. By the time he removes its lens protector, the jeep is far behind us.

"We usually don't have people hanging from cars in the capital these days," Agastaya says with a hint of hometown pride. "Gangtok is pretty strict about these things. You don't see fifteen passengers populating seats meant for nine."

Prasanti, Manasa, and I are packed in the rear of the vehicle.

"His camera is the size of a TV."—Prasanti.

"Even I have a camera that big," I say.

"But I am sure you don't know how to use it." —Prasanti.

Manasa and I burst out laughing.

Manasa then screeches, trying not to fall off her seat when the vehicle turns at one particularly sharp bend.

"What's so funny?" Aamaa asks from the front seat.

"It's Manasa and Ruthwa being idiotic," Bhagwati, sandwiched between Nicky and Agastaya in the middle seat, informs her. "They need no reason to laugh."

It's D-Day. The grand old lady of the house turns eighty-four today. She wants to make early-morning visits to the temples and the monastery. That's what these special days do—they force nonreligious types to embrace faith for a day. The two-temples-and-a-monastery trip is a Gangtok tradition. The temples don't have much history or significance but have become tourist destinations on account of their beautiful locations—the Hanuman one is swaddled in greenery while the Ganesha temple looks out to the length and breadth of my city. Both temples are clean—I don't mind going barefoot in them. Of all the monasteries around Gangtok, the Enchey Monastery, our third stop, I think, has the least tourist appeal.

Alpine vegetation abounds as the altitude escalates. It's a beautiful part of Gangtok—undeniably lush and unspoiled—but Nicky's camera likes the stray dogs better.

"One of those dogs will jump on him."—Prasanti.

"You want to jump on him."—Manasa.

"Did you chug a bottle of vodka this morning?" Agastaya asks Manasa.

"The priest didn't come yesterday. He said he'd be there early this morning."—Aamaa.

"Let him wait."—Manasa.

"Yes, let him wait."—Prasanti.

"Yes, let him wait," I say.

Manasa laughs. Bhagwati turns back and sniffs Manasa's breath.

"It's begun getting chilly."—Aamaa.

"I love the way you guys speak. Maybe I should learn Nepalese. I wonder how long it'd take me."—Nicky. *Click. Click.*

"How many languages do you speak?"—Manasa.

"Half of one—English."—Nicky.

"You can easily learn how to speak Nepali," I joke.

"Speak and write both."—Nicky. *Click.*

"Writing is even easier."—Manasa.

The four of us siblings laugh. Despite being somewhat proud of our written Nepali, we have no fond memories of maneuvering our way around the *raswa-dirgha* dichotomy that causes so many people of my generation to detest the language—I have, for instance, never figured out when to use the small *ee* as opposed to the big *eee* and the shorter *oo* in place of the longer *ooo*. Disentangling the verb-gender enigma and suffixing the cases are even more complex. The obsession with English has atrophied our Nepali reading and writing skills.

"It's a beautiful language," I say.

"It is."—Agastaya.

"So expressive. I love that slash on top of every word."—Nicky. *Click.*

"That's Nepali," I say.

"That's Nepali."—Manasa.

We have now become a family of Nepali-speaking people from everywhere.

Kalimpong, in the troubled Darjeeling district, where hope should have reigned supreme in "Jai

Gorkhland" but has over the years been edged out by desperation.

Nepal, where my mother was from and where Manasa was married.

Gangtok, the capital of Sikkim, our home.

Bhutan (well, sort of), where Bhagwati married.

We now are from America, from England, from everywhere.

People from different places speaking the same language across seven seas.

I: citizen of the world? Not quite. Nepali-speaking Indian. Indo-Nepalese. Indian of Nepalese origin. Gurkhali or Gurkha or Gorkha—terms gaining rapid popularity to describe the Nepali in India, words embraced to chisel out our identity, to distance ourselves from Nepal. Old words with new meanings. Words meant not to confuse our ethnicity with our nationality. Hoping the association that comes from sharing our new name with those valiant soldiers doesn't spawn a different kind of identity conundrum.

Agastaya: an NRI, a Non-Resident Indian. Indian about to leap over. Insufferable green-card holder—poster boy of upper-middle-class South Asian aspirations. Impatient bearer of an Indian passport that will soon be replaced by an American one, the former to be hidden but promised to be turned over to authorities, to be flashed on trips to Bhutan, where being non-Indian means having to shell out a pretty penny.

Bhagwati: Nepali-speaking Bhutanese. Lhotshampa. Nepali-speaking former Bhutanese. Nepali-speaking refugee. Formerly Nepali-speaking Indian. Now Nepali-speaking-refugee-who's-almost-American-and-travels-on-Refugee-Travel-Document.

Manasa: Nepali-Nepali. Formerly Nepali-speaking Indian. Now Nepali. Nepalese. Anglicized or Sanskritized, one and the same thing. The holder of a nonelectronic passport. But almost a Brit—soon to be owner of the powerful, powerful burgundy passport with the fancy, fancy coat of arms.

And Aamaa: with no passport but voter's IDs in Gangtok, in Kalimpong, and in Darjeeling. One person who votes in three places, two states. Just in case.

It's only taken eighteen long years for all of us to be together in one vehicle.

Aamaa wants to know if we are explaining the significance of everything to Nicky.

"There's nothing to say about the temples. The royal cremation ground has more history, and I haven't ever been there."—Manasa.

"Tell him Ganesha is the remover of obstacles." —Aamaa.

Manasa translates that for Nicky.

"And Hanuman is the monkey god, the bachelor god."—Aamaa.

Manasa does what she has to.

"Oh, yes, Agastaya, remember on our taxi ride to the airport? He was right there—on the dashboard." —Nicholas.

"Isn't that where we met? These shared cabs to airports are such a boon."—Agastaya.

"Whatever."—Nicholas.

We get off outside the Enchey Monastery. Nicky can't stop himself from spinning the series of prayer wheels lining the path to the monastery.

"This is where I brought my husband on our first date."—Bhagwati.

"That's so romantic. Wait, you didn't have an arranged marriage?"—Nicky.

"No, we eloped—sort of."—Bhagwati.

"That's even more romantic."—Nicky.

"If you say so."—Bhagwati.

"Ohmygahd, we need pictures of this place."—Nicky.

"Aamaa, this is where Ram and I came on our first date," Bhagwati tells Aamaa in Nepali. "Remember he had come to interview you?"

Aamaa stiffens.

"You don't want to talk about it, do you, Aamaa?" Bhagwati asks.

Nicholas clicks away.

"No."

"Well, here's something you should know. I didn't run away to get married. I ran away because I had failed the boards." *Click-click-click.*

Aamaa stares at Bhagwati, unbelieving. This is news to all of us.

"And it later turned out I hadn't failed."—Bhagwati.

"You ran away because you failed?"—Agastaya.

"Yes, so don't think I ran away to get married, Aamaa. I ran away because I was afraid of the consequences of being a failure who was also Chitralekha Neupaney's granddaughter."

"But you eventually married him."—Aamaa. *Click. Click. Click.* She breaks into a forced smile for one of the clicks.

"I haven't regretted a second of it—so neither should you." *Click. Click. Click.* "I never want you to bring up the issue of his caste again."

Aamaa opens her mouth to say something. *Click.*

"No, Aamaa, it's your birthday. That's your promise to me."—Bhagwati.

Sometimes, Bhagwati delivers the biggest surprises of us all.

Click. Click.

•

It is a good day to be Aamaa's birthday. It falls on the most unimportant day of a most important festival, right between the Lakshmi *Puja* and *Bhai Tika*, so all the invited guests will turn up. Today is the Goru *Puja*— the day for the worship of oxen. It is a dull day until late at night, when the *Deusi* "players," whose female counterparts sang the *Bhailo* yesterday, will go from house to house singing *Tihaar* carols and assaulting people's sleep.

The first of the three hundred guests who have been invited for the *Chaurasi* start trickling in as early as ten in the morning. Neighbors and close relatives, halfway between immediate family and formal guests, are here to run errands. They'll mingle, eat vegetarian food (because we are, technically, a vegetarian family and also because the *Chaurasi* is more or less a religious event—one that involves a priest), and drink tea, coffee, and orange juice while secretly lamenting the absence of alcohol.

Celebrations in Sikkim are big affairs—community affairs, public affairs. A wedding is judged by the number of people who attend it.

Throw intimacy out the window.

Invite the street, the neighborhood, the town, and the entire damn state—that's what makes a proper party.

As the *Chaurasi* graduates from a sedate religious function to a full-blown networking event, Nicholas's prominence soars. He could be an uneducated charlatan, a sex offender, a murderer, but he outshines everyone at the party.

It's been decided that he will stay with us for the next few days. The inroads one makes as a Westerner in the East! Right after he surfaces from his car, a cousin's cousin relieves Nicky of his suitcase, and the priest—one moment deep in incantations around his fading fire and the next, hovering by the foreign guest's side—asks him questions in his *tutey-futey* English.

"Tell me about the American visa for holy men," the pundit implores Nicholas.

"I am just an ignorant American," the charmer replies. "I know nothing about visas. You may want to ask Agastaya."

The uncomprehending priest returns to his domain and chants mantras while breaking twigs to throw into the crackling fire.

Fathers of women of marriageable age hunt for Agastaya.

Women of marriageable ages eye me.

Aamaa's birthday, according to the lunar calendar, coincides with October 24, her birthday on the solar calendar. The overlap is a rarity, the priest declares. He also predicts that this—along with the alignment of a few stars—will keep malefic events at bay.

Already, even before the more important guests have graced the Oasis with their presence, a profusion of bouquets and bouquet-printed wrapping paper that holds presents hounds my vision. All the presents will be tea sets.

Tomorrow, the flowers will be fed to some village cows. The gifts will be recycled for all the weddings to which Aamaa will be invited once the winter marriage season sets in. The amount of each monetary offering will be meticulously jotted down in a notebook against the name of the person who gave it.

Soon the VIPs will be here for all of us to suck up to. Manasa has warned me to dress up for the occasion. My uniform of shorts and a T-shirt won't do. I ask Prasanti to hunt for something decent to wear.

"Wear my *kurta*, you *chakka*," she says. "I haven't forgotten that you won't help me when you don't have stories to dig out of me."

"Please, get me something."

"Wear your brother's pajamas, but he's the size of a buffalo. I am busy. Look at how many people there are. Go bother somebody else."

"I am writing a book about you, and you treat me this way?" I plead.

"So, Manasa was right?"

"Yes."

"You'd better write good things about me. I've heard that you wrote bad things about Aamaa."

"What bad things?"

"Like that she was stingy and didn't give you enough to eat."

Prasanti scurries out of the house and then dashes back in. She calls the Brahmin useless, plucks out a bud from a tree, and walks to the balcony, from where I am studying her movements, to talk to me about the priest. She's busy doing nothing.

"I hate him—gives all Baahuns a bad name," she says.

"What about you? Do you give Brahmins a bad name?"

"I am a *hijra*. I was once Muslim. By the way, don't write about the Muslim part. Aamaa doesn't know.

She will drag me out of this house by my hair if she finds out."

"Are you sure she doesn't know?"

"You think she'd allow me to work here?"

"She didn't object to the white man desecrating her place."

"But he's Christian, and I am Muslim." Prasanti laughs. "Man-woman, Brahmin-Muslim—who am I?"

"You are unique," I say.

"And you are a sweet talker, *condo*. You have the Goddess Saraswati in your mouth, but I am not going to find you anything to wear."

A wedding band trudges up the driveway playing a Bollywood song.

"Who organized that?"

I don't get Prasanti's reply because the drumming of the *dhol* player is the only thing I—or anyone else—can hear.

"What?" I shout.

"I did," Prasanti says. "Aamaa approved."

The grandeur—the tacky grandeur—can match a wedding's opulence—a tacky wedding's opulence.

Where you have a band wielding trumpets, trombones, and saxophones, a lone priest is bound to be ignored.

"Not now!" the poor priest shrieks. "Music only after the *puja*."

The band starts playing another Bollywood wedding song. The priest shouts at the bandmaster. Prasanti demands that the band play a different Hindi number. The bandmaster doesn't listen to the eunuch. Prasanti yells at the priest. The priest yells back.

"Who's that man who keeps staring at me?" I ask Prasanti.

"Oh, the minister from next door. Aamaa and I didn't think he'd come. He hates Aamaa because she used my skills to prevent him from building a rooftop restaurant. He's coming to us." Prasanti sprints away.

"You are the younger one, aren't you?" the minister says. "Some kind of a writer, aren't you?"

"Yes, I am."

"You see that house?" He points to the building in front of me. "That building couldn't be completed because of your Aamaa—quite a woman of substance, she is."

"I am sorry."

"The restaurant on the terrace had already been planned."

I move away.

Nicky hurtles from one end of the garden to the other taking pictures. The cousin's cousin—who had once told me that he wanted to be a writer but is now, like everyone else, an engineer—fills him in on Prasanti's quarrel with the priest.

Aamaa is getting ready so no one arbitrates the dispute between the pundit and Prasanti.

A heavily made-up Manasa joins me at my vantage point.

"I feel like a queen up here," she says. "Is that why you've chosen to stand here on the balcony?"

"A queen wouldn't cake her face with that much makeup," I reply.

"Why aren't you dressed?"

"I have nothing but shorts and T-shirts, and I sort of want to maintain a low profile."

"Shorts and tees are a surefire way to attract attention here, Ruthwa. Go look for something nice."

"Where would I find something nice?"

"Ask Nicholas. You could wear something he has."

Nicky does have clothes—lots and lots of them. He had shopped for *sherwanis* in Delhi, and while some are ornate—the kind only royalty could get away with—others are all right. The Neupaney Oasis's favorite guest is only too willing to lend his clothes to the Neupaney Oasis's most hated guest.

Bhagwati looks ravishing in green. God has given her 80 percent of the family's looks, me 15 percent, and divided 5 percent between Agastaya and Manasa, with Agastaya taking the bigger piece of the pie, no doubt.

Agastaya wears a red *kurta* that mirrors Nicky's red kurta.

Prasanti complains that she's too busy to change, so she appoints me the temporary custodian of a bunch of keys in her absence.

"Where's Aamaa?"—Manasa.

"Where's Aamaa?"—Agastaya.

"Where's Aamaa?"—Bhagwati.

"Where is she?" I ask.

Aamaa's entrance into the garden is almost anticlimactic. She is dressed the way she usually is: the end of her white sari covering her head, the quality, hue, and lack of patterns on her white blouse no different from the one she wore the day before.

She spots Agastaya in the crowd. "Why aren't you all in proper Nepali outfits?" she asks. "You could have acquired them from the factory and . . ."

But she's swarmed by people before she can finish voicing her thoughts. Like a queen acknowledging her subjects, Aamaa joins her hands in a perpetual *Namaste*, only unjoining them to accept presents and colorful *khadas*, silk scarves that she doesn't wear around her neck.

"Where's Prasanti?" Aamaa asks. "Is Prasanti dead? I need someone to take the presents inside."

"I can take them in." I run down, and Aamaa passes me a few boxes without looking at me.

"I told you all not to bring presents—this is what happens when you don't obey me," Queen Neupaney croons to her disciples.

At the *jagya*, where the fire is hissing away, Aamaa returns the greeting of the pundit and sits down.

"They started playing those vulgar Hindi songs even before the *puja*," the pundit complains.

"Keep it short," Aamaa repeats to the priest. "Make the ceremony really succinct, Pundit-*jee*."

Nicky the white guy holds court with a group of brown people at the buffet. He has on a plain Gurkha hat—black, patternless—while people around him bask in the glory of an American honoring their culture by deigning to wear a Nepali hat. He funnily pronounces *bhaat khaanchu*, the Nepali words for "I'll eat rice," while all those clamoring for a piece of him beam about the permeability of their damn language.

Nicky garbles something about the piquancy of the *dalley* chili a total of ten times. Each time the audience response is more raucous than before.

"Your grandmother is like a queen," the American says to me when I amble up to his circus. "Look at how regal she looks."

"She doesn't look any different from the way she did yesterday," I say. "You look more regal than she does."

"I'll take that as a compliment," Nicky replies, blushing.

The priest keeps the ceremony short. He requests Aamaa to sprinkle spices into the fire.

"Amazing." Nicky changes the settings of his camera from video to still and back to video. "Amazing. Such a rich culture."

Once the *puja* is over, the band plays some more songs.

"I feel like a bride—a widow bride," Aamaa says. "Who authorized the band?"

"Prasanti said you gave her permission," I say tenuously.

"That liar," Aamaa replies, and then, realizing that she has spoken directly to me, repeats "liar" louder. "Prasanti is a liar," she finishes.

The queen's subjects laugh. Nicky stares in amazement. I wait for her to deliver the speech.

When you expect three hundred guests, not everyone is invited to attend the celebration at the same time. You choose various slots to accommodate invitees' social prominence and political leanings—although a steady influx of people will be flowing in and out all day. It is unlikely that Aamaa will make a speech every hour—that would dilute her brand. Our friend Nicky has done his bit in contributing a new malady that will sweep this culture. Soon, everyone in Gangtok will make speeches left and right.

Aamaa chastises friends and family for bringing presents, censures the band for being too loud, nibbles on a snack here or there, but she doesn't make the speech.

"Has she forgotten about it?" I ask Agastaya.

"I don't know," Agastaya replies. "I wonder why Nicky even made that suggestion."

"Yes, I wonder why he's even here."

"Exactly my point." Agastaya looks away from a shutter-happy Nicky.

Some guests want to take pictures with the American. He happily obliges.

"He looks so good in that Indian outfit," a woman remarks.

"I know—it suits him so well," another opines. "The Nepali *topi* makes him look even better. He looks like a younger Bill Clinton."

Manasa escapes a circle of snarling women who ask her when she'd give them the good news of her pregnancy.

"Never." She heads my way.

"Babies?" I ask.

"Yes. Have you had enough marriage questions already?"

"None so far."

"Because they've all been directed at me."—Agastaya.

"At least the relatives don't look at you with a mixture of shame and pity the way they do at Bhagwati," I say.

"She's handling it so well." Manasa points at Bhagwati, who looks dignified and distant with a group of people.

"She's used to it," Agastaya adds, then shuts up when Bhagwati joins us.

Nicky wants to take pictures of the entire family. He perches Aamaa on a plush red chair meant for Subba, the chief minister, and requests that we all stand around her. The legend and her future. The queen and her imperial brood.

"The happy family. What a good-looking family." —Nicky.

"I know. Model good looks."—Manasa.

"One more picture." Nicky takes another shot. "If only the partners were all here, this would have been a complete picture."

Sirens far away announce the arrival of important men. People stand up to hail said important men and their women. Only Aamaa remains seated. The important people come to greet her and gift her.

The loudest siren, the most piercing one, is soon sounded. Subba grants everyone a collective *Namaste* as his minions queue up to offer him *khadas*.

"Is he, like, the king of Sikkim?" Nicky asks me.

"No, the emperor," I correct him. "The elected emperor."

"Nice job you've done with the steps—the road looks amazing," Subba says to Aamaa. "It saved me a long walk."

"I know," says Aamaa before they cower and whisper.

Oh, yes, this is when she will make the speech—when the most important man is finally here.

A microphone is arranged for, the band is asked to stop whatever perky song it is playing, and Nicky, our self-appointed master of ceremonies, speaks: "Thank you for coming, everyone. And now Aamaa will give a speech."

Guests laugh.

Aamaa's speech is impressive in its length.

She thanks everyone. She starts with her family— her grandchildren—although she doesn't name names. She thanks Subba and his council of ministers. She thanks the factory in Kalimpong and the workers there. She thanks those who help run her hotels.

She thanks Prasanti, who isn't anywhere in sight.

Her last note of gratitude is for God. She receives a standing ovation (but that could be because half the attendees were already on their feet when she spoke).

A shout from Prasanti interrupts the applause.

"Aamaa, phone!" Prasanti screams as the cheering weakens.

"Now?" Aamaa says. "Tell them to call tomorrow."

Everyone—including Subba—laughs.

"He says it is very important," Prasanti says, handing the cordless to Aamaa.

All eyes are now on my grandmother.

"Hello," she says, and she listens.

Then she faints.

•

I first notice the rapid yellowing of her sari. I try to think of a suitable metaphor but can't. Even a senseless analogy escapes me.

Aamaa has lost control of her bladder. The woman who has always been in control has lost it. It is as though Aamaa's hardy, tireless, resilient soul no longer inhabits her frail, urine-soaked, unconscious body.

The doctor grandson and his friend try resuscitating her while working in perfect tandem with each other. One holds her wrist; the white friend kisses her on the mouth.

Nicky says we should call an ambulance.

"Take my car," Subba says.

Agastaya asks the CM's security guards to help him lift Aamaa and deposit her in the backseat of the waiting Pajero. He gets in with her.

"Should we follow you in another car?" Nicky asks Agastaya.

Agastaya says nothing.

Nicky and Bhagwati get into a waiting car. A bawling Prasanti jumps into the front seat two seconds later.

Manasa and I look at each other.

"What should we do?" I ask, as if she'd know the answer.

"Talk to Subba, I guess."

So we seek the advice of Subba, the most powerful man in the state, who reasons that everyone should go home.

"All the food will go to waste," Manasa says. "Shouldn't those who haven't eaten eat first?"

Subba announces that people should eat before leaving. For once, nobody obeys him.

"It'd be so nice to be alone right now."—Manasa.

Well-meaning guests linger, deliberating Aamaa's mortality among themselves.

"If you're all staying, at least eat," Manasa requests. "You must be hungry."

Once Subba grabs a plate, a few people follow suit.

"Herd mentality."—Manasa.

"Glad you can still make such astute observations," I reply.

"I don't get it—these guests are well-intentioned, but who wants to be surrounded by this many people in a moment of crisis?"—Manasa.

"Think she'll make it?" I ask.

"She will. What do you think?"

"She will. She's tough. Didn't you see how relaxed Agastaya was?"

The cordless rings. I pick up.

It is Bhagwati. "She's come to. Agastaya says she's fine. They're still going to the hospital to get her checked on."

I give Manasa the good news.

"Thank God," we say in unison.

I request Subba to make the announcement that Aamaa is conscious. There's a polite smattering of applause.

"So, why did she faint?"—Manasa.

"How do I know?"

"Let me call Bhagwati."

She does. She's quiet. She listens. Her face falls. Her cheeks turn red. She hangs up.

"What is it?" I ask.

"The Kalimpong factory has been razed to the ground."

"What do you mean?"

"Burned."

"What the fuck? Was there an accident?"

"Apparently, Aamaa's grandson wrote a column telling people not to wear traditional clothes and making fun of the *Gorkha Jana-shakti Morcha* leadership. It was Aamaa who asked Moktan to mandate the traditional clothes. It was our factory in Kalimpong that was supplying them. The *Gorkha Jana-shakti Morcha* thinks it was a setup: Aamaa suggests something, so her grandson can ridicule it. *The Gorkha Jana-shakti Morcha* is afraid it has lost all credibility. Moktan is furious."

•

Reunion—the word has such a ridiculous, Western ring to it. When Agastaya refers to the *Chaurasi* as a reunion, I laugh a little at him. People in the West keep themselves busy during reunions—they play sports; they drink. We do neither. We sit around and squabble and pretend everything is all right.

It's as though calling the *Chaurasi* a reunion instantly glamorizes it, takes the tedium out of family.

This reunion was strange, but I wasn't expecting anything different. There'd be big, uncomfortable silences, I had conjectured. There were. Awkwardness. There was. Reminiscences. There were. The revisiting of past follies and passions. There was. Vindictiveness. There was. Vindication. There was.

And fuck-ups—the largest of which I was, again, responsible for.

"I did it again," I tell Manasa as we go downhill to the Central Referral Hospital.

"Yes, you did."

"But my intentions weren't bad. I don't expect you to believe it."

"You claimed they were good the last time, too."

"Nah. The rape story, I wrote because I knew it'd be an instant bestseller."

"How you underestimated it. It also became a critical success."

"And I don't begrudge that."

"I don't expect you to."

"Even if I had known what would happen, I'd have written the book. I'd still have included the rape."

"You are a bastard."

"But I'd not have written this article. It was a mistake."

"Don't expect me to believe that, Ruthwa. It was your way of being noticed. The world had forgotten about you, so you chose a topic that would get a rise out of those stupid separatist leaders."

"All three of you encouraged me to write it."

"Oh, now, we are to blame?"

"I swear, I had no intention of causing this."

"You failed. Whatever your intention, the end result was damage. That's you—you destroy everything you come close to."

"Think she'll forgive me?"

"No, she won't. Nobody will. I know it's not my place, but I think you should get the hell out of here and go wherever the hell you can go where your family will not be destroyed by you."

"C'mon, Manasa, I didn't know that the nothing article would result in a fire."

"You've been gone too long, Ruthwa, and you're better off gone. You don't understand this world."

"For God's sake, Manasa, nobody, no-fucking-body, knows it was Aamaa's rape I described. No one besides our family."

"You won't convince me about your good intentions, Ruthwa. I consider myself to be the most evil person in the world, but I think I am slightly less evil than you."

"That doesn't even make sense." I bitterly laugh.

"Nothing that doesn't cause damage makes sense to you."

•

Nicky is on his way out of the hospital. He nods at us, but we don't exchange words.

Aamaa is in a private ward—weak, small, defeated. Her sclera is watery, her pupils dilated. She isn't wearing the robe the hospital wants her to. She doesn't open her mouth as wide as the doctor asks her to. She can't talk. Or she won't talk. The doctors say she's in shock. She has suffered a mild stroke.

Prasanti stands guard, her eyes swollen from crying. I ask her if she is okay.

"What will happen to all that *sel-roti* now that the *Chaurasi* was canceled midway?" she sobs. "I thought she was going to die. What would happen to me if she died?"

Prasanti tries feeding Aamaa some *jaulo*. Slowly, Aamaa chews on the rice. She looks at no one.

"It was half truth," Aamaa says with effort. She appears smaller when she talks. "It was half lie."

"Aamaa, you don't have to talk now."—Agastaya.

"The rape story was half a lie—do you think I'd have allowed him to?" She looks tiny when she confesses— more so than when she first spoke.

"Why would you?" Manasa asks, shrugging off Agastaya's signals not to stress Aamaa out. "Why would you burden us poor children with a half-truth so heinous?"

"He tried. He tried very hard. But I wouldn't allow him to. I kicked him. I nearly stabbed him. He was no match for me."

"We know. No one is a match for you."—Manasa.

"It's my story, my suffering—I can tell it any way I like." Aamaa coughs and asks for a bowl to spit into. Agastaya tells her it is okay to stop talking.

She needs to rest. We all wait for what is to come next.

"Everyone who read the book knew I was the person described in it." She speaks in labored tones. "Everyone. People actually thought I was raped. Now my factory is useless. You all used to make fun of my driveway—had I not replaced those pesky steps with it, you'd have had to carry me all the way to the main road. It'd have taken fifteen minutes. I'd have been dead." She's falling asleep.

"We know. We should never judge your acumen."
—Bhagwati.

"It was the factory owner—my childhood neighbor,"
Aamaa whispers. "We called him *Mama*. My mother
put *Bhai tika* on him—that's how close he had been to
my family, to me. He had seen me as a baby. I had my
revenge. I bought the factory from him at a quarter of
what he wanted. He deserved it—he deserved every bite,
every scratch, every kick he got when he tried undressing
me. It destroyed him. It killed him. It served him right. I
killed him. And now the factory is dead. It's gone."

"I killed the factory," I say. "I am sorry, Aamaa. Nothing I do is right. Nothing."

My grandmother is falling asleep.

"I am leaving," I say. "You look beautiful, Bhagwati,
even when you're sad."

"Thanks."—Bhagwati.

"Don't write a book about me, you murderer."—Prasanti.

"I won't, Prasanti—you're too boring to write a book
on," I reply.

"So, this is good-bye?"—Manasa.

"Where are you going?"—Agastaya.

"Fleeing—like I always do," I say.

"Like we all do."—Bhagwati.

I leave. Nobody stops me.

EIGHT

Life

After bidding good-bye to Nicky, which Agastaya tried to make bittersweet but which only left him feeling bitter, and trying to summon tears on command, at which he didn't succeed, Agastaya walked the circuitous loop from the taxi stand to the town square and headed for Baker's Café. There, he ordered a coffee and looked at his watch.

Nicky had summed it up simply: "We are just from different worlds, Agastaya. I have seen your world, and you've seen mine—we can never belong in each other's life."

Nicky said he'd have moved out of the apartment, along with Cauffield, by the time Agastaya returned to New York. Agastaya wondered whether Nicky would provisionally move in with Anthony and Anthony Two and if he'd rekindle his romance with Anthony Senior. Nicky canceled the Agra-Jaipur trip. Agastaya would stay in Gangtok another day or two to play nurse to Aamaa while she, a vegetable version of her dynamic former self, conspired against the world.

Shivani was late arriving, but then, she hadn't lived in the West. And she was female. She perhaps didn't want to appear overenthusiastic. He had decided to see this woman because no one asked him to anymore. Shivani was a doctor and the daughter of two doctors. She had gone to Tashi Namgyal Academy when the Gorkhaland insurgency in the eighties had forced her and many like her to switch from St. Joseph's Convent in Kalimpong.

She was a petite woman. The length of her nails unsettled Agastaya. There was no way those nails didn't scratch or hurt babies when the pediatrician handled them.

"Hello," she said.

"Oh, hi." He put his hand forward, which she loosely took.

This was a meeting that the elders had coordinated with the explicit purpose of marriage in mind. She knew it. He knew it. It seemed the world around them knew it, too. Tomorrow, the entire town would be bustling with talk about Chitralekha Neupaney's grandson drinking coffee with Dr. Dhakal's daughter.

"Have they been forcing you to see men?" Agastaya asked, in Nepali, as Shivani took her seat.

"They've been pretty understanding—*meh*," Shivani said, in English. "It's the relatives who are the instigating type. They talk about the ticking clock like there's nothing else to talk about. My parents are the understanding type."

"I am sorry if you didn't want to see me," he said, genuinely. In Nepali.

"No, that's okay." She asked the waiter for a glass of Orange Crush in English-accented Nepali. "I don't mind it. Do you?"

"A little bit." He sugared his coffee. "I mean, I don't know what the woman is thinking. I am afraid she's been forced to see me by her parents."

"We aren't living in the forties," Shivani said, finally in Nepali, and then quickly switched to English: "If a woman doesn't want to see you, she will tell her parents so. No one's being forced here. Sikkimese parents aren't the forceful type."

"Still." Agastaya stirred his coffee gently and hoped Shivani's drink would arrive soon.

Silence—the kind that amplified the swishing of doors, tinkling of spoons, and the shuffling of waiters—followed.

"So, you gave the USMLE, right?" she said.

"Yes, I *took* it," Agastaya responded, emphasizing the correct verb and feeling like Ruthwa. The medical licensing exam had been easy after the rigors of a degree from JIPMER.

"Would you recommend it for me? I am already specialized. It will be a step behind—backward type—don't you think?"

Her Orange Crush finally arrived, and he gulped his coffee right after she took her first sip. It was cold.

"It depends on what you want," he said.

She asked him to elaborate.

"If you want to live in America, you have to take the medical licensing exam even if you've specialized—you probably already know that. Would you like to settle down in America?"

She looked at him, and he at her. It was a question with too many layers, too many implications.

"I don't know. At twenty-seven, I thought I'd have it all figured out, but I know nothing. I sometimes feel I am still the teenage type."

"Is *type* your favorite word?" He smiled.

"Do you mean my English isn't good?" she asked.

"No, you speak excellent English. How do you like your job?"

"It's a job—am I supposed to be passionate about it?"

"Wouldn't it make a difference if you were?" he asked. He liked his job.

"I work at the STNM government hospital. I do my thing. I don't find it rewarding or anything. It's work. I am not the devoted doctor type."

"Someone's a cynic."

"I've done this so long. I want to take a break from it all. Perhaps paint. I am the creative type."

"Can't you do that on the side?"

"No. I want to be a hundred percent committed to painting. But you know what the world will say—'If she didn't want to become a doctor in the first place, she shouldn't have claimed the Sikkim quota for a medical seat. Someone else could have gone in her place.'"

She said the world's part in a squeaky voice, which provoked hushed giggles from the teenagers at the table next to theirs.

"Why do you care about what the world says?" Agastaya asked.

"This isn't America. It's society."

"We are such different people," he said, his eyes on the ant that was drowning in a sea of ketchup by the window.

"I know," she replied. "By the way, I am not a virgin."

He. Didn't. Need. To. Know.

"I never asked you if you were."

"I've read that all you America-returned types want virgin brides because you find none there," she said offhandedly. "I am not one of those Sati Sabitri types. I have a past."

He, too, had his.

"I don't expect girls to be virgins—not in this age. Have you had a lot of serious relationships?"

The waiter hung around them in the expectation that their order would go beyond two drinks.

"Two serious ones. You?"

"Yes. I am just recovering from one."

"Indian? Nepali?"

"Neither." He was speaking the truth.

"A foreigner? Dream conquest?"

"It was more than simply conquest," he said. "We lived together."

"Live-in?" she said, with the shock that was the preserve of the Indian bourgeois. "You're totally American. What happened?"

"We broke off recently. There were too many fights. Different worlds."

"That's what I keep hearing from all Indian men who go abroad."

"The breakup was hard. It still is. But life goes on."

"How's your grandmother, by the way?" she asked.

"She's all right. She still doesn't talk a lot, which is not very characteristic of her at all."

"We were all dressing up to go to the *Chaurasi*. We were late."

"Yes, we couldn't even celebrate *Bhai Tika* the next day. You still haven't told me about your relationships."

"Let's keep it for some other time—maybe tomorrow," she said. "It's boring to share everything at the first meeting."

They exchanged numbers and said their good-byes with handshakes. Agastaya offered to walk her home, but Shivani refused, stating that she had to stop by a friend's.

A little dazed, Agastaya strolled around the square, hoping he wouldn't run into anybody who knew him. In this town of well-wishers, there would be plenty of people inquiring about his grandmother's health. He needed this alone time to mull over life. In the past forty-eight hours, he had gone from being committed to single. He had just met the woman Aamaa hoped he'd get married to.

At Supriya's Bookstore, on his way back home, he purchased a *Debonair*, that Indian magazine that had introduced him—and thousands of boys of his generation—to the world of breasts. Prabin Uncle, the owner, was absent, but the manager glared at him— the stare of a man who couldn't believe that the scion of such a respectable family would read smut—and gave him a copy, which Agastaya, as he did in his youth, rolled into a tube and stuffed into the back of his waistband.

He ran down the stairs of the overpass and down the steps of Zongri, the every-purpose store of his childhood, half of which was now a liquor shop. Before ascending to his grandmother's house, he retraced his steps to the store and purchased a bottle of Smirnoff.

Once the crowd thinned on the non-liquor side, he asked for a pack of condoms, praying the shopkeeper of his childhood wouldn't recognize him.

Condoms, a bottle of vodka, and a *Debonair* in hand, Agastaya returned home.

Thankfully, everyone was upstairs, attending to Aamaa. He slipped into the room of his childhood, where he had smuggled his first condom, his first *Debonair,* and his first vodka.

He undressed, checked himself out in the mirror, tried not to pay attention to the breasts he was sprouting, thought of Prasanti, dismissed her, thought of Nicky, dismissed him, thought of Shivani, dismissed her, uncorked the vodka, took a gulp, grimaced, took another one, opened a sachet with his teeth, put the condom on his flaccid penis while avoiding a look at his groin, and leafed through the pages of *Debonair.*

A photo of a big Indian woman with breasts the size of melons. Her vagina hidden but suggestions of hair down there. Hairy armpits. Hairy woman. Big hair. Hair above her lip carefully removed.

He resisted the temptation to read an erotic story and kept flipping, the condomed dick in the right hand and the bottle of vodka in the other. The condomed dick he let go when a page needed to be turned. Another spread—this one of a blonde. Legs crossed. Breasts covered. Milky-white skin. Blue eyes. Another one—same woman, pointy nipples, staring at him, mocking his refusal to get it up.

When he was fourteen, a few nights after his younger brother informed him about the Disney World that was pleasuring himself, he had tried it for the first time. Now, vodka forgotten on the nightstand, he rhythmically did what he had to, closing his eyes and opening them. At fourteen, while he tried swallowing the vodka that had made him vomit a little, he had rubbed the head of his member with his palm. Now he pinched his nipples, made patterns on them, and inserted a finger into his rectum. At fourteen, he had put his fingers into his mouth, then bitten them one by one. Now, he looked at the blond woman and invoked an image of her moaning and groaning and crying. At fourteen, he had looked at the picture of a different blond woman and imagined the combined nudity of all the girls in his class.

Finally, Agastaya accomplished his purpose. At fourteen, an almost-battered dick and a bleeding foreskin later, he had known something was wrong because the thought of all the girls in his class parading naked around him hadn't done the trick.

He sent a text to Shivani—"Great time today. Fun types. When do I hear all about your relationships? I leave the day after tomorrow"—and added a smiley.

"Snr or ltr." Double smileys followed.

As he cleaned up and redressed himself, he laughed sardonically at having purchased a magazine in this age of Internet pornography, and also at the audacity of every so often dreaming about a life with Nicky.

Outside, workers cleared away detritus of the *Chaurasi* celebration that wasn't to see its end.

•

Bhagwati would tell herself all her life that right before she left Gangtok, she stepped into Prasanti's room so she could have one last look at it, that a comparison between her kind of poverty and Prasanti's poverty would inspire her to get out of the financial doldrums she and Ram found themselves in, that she went into the servant's room to say good-bye.

The truth was that she walked into Prasanti's room with the intention of stealing.

Bhagwati placed three pairs of gold earrings in her purse. And a necklace. And twelve gold bangles. She could have even pilfered the money, but the gold would be sufficient.

She then said her good-byes—to Aamaa, who feebly asked her to be safe; to Agastaya, whom she reminded to cash her check and who wouldn't divulge what had gone on at his meeting with the doctor; and to Manasa, who said she'd likely see her in Colorado, right before declaring that getting away from her father-in-law would be tough. She wanted to say good-bye to Nicky, whose CPR skills suggested that he wasn't simply an anthropologist Agastaya had met in a taxi to JFK, but he had abruptly left.

Bhagwati's farewell lingered the longest with Prasanti, whom she thanked for taking such good care of Aamaa and to whom she gave a big bundle of bills.

"But everyone says you have no money," Prasanti said.

"I may not have as much money as they do, but you deserve this."

Prasanti accepted the envelope, visibly moved. "I feel guilty taking your money."

"You shouldn't," said Bhagwati, and she got into the waiting taxi.

"How's your grandmother, madam?" the taxi driver asked.

"Fine," Bhagwati replied. "Recovering fast."

"And the factory in Kalimpong?"

"Not recovering at all."

"Fucking scoundrels—whoever did it," the driver spat out. "Thieves, all of them. Has the culprit been found?"

"No, not yet."

"But we know who did it. It's always the politicians who stir trouble. Thieves—that's what they are. Who sets an entire factory on fire?"

"I know," Bhagwati said. "But they aren't thieves. They didn't steal anything."

"They are thieves—no better than thieves."

"So, in your book, thieves are worse than robbers, murderers, and rapists?"

The driver didn't understand. "How was your *Bhai Tika*, madam?" he asked.

"It didn't happen." It fell the day after the *Chaurasi*. It would have been her first *Bhai Tika* in eighteen years.

"These rascals—do they know what they do to people's families?"

"I'll try to sleep," she said.

"You should. I shall not put on any music."

She knew why she had stolen from Prasanti—because she had pride.

She was too high-minded to steal her grandmother's things. Even nefarious deeds had degrees of heinousness to them—pride guided what was an acceptable monstrous act and what was not. Stealing her grandmother's jewelry would have compromised Bhagwati's integrity.

"Bhai," she said to the driver. "Let's go to Jaigaon instead of Bagdogra."

"You mean Phuntsholing?"

"Yes, Phuntsholing."

"Won't you miss your flight if you go to Bhutan?"

"It's not until tomorrow. I'll go to Bagdogra from Phuntsholing."

Thanks to the open border between India and Bhutan, she didn't really need an ID as long as she restricted her movements to Phuntsholing on the Bhutanese side. A penetrable border in an impermeable country.

She decided on a detour to Bhutan so she could see what she had left behind. Years before, this was the same route Ram and she had taken to start a new life together. Then, she was a young woman running away from home who'd never be accepted by her family again. Now, she was a thief who would never be discovered because of the number of people visiting her sick grandmother. Nobody would think she did it.

As the car traversed the vast, ugly plains of North Bengal, Bhagwati wondered if anyone would recognize her in Bhutan. Once she and her husband had been corralled out of the country, her brothers-in-law had cut off all contact with Ram and her by ignoring their phone calls and letters. But now Ram and the siblings were back in touch because the pariahs had been magically moved to America.

Jaigaon was a filthy town full of stray dogs, stray cows, and stray people. Phuntsholing, on the other side of the border, had fewer people and was more planned and cleaner. The border patrolmen didn't stop anyone. She wasn't a suspect. She wasn't going to disrupt national peace. She wasn't about to stage demonstrations. This was her home before she was kicked out. It was the only home her husband had known. It appeared scared now—as though the entire town was afraid of speaking.

"Where are you from?" a shopkeeper asked.

"Sikkim," she said.

"Oh, Sikkim." There was admiration, the asker from the land of monasteries and Buddhism respecting the asked from the land of monasteries and Buddhism.

"Where are you from?" an Indian shopkeeper asked. Stores in Phuntsholing could be licensed out only to Bhutanese (the bona fides, of course, those who received the chance to continue living in the country) and were then leased out to Indians.

"Nepal," she lied. The shopkeeper looked at her with distrust, with fear.

"Where are you from?" a third salesman asked. He looked Nepali. He was Nepali—one of those lucky few who got to stay.

"I was one of those driven out," she said.

"And you've come back because . . ." He stared inquiringly.

"I want to experience how bad things are. You look so happy—as though nothing has happened."

No ethnic cleansing. No bloodshed. No displacement of over a hundred thousand people.

"How can you be so certain?" he said. "We hate it here. Your kind is so lucky."

"You're delusional. You wouldn't have survived all those years at the camps. You, with the pencil shop, living in this comfortable world, couldn't have done it."

"That'd have been better. Look at where we are now. We can't even smoke in peace. There's a new law against it."

"It's a good law for the environment and for your health," Bhagwati said.

"My cousins were at the camps," he said. "Now they are in America."

"Who were they?"

"Anamika Chettri."

"The pretty woman—I know her."

"Lucky woman."

"Yes, she's incredibly lucky. Her second husband is abusive—beats her every single day."

"Doesn't matter. They are in America."

"You really think being beaten up is all right just because you're in America?"

"You're in the best place in the universe. I'd much rather have been among those ejected."

"Best place? Where? In heaven?"

"Isn't America heaven?"

She'd have visited the palace just to show herself she could travel freely but thought better of it.

"Airport," she said to one of the many taxi drivers flitting like flies around her. "Bagdogra Airport."

"Where are you from, madam?" the polite taxi driver asked once they had crossed the border into India.

"Me? From a place in America called Boulder. Heard of it?"

The driver shook his head to deny knowledge of the strange place.

"It's different from Bhutan. People live freely. People can be themselves."

"And what do you work there as, madam?"

"I am a dishwasher," she said.

"I hear even dishwashers in America make more money than officers here."

"Yes, you heard right. In America, they make a lot of money. *Momo* sellers make even more."

"Do they sell *momos* in America?"

"They do. My husband and I plan to do it, too. We might even sell a Bhutanese dish or two."

•

She apologized to Prasanti because it was the civil gesture to make. Up until her grandmother's stroke, Manasa had considered Prasanti an unnecessary appendage to the household. After the hospitalization and the dedication with which the servant looked after Aamaa, Manasa was compelled to change her opinion. They couldn't have done without the eunuch.

"I know I shouldn't have slapped you," Manasa said. "It's just that so many things—bad things—are happening in my life right now. When I see you so happy and carefree, I wish I could be like you. I am jealous."

"You mean, become a *hijra*?" Prasanti asked.

"No, not become a *hijra*. I wish I had no cares, no stress, no tension. You have an easy life."

"Try running the house for a few days," Prasanti said. "You'll want your old life back."

"You're lucky."

Prasanti made light of the apology, but Manasa could see the spring in the eunuch's steps. It was tragedy's way of unifying a family.

"Now, no mischief from you, Aamaa," she said to her reclining grandmother. "No drugs, no flirting, and no fighting with the world."

The older woman replied with gibberish, but she was smiling.

At the Bhadrapur airport, from where she'd fly to Kathmandu, the daughter-in-law of the once all-powerful and now entirely powerless Ghimirey family wouldn't have to submit herself to the humiliation of being frisked. An old loyal dog worked there. His anxiety at her father-in-law's retirement from active politics was palpable.

"Your Bua did great things for my family," he said. "He was responsible for this job I have now."

A man who had positively changed the fates of so many families had distorted hers. She smiled politely.

"Now we hear he lives in London," the man continued. "That he isn't keeping well. But he doesn't need to be well in the body to contribute to this nation. As long as he's well in the head, he should stay here."

"He's not well in the head, either, Daai," she said. "He had problems remembering things. Some other people have taken over the reins of the party, as they should."

"How can you say that?" It was a gentle admonishment. "Who can take over the mantle from someone as great as your father-in-law?"

"Don't know."

"How about your husband?"

"Himal?"

"I've known him since he was a child," the man proudly said while shooing away the short, dark porter who had been a staple at the airport in Bhadrapur for decades. "Your husband perhaps remembers me."

Manasa gave the porter a ten-rupee bill.

"Why don't you enter politics?" he said. "The daughter-in-law of Madhav Prasad Ghimirey belongs to the country."

"I hardly belong to Nepal. I am not even from here."

"But you got married into it."

That solved matters. Marriage solved everything.

Himal was waiting for her at the Tribhuvan International Airport in Kathmandu. As though by reflex action, Manasa craned her neck to see if Bua was next to him. He wasn't.

"How was the flight?" Himal asked.

"Shaky," Manasa replied. "I could see the cockpit from my seat."

"We have to go to Kancha Kaka's for lunch."

"Right now? Straight from the airport?"

"Sorry," Himal said, as though a quick stop at his place in Baneshwor, so close to the airport, would derail the entire lunch. "We have to go now."

Manasa was quiet in the car while the new family driver stole glances at her in the mirror. Feeling violated and ambushed (both by this strange driver and her husband), she stared out at the city stretching out around her. The driver shifted to the side-view mirror to check her out.

It had been such a beautiful city. Nature had been bountiful. Man had been uncharitable. Manasa could see the mountain range behind her. Beside her and in front of her, she saw lofty hills of trash. The car didn't move because the traffic was unbearably bad. Dendrite-sniffing five-year-olds exchanged their tubes of adhesive with hashish-smoking six-year-olds for the benefit of a foreigner who videotaped them in their natural habitat.

This city had become uncontrollable. People were moving into the valley because of the relative stability here. Such a small place, and so many people—it would continue growing. Tomorrow there'd be a strike, and a hundred new families would migrate into the capital. A natural disaster somewhere, and a few more would adopt the city. Some faction of the Maoists would murder some family member, and the rest of the deceased's relatives would move in.

Kathmandu was the easiest escape route, sometimes a long-term layover on the way to the greener pastures of Abu Dhabi, Heathrow, and Houston. Until the country became stable, Kathmandu would burst at its seams with newer migrants. Once the country became stable, Kathmandu would inflate with newer migrants. It was a city that wouldn't stop gaining weight.

"Aren't you going to ask how he is?" Himal asked.

"No," Manasa said.

"I think he misses the way you take care of him."

"I am such a fine nurse."

"Don't be cynical, Manasa. Everyone is very excited to see you."

Before entering Kancha Kaka's, where the drive-way wound to a gigantic mansion whose multicolored exterior gave it the appearance of a cheap, house-shaped cake, Manasa covered her head with her shawl, a gesture that attracted her husband's gratitude.

Himal's uncles and aunts were gathered in the sitting room with Bua. Manasa touched the feet of all the women with her head.

"The youngest daughter-in-law in the house," an aunt quipped.

The token separation between genders occurred once greetings and blessings were dispensed, with the men sticking to the sitting room while the women congregated in the kitchen.

After the youngest aunt went on an ignorant spiel about how beautifully Manasa spoke Nepali despite having been born and brought up in India, Manasa excused herself to go to the bathroom. There, she inserted her finger into her throat and vomited loudly, forcefully.

"I just threw up," she said to the bevy of females in the kitchen. Pregnancy, their favorite subject, was staring them in the face.

"Is it true—the good news?" her father-in-law asked her on their way home.

"I don't know, Bua. I haven't tested myself. It might be something I ate."

"I hope it is good news. It's about time. I need a little boy to play with."

"And what if it's a daughter?" she asked.

"When the first-born is a daughter, she's Lakshmi," her father-in-law said unconvincingly.

Once home, she fed Bua some porridge, washed his face, brushed his teeth, and put him to sleep. Five minutes later, he shit all over the bed. The servant was out, so Himal cleaned Bua while she changed the sheet.

In bed that night, Manasa asked Himal if his ear was better.

"Not better or worse than when we left London," Himal replied.

"Himal," she softly said.

"Yes, honey." He was equally soft.

"I can't go to London."

"Will you stay in Kathmandu with Bua? He has been talking about sticking around a little longer."

"Aamaa had a stroke. There's no one with her."

"What about Prasanti?"

"She's not family."

"And the others?"

"No, Himal. I looked after your father all these years. It's time for me to look after my grandmother."

"When will you be back?"

"When she's better."

"What if she's never better?"

"Then I'll stay until she dies."

"I can't look after Bua alone—you know that." Voice a little louder.

"I'll look after Aamaa alone. You should try it."

"I have a job."

"I had one, too, before I started looking after your father."

"Please, Manasa."

"It's not to get back at you, Himal. It's the way things happened. I have to go. Hire a home-care aide—some Gurkha's daughter or son. I know of someone called Gita. I'll put you in touch with her."

"What will the relatives say?"

"They are your relatives, Himal."

"And what if you're pregnant?"

"I vomited on purpose to get away from Kancha Kaka's house."

"So, you aren't pregnant at all? Should we try to have a baby?"

"Earlier I'd have said I am already looking after your father, Himal. Now, I can't say anything until Aamaa is better."

"I wasn't expecting this."

"I wasn't expecting Aamaa to have a stroke. I am leaving tomorrow. Please get your ear surgery done."

She had already made peace with Prasanti. Now she'd have to learn to live with her.

•

Prasanti hadn't been this busy in years. Aamaa's appetite had taken a nosedive, which the doctors said needed rectifying. Force-feeding her mistress was no easy task now that everyone, especially Manasa, was gone. Manasa had known how to deal with Chitralekha when her grandmother was being difficult—the tyrant thrust the spoon of rice into Aamaa's mouth. Aamaa would spit it out, mutter something about being treated like a disabled baby, but Manasa had carried on unfazed. Before long, the old woman was grudgingly chewing away. When Prasanti attempted to imitate Manasa's militant method, Aamaa, weak as she was, nearly slapped her.

Agastaya, the last person to leave, had asked Prasanti if he could help her with anything before he left later that day, which she thought odd.

"If you want to work, go wash your sheet, *condo*," Prasanti had remarked. "How will a man know how to do a woman's job?"

To her surprise, Agastaya actually washed his sheet.

"You must really like to work," Prasanti said. "What an idiot."

Agastaya's good-bye message to her was not to work too hard.

"You do all the chores inside the house," he said. "Let Nirmal Daaju do the rest."

"That stupid driver knows nothing—all he does is stare at my *condo*."

"I have spoken to him about it," Agastaya said. "He'll do all the man's work."

"There's no man's work to do here. Let him do all my work, and I will do the man's work. Then, I'll get to relax all day."

"This is for you." Agastaya gave her an envelope.

"I hope the money you'd have given me for *Bhai Tika* is included in this," Prasanti said. "Your *condo* white friend didn't give me anything."

"He's from a different world. He doesn't know better."

"Never be friends with stingy people. Even that stingy Ruthwa left money on my bed—it's only two thousand rupees, but I wouldn't have expected the person who nearly killed Aamaa to leave me anything."

"I thought you said you wanted nothing to do with Ruthwa," Agastaya teased. "Why take his money?"

"It's money, you *condo*. Why should I say no to money?"

"And thank you for everything you do for Aamaa," Agastaya said. "You're the reason she's lived so long. You take excellent care of her. She's so much better now. With your care, she'll be even better."

"I run this *condo* place. One of you should now come back and stay here. What will happen when she dies? I alone cannot look after this house."

"It's your house as much as it is ours. Of course you will look after it if Aamaa isn't alive. But don't talk that way. Aamaa will live for many, many years."

"If you all don't bother her so much," Prasanti said, happy that she had received yet another doctor's reassurance about Aamaa's health. "At least you went to see that ugly girl."

"Aamaa is stable now. If she were still in danger, I'd have stayed."

"Liar." Prasanti laughed, relieved. "You tell me she's stable only because you want to get out of here."

"Thank you again, Prasanti. You're a real sister."

"Now, talk to your real sisters about one of you moving back here. Aamaa would like that."

Agastaya's taxi trundled down the driveway, belching smoke on her. Everybody came and everyone left. Only she stayed behind with Aamaa.

Prasanti was a day late for her weekly inventory.

First, she counted the cash. With the addition of the monies left behind by the siblings, she was up to 60,000 rupees. This was a lot of money, and her room wasn't safe—she needed to talk to Aamaa about starting a bank account. Aamaa repeatedly told her to deposit her money in the bank, but Prasanti was afraid that her mistress would question her about the mostly illegal means by which she, a servant, had accrued that big an amount. The money in her *Godrej*, therefore, kept piling up. Aamaa had a right to be suspicious. A lot of the cash Prasanti had stolen or shortchanged. But she was a servant, Prasanti reasoned, and servants stole and shortchanged.

She was a rich woman. Forty thousand rupees more, and she'd be a *lakhapati* in money alone. If she counted all her assets—the jewels she had amassed along with hard cash—she was a *lakhapati* four times over. She peeked into the safe-deposit box where lay her jewels, many of which she had acquired by one genius act of thievery.

At Manasa's wedding, after Aamaa presented her granddaughter with a boxful of jewelry, Prasanti had seen her mistress throw some bangles, a necklace, and earrings into a trinket box. Aamaa didn't wear any jewelry, so Prasanti asked her whom the gold was for.

"Only after my death should that Damaai be given these," Aamaa had said. "That destroyer of my family's name doesn't deserve even these."

That is how Prasanti came into possession of many of those precious ornaments—she had stolen what was meant for Bhagwati. Prasanti, not that she needed to do it, had replaced the gold ornaments in Aamaa's box with trinkets that hardly looked like the real things. She knew Aamaa wouldn't revisit the box's contents. Even if she did—and Prasanti was caught—her mistress would dismiss the theft as a casualty of servant keeping. The jewelry would be confiscated, and Prasanti would be forgiven.

Right now, though, the little bag that should have contained her wealth lay empty. Prasanti removed all her clothes from where they were stacked, dropped them on the floor, shook them out, and turned them inside out. She checked under the bed, under the mattress, and under the pillow. She hurled the blankets on the floor and then spread all her clothes about. She looked inside the sleeves of her *kurtas*, the pants of her pajamas, and the cups of her bras. Finally giving up, she went about the chores of the day, assuming some guest from the *Chaurasi* had stolen her prized possessions.

She couldn't talk to Chitralekha about the missing pieces because she would then have to confess her crime. She couldn't talk to anyone. Chitralekha could barely walk, and Prasanti was afraid of the shock her disclosure—of her original theft and of the theft of her theft—might cause her mistress. Prasanti understood, though, that it made no sense for the money to remain in her room. If her jewelry had been stolen, the money wasn't safe here. She'd have to ask Aamaa about a bank account.

"Aamaa," Prasanti said to Chitralekha, who was lying down. She was always sleeping since her hospitalization. "Guess how much money I have accumulated?"

Chitralekha's eyes danced a little. With effort, she said, "Twenty thousand?"

"More."

"Thirty?"

"More."

"More than that? Have you been stealing?"

"No. Bhagwati and Manasa gave me four thousand each. Agastaya gave me ten thousand. Ruthwa gave me two thousand, but I didn't take his money."

"Liar," Aamaa said. "Like you'd say no to money."

"No, I didn't take anything from him."

"Stupid girl—nobody says no to money."

"Okay, I took it." Prasanti giggled.

"So, how much do you have in all?"

"Sixty thousand," Prasanti said, hoping Chitralekha wouldn't be suspicious about the origin of half the amount.

"That's a lot of money," Chitralekha said.

"Yes, I want to deposit it in the bank."

"You should. The money in your account must have matured."

"What account?"

"I started an account for you when you first came to live with us."

"You mean I have more money?"

"Yes, you are a rich woman." Aamaa coughed hard. She was still weak.

"More than sixty thousand?"

"Yes, a lot more than that."

"How much?"

"You could build a cottage with it somewhere if you decide you've had enough of me," Aamaa said.

"This is my house," Prasanti replied. "Why do I need another house?"

"I know," Aamaa said. And with that, she fell asleep.

Downstairs, the phone rang.

"Aamaa," Prasanti said, flustered. "Manasa was just on the phone."

"Has she reached Kathmandu?" Chitralekha slowly rose.

"She has, and she's coming back. She's in Rangpo. She wants me to cook some rice for her."

"Why is she coming back?"

"She didn't say."

"I knew she'd be back. I am surprised she even left."

"What do you mean?"

Chitralekha didn't answer. "Help me to the terrace," she said, taking baby steps. "Go, clean my office. Remove all my pictures from there."

"Why?" Prasanti supported Chitralekha's frail body.

"Just do what I ask."

"Okay."

"And hang Manasa's diploma—the frame on the windowsill in the sitting room—on one of the office walls."

"All right."

"And on the table, lay the dirtiest sheet you'll ever find—let it be filthy, full of holes, old. Hurry up. It will be fun to watch her ugly face react to the sheet."

Outside, the sky was blue, and the sun flexed all its muscles. Soon, it would only reticently appear from behind the clouds. The Kanchendzonga was partly visible. In front of Prasanti and Chitralekha, masons were laying the foundations for the seventh floor of the new hotel. Hammers, sieves, mallets, sand, cement, bricks, bamboo poles, and mortar all came together in clanging harmony.

The doctor had forbidden her mistress from doing it, but Chitralekha puffed on a *beedi*.

Glossary of Foreign Words

Aamaa: Mother
Adivasis: indigenous people
aloo dum: potato curry
Angrez: literally means "English" but is also used to describe foreigners irrespective of where they are from
Baahun: Brahmin of the priest caste
babus: government officials
badhaai hijra: eunuchs who participate in celebrations
Bahuuns: Brahmins
beedi: a type of cigarette
bhaagney-keti: girl who ran away/eloped
bhaat khaanchu: "I'll eat rice"
bhaatey: a heavy rice-eater
Bhai Tika: the Nepali Hindu festival dedicated to brothers
Bhailo: Diwali carol sung by females
bindis: red dots worn by women on their foreheads
bokas: male goats

bokshee: witch
Brahmacharya: celibate
Brahmin: the priest caste
Bratabandha: the sacred thread ceremony
Bua: father or father-in-law
buhaari: daughter-in-law
chakka: eunuch
chattisey/chattis: "chattis" is the number 36; "chattisey"
          means 36 strokes of the penis, as in masturbation
Chaurasi: the number eighty-four; also the term used
          for one's eighty-fourth birthday
chela: disciple
Chettris: the warrior caste
Chewar: the tonsure ceremony
chori: daughter
chunni: scarf
condo: butt
daal: lentil soup
dalley: a type of round chili
Damaai: the tailor caste
dara: cuspid
Dashain: the Hindu festival that celebrates the victory of
          good over evil
daura-suruwal: Nepalese outfit for men
Deusi: Diwali/Tihaar carols sung by men
Deusurey: a chorus
Dhaka: a type of cloth
dhol: drum
dhoti: a traditional outfit; also a derogatory term for
          Indians
Diwali: the festival of lights; also known as Tihaar
Doars: a place on the India-Bhutan border

galala: an onomatopoeic Nepali word that could roughly be translated to "uproariously"

Ganesha: the elephant god

Ganesha Mantra: a hymn addressed to Ganesha

gas: one's significant other

Gayatri Mantra: a chant

ghar-Aamaa: lady of the house

Gita: the holy book of the Hindus

Goddess Saraswati: the goddess of learning

Godrej: an Indian brand

gorey: white man

Gorkha Jana-shakti Morcha: a fictional political party

Goru Puja: the day for the worship of oxen

gotra: clan

gundruk: a mixture of fermented mustard, cauliflower, and radish

gunyu-cholo: Nepalese outfit for women

Haat Day: market day

Hanuman: the monkey god

Hanuman Chalisa: a hymn addressed to Hanuman, the monkey god

Hijra: eunuch

Illam: town in Nepal

jagya: holy fire

Jaisi: a Brahmin sub-caste

jaulo: porridge

-jee/Pundit-jee: an honorific; the same as "jeeu"

-jeeu: an honorific similar to "jee"

jhilimili: full of light

joot-patti: a card game

Jwaii: son-in-law

Kaag Puja: the day for the worship of crows

Kaali: dark-skinned

kakhapati: worth a hundred thousand rupees

Kaundinya Rishi: a sage

Kaundinya gotra: a clan descended from a sage called Kaundinya

Key kuraa gardaichan?: "What are they talking about?"

khadas: silk scarves

kheer: rice pudding

koti: a house where eunuchs live in groups

Kukkur Puja: the day for the worship of dogs

kurta: a loose Indian shirt

lakh: a hundred thousand

Lakshman: a Hindu god, also Ram's brother

Lakshmi Puja: the day of the worship of Lakshmi, the goddess of wealth

laro: penis

Lhotshampa: Nepali-speaking Bhutanese

Lord Rama: Ram, the Hindu God

Maggi: a brand of noodles

maharandi: whore

Maharani: queen

malas: garlands

Mama: maternal uncle

manpari: as you please

momos: Tibetan dumplings

murai: puffed rice

naatini: grand-daughter

Naga: from the Indian state of Nagaland

Namaste: greeting with hands pressed together and fingers pointing upward

nayak: leader

Newaar: the business caste

nirvanan: castration

paan: betel leaf

paisa: a monetary unit; a paisa equals 1/100th of a rupee

Paro Taktsang: a monastery in Bhutan, also known as the Tiger's Nest

phusuk-phusuk: whisper

pundit: priest

pujas: prayers

Raksha Bandhan: the Hindu festival during which sisters tie the Rakhi—the sacred thread—around their brothers' wrists

Ram: a Hindu god

randi: whore

rani: queen

raswa-dirgha: Nepali spellings

Rupiya: rupees, the Indian currency

saahab: sir

Sagotris: of the same clan

Sati Sabitri: chaste

sel-roti: doughnuts made of rice-flour batter

sherwanis: long coat-like outfit

Shiva: a Hindu god, the destroyer

Sita: a Hindu goddess, Ram's wife

shlokas: hymns

soo-soo: penis

tan: a form of "you" often used for intimates and those younger than one

tapaai: a form of "you" used to connote respect

Tihaar: the festival of lights, also known as "Diwali"

tika: blend of uncooked rice, yogurt, and vermilion smeared on one's forehead by elders on the day of the Tika

Tika: the most important day of the Dashain festival; on
    this day, elders offer "tika" to youngsters
timi: a form of "you" used for equals
Tok: a view point
topis: hats
tutey-futey: broken
Upadhyay Baahun: upper-echelon Brahmin
Venaju: brother-in-law
Wai-wai: a brand of noodles

About the Type

Typeset in Bembo Regular, 12/14.25pt.

Originally designed by Francesco Griffo in the 15th-century, Bembo was revived in 1929 by the Monotype Corporation under the direction of Stanley Morrison. An old style serif typeface, it is widely used to convey a sense of classic beauty and tradition.

Typeset by Scribe Inc., Philadelphia, Pennsylvania.